SALT OF THE EARTH

JJ MARSH

PREWETT
BIELMANN

Published by Prewett Bielmann Ltd.
All enquiries to admin@jjmarshauthor.com

First printing, 2023
eBook Edition:
ISBN 978-3-906256-23-8

Paperback:
ISBN 978-3-906256-24-5

I dedicate this book to the medical profession
and in particular,
Prof. Dr. Michael Thiel, who saved my sight

PROLOGUE

Quit tumidum guttur miratur in Alpibus?
(Who wonders at a swelling of the neck in the Alps?)

— Juvenal, 'Satire No. 13'

August 1901

The one thing Clothilde could not stand was pity. Her brother's pinched lips and appalled expression were no more than she deserved. From her older sister she expected outrage, disgust, mortification, anything but pity. Nonetheless, Margot's eyes filled and she reached out a hand. Clothilde shrank further into the cushions.

"Oh, my darling sister," she whispered. "You must not be afraid. Thierry and I will care for you, rest assured. What a thing to happen when you are but a child yourself!"

"A child, indeed!" Thierry's voice was tight with anger. "Whoever took advantage of you will be punished, I shall see to that."

Margot took a handkerchief from the sleeve of her blouse and patted away tears. "Let us not be hasty, Thierry. I know this comes as a dreadful shock, but we have to think of the family reputation. The man responsible might yet be induced to marry her, no? That would solve the problem."

A flash of antagonism superseded Clothilde's shame. "You can neither punish him nor force him to wed me if you do not know who he is."

Her bullishness elicited no reciprocal anger from Margot, whose forehead remained creased in sympathy.

Thierry contained enough furious temper for them both. "If you expect any support from this family, you will damn well tell us his name this instant!"

The volume of his voice and use of a curse word moved Margot to fresh tears, and she moved from the armchair to sit beside Clothilde on the chaise longue. "Please, Thierry," she gasped, "moderate your tone. Not only does it play havoc with my nerves, but the servants will hear."

Thierry paced away to stare out of the French windows, his posture poker straight.

"You are upset, my dearest, and who can blame you?" Margot moved closer. She scooped up her sister's hand and stroked it. Clothilde was powerless to escape. "But now is the time for pragmatism. Do you happen to know, more or less, when the event is likely to take place?"

Her evasive approach rankled with Clothilde. After all, had she not stated the facts quite bluntly so as to avoid misunderstandings? "You mean when is my baby due? I can't be sure, but I estimate February of next year."

"February!" Thierry exploded. "It's now September and therefore you're already in the second trimester. That rules out a medical solution, leaving us with precious few options." He paced the rug in front of the fireplace, his hands clasped behind his back. "The second best way of managing this fiasco is to send you to a sanatorium for your confinement and arrange for the child to be adopted."

"No. I will not give up this baby. Never."

"Clothilde, you are not yet eighteen years of age," pleaded Margot. "You cannot take care of yourself! Even if you were able, how would we explain the presence of a baby in a household of two unmarried sisters?"

"Impossible!" Thierry stopped pacing and fixed them with an implacable glare. "After everything our parents achieved, your bringing shame upon this house is too much to bear. If you insist on keeping the wretch, it will not be under this roof."

"Thierry!" Margot's sobs were the only sound in the room while Thierry glowered and Clothilde took her turn at comforting her weeping sister.

"We cannot turn her out onto the streets!" Margot's words were indistinct. "It's indecent!"

"Yes, well, she would know all about indecency."

Clothilde made to rise, but Margot clutched her arm.

"Sit, my dearest, we will find a way to manage this."

Thierry straightened his cuffs. "There is another way. An office colleague handled a similar situation when his son got a girl into the family way. Farmers' wives in some of the more remote Alpine valleys are willing to take in disgraced females on condition they earn their keep. I shall enquire discreetly. If I recall correctly, the place they sent that girl was in the Matterthal, north of Visp."

"But I don't speak German," protested Clothilde.

Thierry strode out of the door, and just before closing it behind him said, "You will learn."

1

*When we were boys, who would believe that there were mountaineers
dewlapped like bulls, whose throats had hanging at 'em wallets of
flesh*

— Shakespeare, *The Tempest*

March 1916

The bedroom was never silent. Every night was a
symphony due to her mother's restless shifting, sudden
starts from one of her brothers and the movement of goats from
the floor below. Yet Seraphine had learned to differentiate
between night noises and sounds of awakening. For when three-
year-old Henri opened his eyes, she had fewer than two minutes
to get up, scoop him into her arms and hurry him onto the pot.
Not quick enough, and her first chore of the morning was scrub-
bing the floor. Now the mornings were lighter and the temperature a few degrees above zero, he didn't fight as hard. The winter

had been a thankless battle of screams, sobs and wild flailing hands every time she hauled him from his cot.

She understood. It was cruel to be ripped from the warmth of your bed, undressed and made to do your business in the half dark. Only through routine could she hope to teach her brother the necessity of going to the toilet the moment he woke up. She always rewarded him with a kiss and an embrace and another hour in his cot when the ordeal was over. For her, there was no such luxury. She dressed, cleaned out the pot and braced herself for the day. Downstairs in the kitchen, the fire was lit, the pan was boiling and the baby was feeding at his mother's breast.

Seraphine took the pan from the stove and tipped the water carefully over the tea leaves in the copper kettle. Only last year, she had lost her grip and scalded her own shin, which still bore a shiny red patch of burn tissue.

"Good morning, Maman. Did Anton sleep through the night?" she asked her mother, stopping to caress the infant's downy head as he suckled.

Her mother gazed vacantly at the fire, chewing her lip, her chin resting on her neck.

"Madame Clothilde Widmer, your daughter is speaking. The baby slept through, yes?"

Clothilde's face rearranged itself into its normal weary disappointment. "Good morning, *ma fille*. He did. And Henri? No accidents?"

"No, I was fast enough today. He did his duty and went back to bed. I'll see to the goats first then bring him down for some breakfast."

"Only if he's awake. If not, leave him."

"Only if he's awake, of course." She slipped on her jacket, stuffed her feet into a pair of boots and opened the door to the stable. The warm fug of animal bodies and breath greeted her, as did a dozen pairs of rectangular pupils and one black-and-tan canine, wagging his tail. She let the dog out with a ruffle of his soft fur. Then she tore armfuls of hay from the grain store and scattered it along the central manger, trying to distribute it fairly. On her sturdy little stool, she milked their udders, filling pail after pail for the churn. Then she took bucketfuls of water from the rain butt and sluiced the channels of the animals' waste before filling the drinking troughs. Once the goats were fed, milked and watered, she opened the hen house and collected the eggs. The chickens fluffed themselves, clucking and puttering out into the orchard, their beady eyes scouring the ground for worms.

The morning was bright, chilly and clear. Early rays of sunshine lit the mountains, casting a pink glow over the snow-covered slopes. With a promise of good weather and the hope of a day in the meadows with the goats, Seraphine tucked the eggs into her pinafore pockets, took half a pail of warm milk and returned to the farmhouse, the St. Bernard at her heels.

Clothilde was on her feet, the sleeping baby strapped to her back. Without looking up as Seraphine re-entered through the stable door, she poured the tea. Mother and daughter moved like clockwork, intersecting, connecting and passing one another as they prepared the morning meal without the need for words. The kitchen, scented with baking dough and fresh milk, seemed to bolster their spirits. Clothilde's face softened into a smile as they sat at the worn wooden table to eat dark bread with butter and last year's jam.

"Guess," said Clothilde, tapping the jar.

Every year they played the same game. Boiled fruit, sweet-ened with sugar and thickened with dried apple, sat in matching jars in the pantry, preserved throughout winter to sustain them until spring returned. No labels, merely a colour to suggest the flavour. When Seraphine was little, jams tasted red or black. At the age of fourteen, her palate had matured.

"Apricot. Or maybe yellow plum?"

"Quince. Remember Henri got sick eating raw ones while we were picking?"

Seraphine swallowed, her conscience twinging at yet another instance of neglect. She was responsible for her brother, and every single accident or mishap was her fault. "I remember. Poor Henri."

Her mother emptied her cup of milk and untied the cloth holding the baby. "Hold him for a moment while I make the oats." She used her index finger to lift the checked curtain at the window. "Thanks to the Lord, the mists are gone. There's a world out there and we're no longer alone. When Henri is awake and fed, you should take him and the goats up to the pasture. I will take the churns down for the milk wagon." She hooked a cast-iron pot from the shelf above her head and banged it onto the stove.

The baby jumped, his eyes opening in alarm before drooping closed again.

Seraphine gazed at the child in wonder. Both her half-brothers suffered from a common condition known as cretinism. Henri was a deaf-mute with rudimentary abilities who would likely die before his tenth birthday. Anton's misshapen head and slow reactions, just like his brother's, led everyone to assume his development would be equally stunted.

For a woman like Clothilde with a husband called up to defend the Swiss borders, giving birth to two such children was an impossible burden. But what if this baby was different?

"Maman?" whispered Seraphine, scarcely daring to voice the thought. "I think Anton can hear."

Clothilde put down the oats and glared at her daughter. "What are you talking about?" Her anger masked hope and despair.

"When you slammed the pan onto the hob, he started at the sound. It woke him up."

"You're wrong, Seraphine. He's a cretin, same as Henri. No hearing, no speech, no use." Despite her harsh words, she came across the room to gaze at the baby boy.

No one could say he was pretty with his knobbly potato head and asymmetric features, but he had soft skin, rosebud lips and a tiny peach-coloured nose. Seraphine tried none of the communication styles she used with Henri – blowing on his cheek, tapping his shoulder, moving into his sightline – and simply tensed, waiting to see what her mother would do. She forced herself to sit still, not to curl protectively around the infant as she had done so many times with Henri.

Clothilde snapped her fingers near the child's ear. He did not stir. Her face hardened and Seraphine wished she'd kept her observation to herself until she had proven what she suspected. Then her mother clapped her bony hands together with a whip crack loud enough to wake the dead.

Anton's blue eyes startled open and with a jerk, his hands uncurled like tiny starbursts. For a second, he stared into Seraphine's face with a look of the most severe reproach. The wave of love washing over her was irrepressible. She bent to kiss his bumpy forehead, even though his eyes had already closed.

Her mother returned to the oats, her back stiff and uncompromising. "Let's wait and see," Clothilde grunted. "Always be prepared for the worst."

Sounds from above her head alerted the girl to her sibling's movements. Seraphine laid the baby in the bottom drawer of the dresser, the one place where he could not fall out. He gave no reaction to the change in angle or texture, sleeping on without a murmur. His brother, on the other hand, was already rattling the bars of his cot and making the bird-like caws he used to attract attention.

When she entered the room, his eyes swivelled towards the movement and he smiled his crooked smile, yanking the bars as if to wrench them out.

"Good morning, Henri! How did you sleep?" She lifted him out of the cot and onto the floor, wiping his nose with her handkerchief. To her alarm, his throat seemed several degrees more swollen than yesterday. She caught his flapping hands and tried to gain his attention. They had developed a rudimentary sign language which worked fewer than three times out of five. Still, Seraphine kept trying.

If he was crying or agitated, she would point at the affected area of his body and curl over, her face pained. Henri understood how to shake his head for no and nod for yes. If she could just get him to concentrate for long enough, she was able to make an educated guess as to the source of his distress. Today, he was excitable, but the reasons for that could be anything: sunshine, the smell of oatmeal or something as basic as the fact he wasn't lying in his own waste.

She pressed her fingers to his throat, touching the saggy area gently but firmly enough to detect if it hurt. The boy seemed to understand, lifting his chin to enable her examination. His caws and cackles continued without a break, yet Seraphine felt no vibrations through the lump. She took his face in her hands and looked into his eyes. She prodded at her own neck and mimed the pain gesture.

It took a moment until light dawned in his eyes. Then he reached forward to embrace her and stroke her throat. She gave a laugh, half touched and half despairing, then tried again. Too late, his attention span was gone. She helped him dress, noting the powerful body odour, and faced reality. He needed a wash. Cleaning the boy was an enormous effort because he resisted with all his strength. The procedure exhausted them both, leaving her covered with bruises and him in furious tears. But she could not allow him to fester in filth. There was a chance, if it was warm up at the pasture, she could encourage him to splash the stream with the goats. It was better than nothing.

He clattered down the stairs, peeping and squeaking with pleasure on seeing the dog. Barry was officially banned from entering the kitchen, except when he was useful. The shaggy St. Bernard was always useful. He knew his place and took his duties seriously. He assisted Clothilde and Seraphine by guarding chickens, herding goats, watching babies and soaking up tears. His tail wagged as Henri tripped down the final few steps and flung himself at the dog's ruff.

They were at the table, eating oatmeal in silence when Barry's head lifted from the hearth. The dog's head cocked sideways and a low grumble emanated from his throat. Clothilde put down her spoon, her eyes hooded with suspicion. From the track below the farm came the creaks of cartwheels, the bray of a mule and the unmistakeable sound of a man yodelling. Seraphine rose, taking care not to transmit her trepidation to Henri, and went to the window.

A figure was waving some papers in the air. Pointing to the post box, he slipped the documents in and returned to his contraption with a jaunty salute. Seraphine fluttered her hand in response, keeping her back to the kitchen so as not to attract Henri's attention. Barry stood beside her, waiting for instructions.

"A post delivery! The first one in weeks," she murmured to her mother. "From here, I cannot see who that is. Shall I go down and see what he has brought?"

"Wait till he is gone," hissed Clothilde. "Those people thrive on gossip."

The man and his mule navigated their way further up the rustic lane. When he was no longer in sight and his yodels became distant, Clothilde gave a twitch of her head, like a blackbird eyeing the sky for hawks. It was the signal her daughter had permission to move. To minimise disruption, Seraphine opened the cupboard and dropped a few raisins into Henri's bowl. He began his excited squeaks, prodding the dried fruit with his spoon, and Seraphine knew she was safe to slip into the barn. She let Barry go ahead and heaved on her boots only after the kitchen door closed.

The cloudless morning doubled the sun's strength, brightening scenery long hidden by clouds and mist, heating her black hose so she felt warmer outside than in. Even Barry embraced the change in weather, strutting down the farm track like a proud pony, his tail a ceremonial flag. Yet the fear of what the post box contained dampened Seraphine's spirits. Communication from the outside world brought bad news more often than good.

Since the army had summoned her stepfather to defend the Swiss border, telegrams or letters bore particular significance. His unit had formed part of the armed resistance, not active in battle up till now. But that could have changed weeks ago and neither Clothilde nor Seraphine would be any the wiser. Nerves slowed her steps. Her gaze bored into the post box as if she might divine what was within. Used so infrequently the key was long lost, the metal container froze shut in the winter and gathered cobwebs in autumn. Barry stopped at the road, waiting to gauge her intentions. Proceed to the village or return home?

The box was unusually full. She withdrew each item individually, scanning postmarks for clues. A letter from Basel, a heavy envelope from Sion, two handwritten notes posted locally and a hessian-wrapped lump the size of a sock. Seraphine gathered everything in her arms and whistled to Barry, who was sniffing around the postman's footprints. She looked up to see her mother's face in the kitchen window, her expression impossible to read.

. . .

From hard-won experience, Seraphine knew eager anticipation and keen interest in the post would make her mother retreat like a turtle. Clothilde only shared relevant news when she had digested the information herself. As for her little brothers, Anton continued to sleep in the drawer and Henri, having eaten his breakfast, was now tapping his face with his spoon.

"Come on, *mon petit chou*, we're going up to the pasture with the goats." Even though she knew he heard nothing but vibrations from her chest when she sang him to sleep, she always spoke aloud to accompany her gestures, in the vague hope he might learn to lip read. She held out a hand and widened her eyes to convey excitement. The boy responded with a huge grin and slid from the bench. His short trousers exposed his knees, a ridiculous tradition when they were going out into the mountain breeze. Henri reacted badly to the cold, his lips and fingertips turning blue in a matter of minutes. While her mother sorted through the pile of post, Seraphine slipped a pair of undergarments from the drying rail and stuffed them into her pinafore. The scolding would be worth it as long as her little brother stayed warm. She placed a kiss on Anton's brow, took Henri's hand and whistled to Barry.

"Seraphine?"

"*Oui,* Maman?"

"This letter. It's from the canton. You have to go to school this year."

Seraphine stopped, her hand on the barn door, wilfully misunderstanding. "I already go to school. Most days during term time, I walk to the village, even in the worst snow. I like school."

"You know what I mean. Not in the village. From September,

they say you must go to St. Niklaus with the older ones. I already deferred twice, but now they say your time is up. Everyone is required to attend until sixteen to achieve the minimum level of education. No exceptions. Anyway, you're too big for primary and they need room for the next lot of juniors. Things are returning to normal, apparently." She exhaled a sharp breath. "Nothing normal here. What with the farm to manage, your father bringing nothing home but dirty washing and two idiot sons, how am I expected to manage alone?"

All the air sucked out of Seraphine's lungs. School was her sanctuary, a safe haven and the only time she could breathe. She prayed every night to be allowed to take the bus to St. Niklaus and join her classmates. Her prayer was instantly contradicted by another: her wish to protect her brothers and support her mother. Her salvation would be her family's destruction. An impossible conundrum, but now it seemed the decision was no longer theirs to make.

"September is a long time away. The war might be over by then and Papa can come home. Let's wait and see, *hein*? Henri and I will herd the goats up to the pasture today. Maybe I should take some bread and cheese so we don't need to come down till sunset."

Her mother watched her every move as she wrapped half a loaf of bread, some chunks of cheese, a few pickles and two wizened apples in a cloth. They could drink water from the stream. By the time they returned that afternoon, her mother might be ready to share the content of the other envelopes and what was wrapped in the sacking.

"You took a pair of *Unterhosen* from the rail, didn't you? I'm not stupid."

Seraphine removed the garment from her pocket but did not relinquish her hold. "When he's warm, he will walk. When he starts to shiver and cry, I have more than the goats to herd."

"The boy is soft. He needs to toughen up for a life on the mountain. Treating him like a pet will make his life harder."

"Harder than it already is? He cannot hear or speak or take care of himself. Henri could not survive without ... us."

Clothilde pounced on her hesitation. "Without us? Without *you*! That's what you wanted to say, is it not? Both boys would be dead were it not for their doting sister. How is it possible everyone knows best except the woman who bore them? You cosset and coddle the child like a lap dog. Alice from Dijon sends me a guaranteed cure for my son. His father says he is a runt and should be drowned. Take the damned *Unterhosen* and leave me in peace!"

It was dangerous to probe further, but Seraphine had to ask. "Our old neighbour Alice? Does Dijon please her? Is she well?"

"She's alive, that's all I can tell you. Still as much of a gossip as ever. There's a cure, she writes, a special chemical they put in salt. She sent me a jar. Seems you're not the only one who thinks I'm stupid. Take this and throw it in the compost." She thrust the hessian sack at Seraphine and heaved herself to her feet. "Do you want to make the most of the morning or sit here all day?"

Seraphine took the sack and Henri's undergarments into the barn, ears cocked for a last-minute change of heart. It never came. She put everything in her rucksack, retrieved her book from its hiding place on the rafter and set off.

The walk to the top pastures usually took an hour, but because Henri's short legs necessitated regular stops, the sun was high in the sky before they found the perfect spot. A long sloping meadow lay around half a day's climb below the snow line where the goats could roam and graze, their bells ringing in irregular tunes. On carefree days, Seraphine improvised a joyful melody to accompany their chimes, her voice reedy in the clear air. Today, she was not in the mood for music. She sent Henri to collect stones, which would keep him occupied for a little while.

Barry took up position at the other end of the meadow and stretched out on a long rock from which vantage point he could survey the herd.

Seraphine counted the goats again, more out of habit than concern, because her faith in the dog was absolute. She spread a threadbare blanket on the grass and opened her book to return to Joggeli and his pears. Her mind wandered, returning to the troublesome issue of school. Somehow, she had to persuade her mother that her attendance was of the highest importance. School and the books she borrowed were the only things Seraphine had for herself. She loved her family, her brothers, the animals and their pretty little farmstead in the foothills of the Alps, but that surely could not be the sum total of her life.

She wasn't one of those women her aunt was so fond of describing, the fearless types who wanted to climb mountains or travel the world as if they were men. In any case, women like that had wealthy families and free time to devote to such expeditions. Aunt Margot meant well, she knew that, but her attempts at fanning any flickers of nascent ambition in Seraphine demonstrated how little she understood. Not only was it insensitive to tell a fourteen-year-old girl she did not have to follow in her mother's footsteps, but it was also fundamentally unrealistic. Both her maternal aunt and uncle enjoyed a comfortable existence with time to pursue activities such as reading or travel, whereas Clothilde had weathered more than her fair share of unlucky blows. No wonder Maman bore little love for her affluent siblings.

Even so, Seraphine longed to see a little more of Switzerland than her own backyard. People from all over the world travelled to climb her magnificent valley, bringing stories of city life or journeys over the ocean from distant lands. Other countries intrigued her but none held more attraction than her own. Strolling the boulevards of Geneva or Lausanne, visiting the capital of Bern to see the bears, crossing the Gotthard Pass and descending into Ticino, or simply travelling the railway down the valley from Visp to Sion would fill the wells of her imagination.

It was not healthy to dwell on such topics and Seraphine brought herself back to the here and now. Henri's constant background sounds of clucks and squawks had fallen silent. She scrambled to her feet and scanned the meadow for the boy. The field was resplendent with brilliantly-coloured flowers and swaying grasses; the rush of the brook, swollen with snow melt, whispered of sunny days to come, tinkling goat-bells and the presence of the benevolent St. Bernard all offered reassurance, but nowhere could she see another human being.

Panic took hold in an instant. Seraphine envisaged pulling his body, face down and sodden, from a mountain pool no deeper than a puddle. Or peering over the cliff drop to see his crumpled form smashed far below against jagged stone teeth. She ran uphill, powered by terror for her charge, refusing to acknowledge the selfish spark of hope that he had indeed met a sudden and peaceful end. For everyone's sake.

Blinded by premature tears of grief, she failed to register the slight depression in the grass the first time she sprinted along the stream. From the tree line, it was easier to spot. Barry was already loping in her direction and the two met at the same point, where she found her brother asleep in the grass, each of his small fists clasped around a pebble. His open-mouthed snores reverberated so loudly Seraphine wondered how she could have missed him. She fetched the blanket and draped it over his sleeping body. She walked around the herd, her pulse returning to normal, and with Barry at her side found joy in a moment of peace.

All was well.

To her left, the valley unfolded beneath her feet, tiny houses dotted in clusters. To her right, mountain peaks cut sharp silhouettes in midday sunshine, throwing no shadows. The goats had sufficient grass to dissuade them from straying, Henri was exhausted from the climb and as for her worries, everything could wait until tomorrow. From her pinafore, she found a piece of dried pig's ear and offered it to Barry. He took it with as much delicacy as a French king and returned to his throne. She unwrapped the hessian sack and stared at the contents. A glass jar with a cork stopper tied with string, containing innocent-looking pinkish crystals. A guaranteed cure? The wildest of chances, but then again, nothing more than salt. If it made the smallest difference to either of her brothers, she had to try.

Today, all was well.

2

I am satisfied.
I have seen the principal features of Swiss scenery– Mont Blanc and
the goiter–and now for home.

— Mark Twain

July 1916

Every soldier dreamt of an end to the war. In early August 1914, all Swiss men of fighting age were conscripted and called to defend their country. General Wille, the commander-in-chief of the armed forces, was charged with protecting Swiss sovereignty and neutrality. Troops occupied the country's north-west, defending itself from invasion by its warring neighbours and preventing belligerent armies from sidestepping the Franco-German frontline. Men were deployed in continuous rotation, on duty for months at a time.

Grenzbesetzung or armed resistance at the borders meant long periods of inactivity and reinforcement of defences punctuated with regular false alarms of an incursion. On subsistence salaries with nothing to send home, many men yearned to burst out of their bleak circumstances and confront the warmongers. Even a hedgehog must eventually come out of hibernation. Small wonder the willingness to fight for one's country had faded to boredom or flamed into its own belligerence.

One day, they told each other, *this will be over*. Amid the relief at permanently leaving the line of defence, men dreamed of picking up the pieces of their lives. *What will you eat for your first meal at home? Can you imagine wearing your own clothes and drinking a beer again? Who's going to propose to his girl?* Such scenes filled their imaginations as they lay awake in rough trenches or rudimentary bivouacs, guns by their sides, ears alert for a siren or the final dismissal. Across all ranks, they longed for the big announcement; that the aggressors had come to a diplomatic resolution, swiftly followed by an order to stand down from military service.

When it happened in reverse, no one knew how to behave.

A troop of fifty men were eating a breakfast of bread, cheese and cured bacon in a dimly lit tent when the captain read out a dozen names. One of those was Favre, Bastian.

"The men I mentioned are to return to your role in society with immediate effect. Gather your things and muster at 10.00 to join the military trucks. Those remaining will be redistributed to surface camps and should wait for instructions. Thank you for your loyalty to our country and the Swiss Army. We moles are coming out of our holes."

The men cheered, as was expected, but not with the untrammelled joy *they* had expected. A unit that trained, lived, ate and slept together for months was now divided into useful citizens and soldiers. How could any of them rejoice?

Farewells were muted and uncertain when Bastian left his

makeshift dormitory, the only one of his company summoned to normal life.

"Good luck, even if you don't need it."

"Drink a beer for me and make it a large one."

"Go, be a great doctor. You were a shit soldier, so you'd better shine at something."

He laughed and shook his colleagues' hands. "We should be getting out of here together. You taught me how to grow up. I wish ..."

Gubler snorted. "You have a long way to go before you grow up. Get out of here and do something that makes us proud to say, 'I knew that onion before he sprouted'. If not, one of these days we'll find you."

Bastian cast one final look around at men he knew like brothers and gave a professional salute. Then he shouldered his baggage and climbed the slope into the sunlight.

T he truck drove them to a holding station where he and his fellow militia men were 'processed'. An officious individual barely a year or two Bastian's senior stamped his papers and glanced over his glasses. "You're going to university in Zürich?"

Humility was Bastian's default position. "I hope to return to my studies, yes, sir."

"Watch out for the radicals. That city is spilling over with men who are full of talk but have never seen action. Take your papers and good luck. Next!"

Another smaller truck contained only two soldiers and a sergeant. By now the sun had set and all he could see of his companions' features were shadows and planes above their uniforms of field grey. Bastian saluted as he heaved his pack and gun under the tarpaulin, offering a greeting in German and French.

The sergeant spoke in German, his voice gravelly with tobacco. "We're all equal now, my friend. No need for salutes or any other form of deference. Once again, we're civilians. Cigarette?"

The other two soldiers accepted eagerly but Bastian shook his head, preparing his usual excuse of a lung condition.

"Of course not! You're the doctor, I recognise you now." The sergeant tucked his cigarettes into his breast pocket, his eyes glinting in the match light as he inhaled. "You did a good job on two of my men. One with a rotten tooth and the other had a broken thumb, remember?"

Bastian had attempted to treat dozens of minor injuries with varying degrees of success during his stints with the military. Neither of the incidents cited by the sergeant sprang to mind. "As I'm sure I said at the time, I'm not yet a doctor. Nothing more than a medical student willing to help his fellow soldiers. To be honest, we had a veterinarian in our company whose treatments were far more effective than mine. Are both of your men recovered?"

The truck listed to the left as the driver got in, shouted something incomprehensible and started the engine. The men secured their packs, bracing themselves for another bumpy journey.

"Where are we going?" asked the younger of the soldiers.

"Baden." The sergeant's cigarette glowed in the half-light. "From there we catch trains to our home towns." He jerked his chin at the thin man sucking on his smoke. "Where are you from?"

"Winterthur, sir. My family and I grow fruit."

"And you?"

"I'm a wood merchant from Brugg. Whether there's anything

to return to, we'll see." The man's voice sounded so hopeless, Bastian feared to look at his face.

"What about you, Medicine Man? Your French sounds better than your German, so I reckon you'll head west."

If the Brugg timber man's voice was flat, Bastian Favre's was unstable. "I come from Fribourg, and yes, French is my mother tongue. It's where my family and friends live, where I grew up and the place I feel is my home, I suppose. Until reporting for duty, I studied there, at the university. The papers I received today state my medical training must continue in Zürich." His voice was close to cracking, so he turned to look out from the rear of the truck at the receding scenery. Sadness settled upon him, perversely regretful at saying goodbye to a period of his life he had only ever prayed to be over.

The truck bumped and wobbled down country roads before finding a smoother surface and picking up speed. Engine noise and wind whipping through the tarpaulins required more effort for casual conversation than any man had energy to sustain, so the journey progressed in silence. Night was falling by the time the army vehicle deposited them at Baden station. The two soldiers bade their colleagues hasty farewells and pelted away to find their respective platforms. The sergeant shook Bastian's hand and fixed him with an intense stare.

"Do not dismiss Zürich, young man. It is a city of learning, thought and ideas, some pompous and farcical, others earnest and naïve. Know your principles. Listen and educate yourself. Do not, and by this I mean never, succumb to the wildest fringes of immature ideology. You are a scientist and any theory always requires proof."

His speech disconcerted Bastian. "You asked each of us our professions, sergeant. You did not share yours. If we are equals, may I ask which profession is ready to welcome you?"

The sergeant tilted his head in acknowledgement. "I was a

primary school teacher. I have an eye for aptitude. My train leaves in eight minutes so I bid you goodbye and good luck."

Bastian watched him go, his eyes floating upwards to the announcement boards. A train to Zürich was leaving in half an hour. As an army man, he required no ticket. He wandered through the station, searching for something affordable to eat. At a little stall, he queued, counting his coins, and ordered a small plain pretzel. The woman ignored him and filled a large one with ham and cheese, refusing his money. A man behind him handed over some coins and bought him a beer. Shy glances and respectful nods carried him all the way onto the train and into the city. Switzerland appreciated the sacrifices made by its army. For the first time, and hopefully the last, Bastian was glad to be a soldier.

The University of Zürich sat beside *Die Eidgenössische Technische Hochschule*, known as Das Poly to its students. Such seats of learning occupied an impressive swathe of land overlooking the city of Zürich, deserving of their lofty location. Below lay banks, financial companies and other sites of commerce, where a constant stream of workers ebbed and flowed according to the time of day. High above their heads at the foot of Zürichberg, future scientists, engineers, chemists and doctors tailored their timetables around lectures and experiments. When fine young minds had the opportunity to visit the city streets and sample its offerings, it was often a relief to leave it behind and board the Polybahn, a funicular railway creaking heavenwards from the daily grind towards the arch perspective of the ivory towers.

Only to be humbled by nature.

At the end of Lake Zürich towering mountain peaks reminded all inhabitants, from street cleaner to history professor, of their insignificance. In the end everyone was an ant, striving, building and working to survive, forever battling the inevitable. Science could merely attempt an understanding of how the world worked and dream of influencing it.

Philosophical introspection was a pleasant way to pass an afternoon, but Bastian had work to do. An hour ago he had sat down at his desk with the firm intention of writing to his mother. On paper, he had penned fewer than four lines.

Dear Mama

I write with the greatest possible news. Released from military service, I am permitted to resume my studies. Contrary to expectation, my former place in Fribourg is no longer an option. Instead the Board of Education has elevated your son to the University of Zürich. Whilst appreciative of the honour, I ...

How to express the dichotomy of privilege and loss? Every attempt he made sounded churlish and disrespectful of his family. Disguising his enthusiasm was impossible even via a simple chronicle of his journey and bare statement of fact. Yet Bastian was free and unable to conceal his dizzy gladness. At this institution, in this city, at this time, circumstance afforded him unbounded opportunity. All he had to do was take it.

He took it. Especially the light.

Months spent mostly moving overland in darkness or through ditches by daylight made Bastian greedy for sunshine, hungry for skies with or without clouds, high windows and extended vistas. Each morning in his narrow student room he woke with the dawn, allowing the colours of another day to fill his heart. His shutters never closed for fear of missing a moment of dusk, dawn, midnight stars or unrelenting fog. He soaked it all in. Bastian craved rainbows. A man could stay in bed the entire day and witness wonders.

Yet staying in bed was not an option. Lectures, luncheons with fellow practitioners, practical demonstrations, afternoon walks in the woods, and informal soirées in the old town to converse on new science or old politics absorbed every moment of Bastian's day. He raced to keep up with the number of ideas he encountered and maintained a journal, concerned he would forget a chance comment or radical concept. There was simply not enough time to think.

On Sunday mornings, he went to church. Nowadays one's faith was a matter of dispute, so he attended the service at Fraumünster for no reason other than to drink in the art. A stained-glass window behind the organ, created by an Englishman called Heaton, and centuries-old frescoes elevated him to a level above prayer. Bastian had faith, most certainly, but it took the form of optimism. He and his contemporaries could shape the future, change lives for the better, progress rather than retreat. On leaving the green spire to cross the Limmat, he heard the choir still echoing in his ears and jewel-bright colours danced in his eyes.

M en dominated the lecture halls at both UZH and ETH, but female faces were not uncommon. Among Bastian's acquaintance were ladies from Russia, Hungary, Scotland, France and Italy, as well as the obvious Germans and Swiss. It took some time to adjust his demeanour from soldier to student, but one thing he had learned from his stints with the army was to adapt to his circumstances without complaint. Here, he could choose to spend time with anyone who interested him, rather than exchanging complaints with the man in the next bunk. Bastian dined, debated and discussed, or simply meandered through the old town with people whose company brought him pleasure. His closest friends were Julius, another medical student from St. Gallen, a Scottish girl named Flora who studied architecture, and Walter, who specialised in nothing other than incessant chatter.

"It's not like being a scientist, I said to him, as if I had any hope of making the man understand. He's an academic with as much imagination as ... as ... one of those." Walter gestured to a passing tram. "Round and round on the same parallel lines, never deviating from the prescribed route. An artist needs time and freedom to find their metier. That changes as the mind develops. To insist on finding a topic of study and sticking with it starves the imagination. Take me, for example."

"I wish someone would," said Flora, lifting her skirt to step onto the pavement of Zähringerstrasse.

Julius gave his echoing bass laugh and offered her his arm. "Now, now, Flora, don't be disrespectful. Let's not forget we're in the presence of an artist."

"Really? I can't recall his ever mentioning that." She tucked her hand into the crook of his elbow.

"You may mock," continued Walter, falling into step beside Bastian, "but I challenge you to deny the truth of my argument. Art is in a constant state of evolution."

"Whereas medicine stagnates," countered Bastian. "That's why we still live in fear of rickets, cholera, diphtheria and scurvy, but thankfully we have art as our solace."

"Far be it from me to deny the work of Pasteur et al. Advances in the field of bodily deterioration are not under discussion. My point is that art gives voice to the soul. As such, it cannot be trained or examined in the same way as a mathematician. His subject is finite. Art recognises no limits. I will give you a demonstration!"

"Spare us!" cried Flora, in mock-querulous tones.

"Fear not, fair lady. I will not subject you to my own creations."

"Because there are none?" asked Julius.

Walter scuttled ahead, head cocking left and right as if he were a pigeon. "Here it is! Spiegelgasse! Come, lady and sceptical men of science. May I introduce you to art at its most radical and revolutionary? Brace yourselves and open your minds, for this is Cabaret Voltaire!"

Bastian peered up the narrow alley and caught Flora's cynical eye. "Might make a change from a *Bierkeller*? Why not?"

"A *Bierkeller* is for peasants," said Walter. "Plain heavy food, strong wheat beer and tired topics of conversation. A cabaret is wild abandonment, an exchange of ideas, protest and beauty entwined. Here we feast on poetry, dance, music and wine! Here we dine on ideas! Here we are free to express ourselves!"

He opened the door and led the way inside.

Bastian and Julius stood aside to allow Flora in first.

She curtseyed and muttered from the side of her mouth to Bastian, "Nothing could stop that man expressing himself. Apart from a firmly applied cushion over his face."

3

In plain language: the hospitality of the Swiss is something to be profoundly appreciated

— Hugo Ball, *The Dada Manifesto*

July 1916

"It's the only place to be, Julius, I'm telling you. Imagine the entire intelligentsia of Berlin and Munich, many of whom are Russian émigrés, relocating to the coffee houses of Zürich. When mingling with our own artistes, the city becomes a crucible. Look over there but please don't stare. The man in white is Alexander Sacharoff, as delicate as a fawn. The grace that man possesses is worthy of applause, whether crossing a street or his legs. I'm pretty sure the arresting creature opposite is his dance partner, the von Derp female, whose reputation stands on its own. Do you remember her? She played the lead in Reinhardt's pantomime, whatever it was called. No, I don't recollect it either. No matter. That pair can turn every head in the room, whether here or at Café Odeon."

Julius allowed his gaze to take in the room, dwelling no longer on Sacharoff and partner than anyone else. "He certainly attracts attention. Not least because he inhabits the space between male and female. Before you mention it, yes, I have heard that rumour and you can spare me the sordid details."

"What rumour? There are so many! Flora, come down to the front near the stage. I want you to get the best seat for when Emmy Hennings comes on. This is why the Dada movement is progressive and radical, because women occupy the same space as men. Her poetry is astounding, often outshining the monologues of Hugo Ball or Tristan Tzara. Where's Bastian? Lurking at the back, I suspect, fearful of the avant-garde."

"Don't be ridiculous, he's gone to the toilet. Talking of monologues, dear Walter, would you interrupt yours and get me a drink? I've a feeling I shall need it."

Julius caught the eye of a waiter and ordered a carafe of red wine and four glasses. "Already arranged, Flower of Scotland, because you and I are of the same mind. Walter says this place is largely populated by Russian and German émigrés. I couldn't care less where they come from as long as they maintain a decent wine cellar. Ah, Bastian, drag those chairs over so we can sit down and enjoy the show."

Walter drifted away to socialise with other audience members, leaving his friends to sit in companionable silence. Julius observed the artwork on the walls with a critical eye and eavesdropped on Walter's gossiping.

"Max, did you know Diaghilev is in Lausanne?"

"Yes, I heard. He's establishing a ballet company and his collaboration with Stravinsky continues."

"What great good fortune for Switzerland!"

"This is what art means to the Russian soul, Walter. We may be displaced yet we never stop creating."

"How true. I may quote you in my next article. Diaghilev is not the only choreographer in the country. Rudolf von Laban teaches a class a little way down the lake."

"I know! Although we are yet to be introduced, I've seen him twice and recognised him on both occasions. Dance is my favourite means of expression."

A man interrupted. "Walter Brunn! We missed you last night at Zähringer. Tell me, what do you know of the Zimmerwald conference?" He dropped his voice, guiding Walter into a dimly lit corner.

Two women placed stools directly in front of their seats, partially blocking their view, talking in High German. Julius leaned towards Flora and spoke in English.

"Have you ever seen an uglier hat?"

Flora shook with silent giggles while the women continued regardless. "Let me tell you who else is here in Zürich. Else Lasker-Schüler! Yes, the poetess. I was astounded to see her at Café de la Terrasse. The usual acolytes surround her and ask endless facile questions about her poetry. She pulls bonbons from her cleavage and tosses them at anyone who annoys, or even pleases her."

"Really? How marvellous! The whole city is replete with eccentrics, poets, radicals, writers, dancers, idealists and composers. A cage of brilliant butterflies, are we not?"

Walter returned, carrying a glass of clear liquid. "The performance is about to start! See the woman sitting on that barrel? No, not her, the one with the wings. That is Sophie Täuber, the sculptress and puppet-maker, who dances like a plume of smoke. My friends, we are privileged to be here."

"I do hope so," said Julius, his head rotating like an owl.

"Otherwise the stuffy room and stench from the sausage factory would make this place insupportable."

"Ssh, here's the first act."

A woman with black paint around her eyes took the stage, a grey wrap barely concealing her curves, and commenced a peculiar prancing and chanting, ending on a repetition of the word Dada. The audience cheered and applauded until the wraith ran off.

Immediately the women in front continued their conversation. "There is a kitchen in our boarding-house, but I find it most disagreeable, crowded with children, cats and foreigners. I am the first to confess it is not the most salubrious *quartier*, what with the garrulous prostitutes chattering at all hours, but the river and lake are a matter of minutes away. Water always soothes the mind."

Julius covered his eyes and wished he could do the same with his ears. When he took his hands away, he saw the bewilderment on Bastian's face. "What can I say? I am as confused as you, my friend. Walter, can you help us understand what that performance was supposed to convey?"

"It's anti-art. Performance as rebellion. Nothing more than nonsense rejecting aesthetics. Art as revolution. Songs filled with protest and rage are the lifeblood of the cabaret. The very essence of Dadaism is expression freed from form. If you are too bourgeois to appreciate it, feel free to leave. I'm staying with my fellow visionaries."

With a gleeful laugh, Flora emptied the carafe into their glasses. "I love performance art. I can sit here with rapt attention all night, suffering the stage vignettes as minor interruptions to the main feature."

The woman with the ugliest hat continued speaking, her voice strident. "On the other side of my very own square live two political agitators. Yes, the very same. A married couple, pleasant enough when one passes the time of day, but in conversation, they tend to adopt a hectoring tone. I suppose Siberia must do that to a person."

Flora disguised a snort of laughter as a cough. Walter took his glass and walked away with a patronising shake of the head.

"The ambience is not to my liking," said Julius. "Bastian? Shall we go?"

"Yes, I'd prefer a quieter corner with decent company. Flora?"

"Hush! I might miss something."

The woman with the second ugliest hat was shaking her head, wagging feathers in the layers of smoke. "Your apartment is paradise in comparison to mine. One would think elephants were running around the upstairs apartment. Would that they were elephants! No, those thunderous feet belong to three noisy, whining children who disturb the entire building, morning, noon and night. I have never regretted spinsterhood, but residing beneath that family makes me give daily thanks for my childless status. I should not mind exotic creatures, because at least they would excite curiosity. Did I tell you about that hippopotamus?"

Flora's laughter was irrepressible and drawing attention. With a wave to the disgusted Walter, Bastian and Julius escorted her outside.

4

In this hard toil I've such a goiter grown,
Like cats that drink water in Lombardy

— Michelangelo, *Sonnet V*

December 1916

Children scrambled out of the junior school building, breathless with anticipation, shouting good wishes for the festive season over their shoulders.

"*Frohe Festtage! Joyeux Noël!*"

"*Danke! Merci! Gleichfalls!*"

Some raced down the hill, some toiled upwards and others jostled one another for a place in the bus. Two years older than her peers, Seraphine stood a few steps from the boisterous knot of teenagers at the bus stop. They meant no harm. In general, Seraphine received more respect than most girls, due to her height, age and patience. The senior class teacher often employed her as an assistant in French lessons, trusting in both her accent and good nature.

Now winter had set in and the government had banned motor cars to save fuel, few vehicles used the roads other than the school bus and agricultural machinery. Climbers and sightseers would be thin on the ground until the thaws of spring, which seemed a long way away. Light was fading when the Postauto creaked through the snow, sounding its horn to draw people from their homes. Seraphine cast a glance over her shoulder to see the lights in the school building had already gone dark. No more school. She sighed, hitching her rucksack higher on her shoulders, reassured by its weight. Her teacher, Frau Fessler, had allowed her to take a selection of books from the school shelves to keep her occupied through the darkest days of December.

The doors of the bus opened and the children bundled inside, eager to get out of the cold. For some reason the rear of the vehicle held the greatest attraction for boys, and competition for the back seats was fierce. Seraphine stood outside and watched half a dozen small bodies elbow themselves into prime positions, the demarcation between genders quite clear. Girls at the front, boys at the back. She usually placed herself somewhere in the middle, a typical peacemaker. Most of the time, it worked.

The noise of twenty-plus excitable children returning home for Christmas holidays was charged with anticipation. After three weeks, the noise of the same eager children returning to school would be even louder. Seraphine wrapped her scarf a little tighter around her neck, boarded the bus, and nodded to the driver. He greeted her by name, trying to catch her eye, but she kept her eyes downcast and sat alone in the middle section.

Her father was coming home. By the time the bus deposited

her at the bottom of the lane he might already have returned, his boots in the hallway, his voice filling the kitchen. She could not decide whether it made her happy or sad. For herself, she felt nothing. For her mother, she was elated, relieved and triumphant. For her brothers she felt visceral dread. Josef Widmer refused to accept that any child born of his loins could be as profoundly defective as Henri or Anton. Despite the evidence of cretinism all around him, he blamed Clothilde and her bad blood. No one dared state the obvious, that Clothilde's child from a previous marriage did not suffer from the same condition. Even if someone had, Josef would ignore the evidence of his own eyes. As far as he was concerned the problem lay with his wife.

Until now, Seraphine had mostly managed to disguise the swelling of her own throat. Many of her classmates bore the same lumps, some barely noticeable, other bulges impossible to ignore. During the winter months, she might be able to keep her slight growth concealed from her father, but nothing escaped her mother's keen eye.

Clothilde knew before Seraphine herself that womanhood was upon her. In a few sharp sentences, mother conveyed the facts to her daughter: it was every woman's burden, Seraphine had a responsibility to keep herself clean and she would be wise to bind her chest. No, it was not like a childhood illness. This would return every month until she was a grandmother. When Seraphine absorbed that information, she gathered her courage and asked how she might treat the swelling at her neck. Her mother had no answer.

The bus heaved itself along the route, little windows glowing in every village, welcoming those returning home. Every time the doors opened to let a child out into the snow, the bus chorused with Christmas wishes. When it was her turn, only the shepherds' kids and the bus driver remained to call a hearty '*Frohe Festtage!*'

She turned to wave with a smile and the bus driver caught her arm as she passed.

"A little something for you." He pressed a package into her palm, squeezing her hand with gloved fingers. "Have a lovely holiday."

"*Merci.* Same to you."

She met his eyes for a second and trod cautiously down the wet steps and out into the cold. Barry was waiting, his coat covered with a thin film of snowflakes. He pressed his nose into her hand and circled behind her, his usual signal to hurry. She trudged up the lane, eyes on the farmhouse, trying to gauge what she might encounter inside. As a precaution, she slipped the little package from the bus driver into her pocket.

She and Barry entered the barn, amid the rustling of goats, where she shook the snow from her coat and took off her boots. She lost her balance for a second, and her shoulder hit the wall holding all the goat collars with bells. She might as well have yodelled her arrival.

The door jerked open and there he was: Josef, Papa, the head of the household.

"Seraphine! At last! Now we are complete." He kissed her cheeks three times and embraced her with conviction. "Come inside. Bring Barry too. He's been the man of the house for two years and at least his presence by the fire will comfort your brother. My arrival has upset the order of things, I fear."

The order of things seemed instantly restored once Seraphine entered the warm and steamy kitchen. Henri stopped his wailing and ran to Seraphine's skirts, grasping her legs and wiping his face against her knee. Her mother gave her a curt nod and without stopping her stirring motion, indicated the rug by her feet. Anton lay in a tin bath, naked and shivering, eyes closed with lips and skin ashen. He made no sound.

"It was coming out both ends so I put him in there. Of all the days for this to happen. See to him, will you?"

Seraphine detached Henri from her skirts and guided him to the hearth, beckoning Barry to follow. Once the boy was nuzzling the dog, she scooped up the bath and took her baby brother out of the lukewarm water, rinsing the filth from his legs over the sink. She dried him gently and tied a napkin around his legs and waist. Then she unbuttoned her blouse and tucked him inside, next to her heart. His little body was freezing, making her gasp as his skin made contact with her own. She wrapped her arms around him and pressed her chin to his head.

"Your father brought mutton! Tonight we fill our bellies and say grace to God for delivering my husband, your father and our protector safely into our arms."

Whether she was supposed to rejoice or pray, Seraphine had no idea. She rocked her brother to and fro, her eyes flickering across the room to check Henri's level of distress. The boy continued to hiccup small sobs, muffled by Barry's thick fur. Her father talked as if no one other than his wife was in the room, sharing stories of violence and aggression which seemed to have little to do with war.

"My record, due to these incidents and others not right for a lady's ears, brought me to the attention of some senior army figures. I have the offer of a semi-permanent military position and impressive wage, plus the chance to command my own unit to patrol our borders. They could not have chosen a better man. I am familiar with every valley, mountain face, town and river between three countries. My French is almost as good as my German and while I could never pass as an Italian, not that I would wish to, I can make myself understood." He punched his fist into his palm.

Clothilde did not turn to her husband but continued stirring. "We must congratulate you. The last years have impoverished us all. To hear you will have a regular wage to support your family is reason to celebrate. Sit. Let us eat. Seraphine, if your brother wants to eat, he must come to the table."

With light gestures, she beckoned Henri to the table, miming food. It was one of the only signs he always understood. She positioned herself between her parents and her brother, aware that Henri's greedy slurping could cause annoyance. They ate with enthusiasm, complimenting the mutton, the vegetables and the bread. After a few mouthfuls, Anton stirred, as if he too wanted to participate. Seraphine sank her spoon into her bowl, just enough to gather some of the rich stock. She unbuttoned her shirt, cupped her hand around Anton's head and dribbled some liquid between his lips. He reacted eagerly, swallowing everything that went into his mouth. The rest soaked Seraphine's undershirt. She repeated the gesture three more times and ate a few mouthfuls of her own, waiting to see if he was able to digest such unusually rich food.

So focused was she on the infant that her father's shout came as a shock.

"No, you imbecile! Never feed meat to the dog!" With a sudden slap to the side of the head, Josef Widmer knocked his son from the kitchen bench onto the floor.

Henri howled in shock and pain. Josef opened the barn door and kicked Barry outside, the dog's head and tail down, although Seraphine noticed his jaws were clenched around his lump of mutton. The chill air from the goat shed filled the kitchen. Anton's mouth opened for more and now two pairs of lungs protested their misery.

"Maman, why don't I stay down here with the boys? You and Papa can sleep upstairs and rest. I have everything I need to take care of these two. I'll clean up. *Bonne nuit, schlaft gut.*"

They didn't need asking twice. Josef drained his soup, while Clothilde cast a disgusted glance at the wretched Henri and followed her husband up the wooden stairs.

She waited until all was silent, righted her brother and gave him the rest of her soup with an added sprinkle of salt. His tears disappeared instantly but the welt on his temple did not. The special salt on which Seraphine pinned all her hopes was concealed within the henhouse. Each morning she screwed a few pinches into a piece of paper, something easy to discard if she was caught. Now she added a few grains to warming milk and fed Anton a half bottle, while soaking some oats for the morning and gnawing on some bones from the pan. She never consumed as much as a grain of salt. In her mind, that would be stealing from her brothers whose needs were far greater.

Calm settled and the boys dozed, so she sneaked open the barn door and smuggled Barry inside. As quietly as she could manage, she gathered half a dozen logs from the outdoor stack to feed the fire throughout the night.

On goatskin rugs in front of the glowing fire, three humans and one canine huddled close. Seraphine draped her coat over her brothers and closed her eyes. Only then did she recall the bus driver's present. With great care not to disturb the sleeping boys, she withdrew the package from her pocket, worked the string knot apart and ran her fingers over a smooth oval. She lifted it into the firelight and saw it bore a monochrome pattern like a chessboard, held by a brass clasp.

One click opened the object into two halves: a compact, powder and a mirror. An object for a lady. Or a painful reminder of her own ugliness. She shoved it deep into her pocket.

The whole time Josef was home, Seraphine lived on a knife edge. Spending too long outside was chilling but she was reluctant to remain indoors. Josef disliked to see her reading and he always found a chore to keep her occupied.

"It's not healthy, sticking your head in a book. If you think yourself a lady of leisure, you can think again. The Devil makes work for idle hands. Go and chop some kindling for the fire."

More often than not she found herself in the barn, Anton strapped to her chest. His health was still delicate and Henri suffered constantly due to the cold. Sleeping on the kitchen floor was not helping the situation yet the idea of getting a good night's rest upstairs was unthinkable. Warmer it might be, but lying awake worrying Henri's grunts or Anton's snuffles would incense her stepfather made the kitchen the better option. She tried several times to ask how long they would be blessed by the paternal presence, to no avail. Then one morning her mother wheeled the churn barrow up the drive, a letter in her hand and a look of scorn on her face.

"Margot invites us for 'a family Christmas'. Ha! I never heard anything so ridiculous! Who looks after the animals while we abandon the place to eat French pastries and *foie gras*? That woman has no more sense than a goose herself. The very offer is an insult. We are working people, with no desire to nibble on crumbs of her wealth and comfort. She has no idea of what 'a family Christmas' would mean if I brought *my* family to visit. Look at them!"

Seraphine looked. Henri rocked to and fro beside the fire, gurgling small meaningless sounds. From the dresser drawer, Anton coughed with the regularity of a ticking clock. Seraphine herself was straining to read one of Johanna Spyri's books by the grey light of a winter afternoon.

"Yes, look at them." Josef stopped polishing his boots, his fingernails black as he scratched his chin with a cunning grin. "Maybe a change of scene beside the lake would do the children good. What a pity we cannot join them, but someone must work the farm. We are grateful for Aunt Margot's offer and a stay of two weeks would be acceptable. Our financial circumstances limit us to one journey for our little darlings. We trust she is prepared to fund their return travel. If not, she is welcome to keep the lot."

For a change, the lash of his words cut mother far more than daughter. Clothilde's face twisted into a mask of pain, visible only to Seraphine since Josef had returned to his boots. She smoothed the letter on the table and composed herself.

"The girl is fourteen, she cannot travel alone. Someone in the village must act as chaperone. I shall write Margot a note for Seraphine to post this afternoon, instructing my sister when to expect her trio of guests. By the time they arrive it will be too late to argue and she can feed them for Christmas. But hear this, Josef Widmer, my children belong here with me. No member of my family takes them away. This is a temporary arrangement. Seraphine, go upstairs and pack what you and your brothers will need for the duration."

For Seraphine, two weeks staying with Aunt Margot and escaping Josef Widmer was a fantasy too far-fetched to entertain. Her two little brothers warm, well-fed and out of harm's way was beyond comprehension. She spoke without thinking. "What about Barry?"

"Dogs don't celebrate Christmas. He's a working dog and stays here."

The daughter of a local tailor travelled with Seraphine and the boys as far as Visp. Their trip began on an optimistic note, in brilliant sunshine. Clothilde waved them off from the end of the drive, a reddening of her complexion the only sign of emotion as they walked away. It was a shame they could not say goodbye to Barry but he was already up in the pastures with Josef and the goats. All the way into the village Henri peeped and chirruped with excitement, making Seraphine smile despite her discomfort. The old mould-stained leather suitcase was heavy, her shoulders strained under the weight of Anton on her front and her rucksack on her back, but they made it to the village in time to take their seats on the Postauto.

Local folk were helpful, lifting her suitcase, smiling at Henri's meaningless chatter and making space for her bags. The tailor's daughter shared one of her apples, the bus left promptly and Seraphine embarked on the longest journey of her life. She had tears in her eyes when the bus pulled away from the stop and turned the corner, giving her a momentary glimpse of the hill where she lived. The farm was no longer visible but she knew it was there. Part of her ached to drag herself back up that track to safety, but that was cowardice talking. In any case, it was too late now.

In Visp, the problems began. The station was crowded with more people than Seraphine had ever seen. The tailor's girl made sure they found the correct platform and bade them farewell. They sat on the bench, gawping at the melee until the train pulled in. The size, noise and sudden exodus of people overwhelmed Henri and he panicked. Screaming in terror, he tried to bolt and lashed out with his fists when Seraphine tried to coax him aboard. People stared at the spectacle, Seraphine lost her grip on her suitcase and Anton began his rasping sobs. Henri writhed and punched, landing one punishing blow after another on her forearms. An evil thought crossed her mind.

She could let him go. Just release his wrists and let him run. In seconds, he'd fall under a train or a bus and it would all be over. No more responsibility. *Let him go.*

From behind her a tall uniformed man scooped Henri under one arm, oblivious to the boy's flailing limbs. With his other hand, he lifted their pathetic suitcase and motioned for her to follow. He wedged Henri into a compartment, stowed the suitcase above their heads and announced himself as the conductor. With a sincere promise to deliver them safely to their aunt, he closed the door. The sudden silence bewildered Seraphine, whose heart rate was racing. As always with Henri's tantrums, this one blew in like a hailstorm and out like a spring breeze. He was already pressing a tear-stained face against the window, making small hoarse noises of amusement. Seraphine repressed the urge to clear his face of mucus for fear of provoking another fury. Instead, she tucked a feeding bottle under her armpit and cradled Anton. While the milk warmed, she sang, as much to calm herself as the boys.

Since they were in a compartment to themselves, she risked sneaking a hand to her inside pocket for a twist of paper. She unscrewed the cap of the bottle and sprinkled three grains of salt into Anton's milk. Her mind flew back to the henhouse, where the magical cure awaited their return. She could have brought the little jar on their journey, but suspected it might yet be useful at home. Judging by the sounds from upstairs and presuming Seraphine's calculations were correct, her mother would fall pregnant in the next few months. Clothilde might have no faith in the medical profession, but Seraphine was convinced. Health by stealth and no one needed to know otherwise.

The train rumbled out of the station and through the valley, providing so much visual stimulation that Seraphine grew weary. By the time the locomotive passed Sion, all three family members were asleep.

A sixth sense woke her, just as it did every morning. Anton needed a change, Henri was due a visit to the bathroom and she ought to tend to her own state of disarray. She lured Henri without too much drama into the tiny toilet with the promise of a dried apple ring. By the time the conductor announced the Montreux stop, she had managed to clean all three of them to a respectable standard. Her naïveté regarding respectability lasted for less than a few minutes.

The conductor assisted them onto the platform and hailed one of his colleagues, who came towards them with a nod. "*Ah, oui, les enfants*. This way, little ones. Your aunt awaits you."

With a hand clasped tightly around Henri's wrist and her eyes fixed ahead seeking a familiar face, Seraphine was initially insensible of the stares. Only when one woman stepped back and uttered, '*Quel horreur!*' did she become aware that their small party was attracting as much attention as a circus. Anton, cradled on her hip, was drooling on her shoulder, his head slack. Henri cackled and whooped at the sight of so many strangers, lurching towards them as if to shake hands.

As if her ears had adjusted to the pressure of descent from Alpine altitudes, she could hear the not-quite whispers.

'*I'd heard the rumours, but assumed it to be an exaggeration.*'

'*Stop staring, Louise, they can't help it.*'

'*Dozens of them up there, apparently, like a freak show.*'

'*Move back, Charles, we don't know if they're infectious.*"

"*Frankly, I'm not surprised. Look how old the mother is!*'

"*Seraphine*, ma chérie! I am so happy you are here!" Tante Margot crouched to her knees, holding out her arms. As always, Henri responded to physical gestures and rushed to his aunt, wrapping his arms around her neck. A uniformed man relieved the conductor of Seraphine's suitcase and she had enough presence of mind to thank the train official. Hands lifted Anton from her hip and eased off the rucksack. Tante Margot cupped her hands around her face and kissed her, her eyes filled with tears.

"My dearest, precious niece, how brave you are to come so far! *Bienvenue à* Montreux, where you are the most welcome guests."

Seraphine cast a glance over her shoulder at the gossips.

"Those awful people deserve not the slightest acknowledgement. You see that look in their eyes? That, my sweet girl, is ignorance. Therefore they should be pitied while you deserve everything good in the world. Come, the automobile is waiting."

"An automobile?"

Something changed on the drive from Montreux station to Tante Margot's villa. Henri pressed his face to the window, Anton coughed and Seraphine's eyes widened. Yet this new landscape and mode of travel no longer frightened her into retreat. She sat upright, absorbing every detail. Streets, trees, ornate gates, city folk promenading in fashionable clothes and the vast expanse of Lac Leman called to her.

On arrival at the villa, a manservant took charge of their belongings while a maid served tea in the library. Seraphine had never seen so many books. Their covers seemed to gleam in the afternoon sunshine, each promising a doorway into another world.

Welcome, they whispered, *all of this is for you.*

I n mid-January, Seraphine returned to the farm with two suitcases and no brothers.

On the very afternoon they had arrived by train in Montreux, Tante Margot summoned a doctor for Anton, concerned by the sound of his breathing. Within twenty-four hours, the baby boy was in a children's hospital, receiving treatment for tuberculosis. He fought on for three more days and nights, before succumbing to the White Plague. Neither Seraphine nor her aunt could see him for fear of infection. His passing was like a sputtering candle, a small life quietly extinguished.

Day after day Tante Margot impressed upon Seraphine that she was not to blame. The disease was transmitted through droplets or direct contact, not neglect or irregular temperatures.

In fact, Alpine sanatoriums were popular places to recover for those who could afford them. Someone must have passed the disease to Anton, and given his existing condition it was a wonder he had survived this long.

Seraphine listened politely but inside she was inconsolable. It was her fault. Slipping the special salt into his food was what had killed Anton, she was convinced. She had poisoned the boy. She vowed from that moment on never again to tamper with Henri's food, or anyone else's for that matter. Interfering with nature never turned out well.

A telegram from St. Niklaus granted permission to bury Anton in the family plot. On a wretched grey day by Lac Leman, the sight of his tiny white coffin touched the hardest of hearts. While Seraphine wept into her pillows each night and prayed for her brother's soul, Henri was oblivious. Fraternal grief and familial loss meant nothing. He was happier than ever before and who could blame him? Sunshine, warmth, comfort, food and endless entertainment filled his world. Seraphine had never seen him more reactive or persuadable. He bathed daily in warm water, splashing and laughing in the huge tub, overseen by a maid. He ate fresh fruit and ran around the gardens with a kite, never releasing it to the sky but cooing and cackling as the colours streamed behind him.

Her aunt extended every generosity to her niece and nephew, indulging Henri's high spirits and giving Seraphine time to grieve. The return of Uncle Thierry – Margot and Clothilde's brother – completed the party two days before Christmas. They celebrated with a visit to church, an informal supper and the presentation of gifts. What they ate and what she received, she could not recall, but she remembered to be unfailingly grateful.

Three days before they were due to return to the Alps, she sat on a window seat looking out at the water, unable to find joy in such beauty or shake off her cloak of leaden hopelessness. Across the room, Henri was dozing on the rug in front of the fire, mouth open, supervised by the maid. At least one of them was content.

Her aunt and uncle emerged from the dining room and invited her for a walk along the promenade. Henri slept on and the maid curtseyed, indicating she was on guard. Seraphine wrapped herself in her new winter cloak and followed her hosts outside into the fresh air.

Sea birds squawked and clamoured as they strolled, competing for space on buoys or rocks, while clusters of sparrows swooped from one bare tree to another.

"Seraphine?" Her aunt's voice was gentle.

"*Oui, madame?*"

"Your uncle Thierry and I, *chérie,* we have a proposal."

Thierry cleared his throat. "This may appear insensitive and sudden after the loss of Anton, and I apologise if what I have to say makes you feel uncomfortable. Most of all, Margot and I would like you to be honest."

Seraphine continued walking, afraid of what they might say. "*D'accord.*"

"In the course of my work, I learned of a hospital in Bern. It's a place where they treat young people like Henri. Trained nurses and doctors care for these boys, studying their development and meeting their needs. This is a government program so no funding is required by the families. That said, you should know I have made a charitable donation."

Margot stepped closer and linked her arm in Seraphine's. "Henri would be looked after by specialists, kept warm, fed three times a day and given the chance to play with other children. Thierry and I will visit regularly to guarantee his welfare. Neither of us is ignorant of how much you care for your brothers. The timing is wretched after Anton, I completely sympathise. What we propose is more of a temporary separation. Like you, we want the best for Henri."

"Maman and Josef ..." Seraphine swallowed the painful contraction in her throat. "It's not my decision."

"If you are willing to give Henri this chance, I can telegraph Clothilde and Josef to explain." Margot pressed a hand to Seraphine's shoulder.

Thierry added his view. "Our sister can be stubborn at times, as we all know, but her son's well-being is of paramount importance to us all."

"I see."

They walked on, turning instinctively against the wind towards the park.

Moments passed before Margot spoke again. "Seraphine, this is not just about Henri, it concerns you too. Thierry and I would like to offer you a home. In front of me I see a bright, beautiful girl who deserves more than a mean existence as her mother's skivvy. You can live here with us, visit Henri whenever you wish, attend school, make use of our library and fulfil your potential."

They walked along the neat paths of the park, side-stepping puddles and greeting passers-by. Her pretty but impractical boots and warm tippet deceived everyone into thinking she was one of them. Imagine their flared nostrils and raised brows once she revealed her neck.

"The hospital sounds like a good place for Henri. I will miss him, of course, but more than anything I want him to be happy. For myself, I must return to the farm. Please do not think me ungrateful. Your kindness to me and my brothers touches me deeply and I will never forget what you did for Anton. You are good people and you have each other. While Josef is away, my mother has no one. Next week, I would like to go home."

5

One hour of right down love is worth an age of dully living on

— Aphra Behn, *The Rover*

Mar 1917

It was not the first time a woman had broken Bastian's heart. At the age of eight years old, Genevieve Dupin rejected him in favour of his classmate, a gangly boy whose name Bastian had eradicated from memory. Her callous gesture cut him to the quick and he swore to have nothing more to do with girls. During his first year in medical school, he wondered if that rash vow in primary school had cursed his future love life. He made female friends with ease but none showed interest in anything more than amity.

In the second year, his flirtations with a pretty waitress at the Café de la Presse were interrupted by the call to serve his country. Bastian Favre, he felt sure, was doomed to die a virgin. That was the first and last time he tried to write poetry. In the event, he learned a good deal about sex whilst in the army. Not first hand, but his fellow soldiers' anecdotal evidence opened his eyes to considerably more possibilities than thus far entertained.

In the spring of 1917, the war was not yet over, but Switzerland's neutrality was respected by both Central and Entente Powers. Fighting would surely not spill onto Swiss soil. The population rejoiced and embraced all life had to offer. Zürich was full of exciting, beautiful characters, confident in their bodies and ripe for adventure. Julius, the handsome swine, could scarcely enter a room without women flocking to him like butterflies. He was courteous and charming but always disengaged himself with urbane grace to join his friends; Bastian, Flora and the ever-loquacious Walter.

"... seen from that perspective who can argue? It is indeed an imperialist war, because the winner will divide the spoils between the capitalist warmongers, leaving the proletariat decimated. Hello, Julius. I thought I felt a draught. Must have been all those batting eyelashes."

Julius kissed Flora's cheeks, shook hands with Bastian and Walter, and sat with his legs crossed and back to the rest of the room. "Are you still spouting whatever Bolshevism you heard in Café Zähringer last night? If so, I'm surprised Flora and Bastian have not yet succumbed to narcolepsy. What are we drinking this evening?"

"Oeil de Perdrix," said Flora. "It's a finely balanced rosé I'd never encountered until yesterday, but now I'm a loyal fan. Bastian assures me it's popular in the west of Switzerland, Would you like a glass?"

"Order a beer, man," scoffed Walter. "Sipping pink wine like effete members of the bourgeoisie, what a disappointment you are."

Julius looked over his shoulder and before he could even raise a hand, a waitress rushed over with a fresh glass.

"*Danke vielmal*," he said, giving her a broad smile. The girl ducked her head, giggled and busied herself clearing a table to hide her blush.

Flora crossed her eyes for an instant. "Does your hypnotic charm also work on men? If so, please cast a spell on Walter and make him change the subject. I'd ask you to shut him up completely but that's beyond even your powers."

Julius poured a little wine into his glass, swirled, sniffed and tasted. If Bastian didn't like the man so much, he would detest him. He was intelligent, thoughtful and open to ideas, challenging their professors with exactly the right amount of polite deference so that they were willing to enter into debate. He sang with the chapel choir, knew the best restaurants, ski slopes and members-only bars, spoke French, Italian and English, and understood subjects Bastian feared, like literature, women and wine.

"It's pleasing, suitable for an *apéro*, but on the sweet side for my palate. Walter, you were opining on the moral probity of this conflict, no? Impertinent as it may be to join a conversation without context, I must remind you there are four of us at this table. Only one of our members has played any role in the war. Flora cannot be faulted for her sex." He took her hand and kissed her fingers. "My father pulled strings to secure me an administrative position, and due to your leg you were exempt from military service. How fortunate are we? For a newly impassioned Social Democrat to lecture an ex-soldier, a member of the proletariat, on how the working classes are cannon fodder for the predatory elite rings hollow, impolitic and downright rude." He forestalled any protestations by reaching across the table for Walter's beer. He drained it in three swallows and smacked his lips. "Property is theft, I believe?"

"Julius, the message I'm trying to communicate to these frivolous dilettantes is in support of people like Bastian. I'm no squeamish pacifist! I believe in armed resistance against the true enemy. The ruling classes are defenceless against the masses of united workers! When the peasants rise up against the nobles, I'm going to be on the front line, bayonet in hand and victory in my heart."

"What about your gammy leg?" asked Flora, an expression of mischief crossing her face. "Will it recover to full strength on condition it's a class conflict and definitely not a bourgeois war?"

Bastian's laughter escaped in a snort and he hailed the waitress for more drinks. The debate dragged on with waning enthusiasm as they drank another two rounds and a decision was required.

"Food!" Flora declaimed. "That raclette place is two streets away and I crave cheese. Who's coming?"

"Me!" yelled Bastian, aware he was more than a little drunk.

Julius stood up, throwing some coins on the table. "Not tonight. I plan to attend one of these political meetings. That Russian exile is speaking and if Walter's not exaggerating the man's rhetoric, I will take much satisfaction in deflating his hubris. *Bis morn, zusammen.*"

He and Walter left the café with perfunctory goodbyes. A cool breeze wafted over Bastian's brow and he faced facts. More wine and Kirsch, with a fatty meal of cheese and potato, would wreak havoc on his digestive system. A wise man would go home to bed.

"Looks like it's you and me, my friend," said Flora, reaching into her beaded bag for her purse.

"Please, Flora, let me get the bill. In fact, I insist, since the wine was my idea."

"Very well. That's most kind of you. Although, you might like to stay on for a while. There's a fine-looking girl sitting by the window who cannot keep her eyes off you. You need do nothing more than wander over and ask her name."

"I can't." Bastian blushed more deeply than the giggly waitress. "I'm not good with women. Anyway, we should go." He fumbled in his pocket for a few francs and heaved himself to his feet.

The cool air of the night was as welcome as a soft hand on his brow. They walked in silence past closed bookstores and lively cafés until Bastian realised they were approaching the Polybahn.

"Flora, you wanted to have dinner. I'm also hungry and in need of sustenance."

She slipped her hand from the crook of his arm and faced him. "Let me feed you. Answer me one question. You say you're not good with women. Is that innocence or experience?"

Trams rattled past and street lights glittered in the waters of the Limmat. Bastian resorted to his typical dodge when he needed time to think. "How do you mean?"

Flora chuckled, guiding him to the funicular railway. "Your romantic interactions so far must have been disappointing. I'm no psychic, Bastian, but I sense you are attracted to the ladies but at the same time, you fear them. If you perceive me as intrusive, you're perfectly at liberty to ignore my pestering."

They took their seats on the Polybahn, Flora's arm linked with his. As the train whirred up the hill, he left something behind. Embarrassment, naïveté, faux-sophistication, all dumped at the bottom of the hill.

Once the other students spread out in the direction of their own dormitories, Bastian spoke.

"You're very observant, Flora. I'm a virgin. I feel as if I'm excluded from a club. Everybody is a member, from the crude to the ridiculous. My God, even Walter had a thing with that dancing girl. But not me. No. I'm on the outside. At twenty-two years old, I've never even kissed a girl. I wouldn't know how."

Flora squeezed his arm. "As every medical student understands, theory is no substitute for practice in the field."

Bastian stumbled to a halt. "I've been drinking."

"So have I. Fortunately for you, I happen to specialise in architecture. Once the foundations are laid, the only constraint is your imagination."

S o it was that he embarked on a new field of study – the heady, addictive pleasures of the flesh. His tutor was patient, alternately encouraging and demanding, insistent on good manners and tolerant of his overenthusiasm. For like a child learning a new skill, he wanted to practise all the time. Flora took him to her bed twice a week, on Wednesday evenings and Sunday mornings when she knew her landlady would be at church. Bastian craved more and thought of little else unless his brain was forced to pay attention to lectures.

Their intimacy, often erotic, sometimes sensual and occasionally tender, was limited to the bedroom. Flora rejected any display of affection in public and gave him to understand their affair was a private issue. In cafés, concert halls or a *Bierkeller*, he was just one of the gang. No matter how minute the distance between their bodies the previous night, the following day she was untouchable and remote as ever.

Hurt by her decision to attend one of Julius's choral performances one Wednesday evening, thereby depriving him of the one thing he desired most, he punished her. He avoided her on the university grounds, taking his meals in a café rather than the refectory, choosing the cinema with the chaps from his hall instead of drinks with his friends. On Saturday, he planned to relent and offer her an olive branch, because he had no intention of missing out on Sunday morning sex. He meant to declare his love, stating his wish to steer their romance onto the public stage. He would be firm. As a young couple in love, it was only natural to spend less time with Walter and Julius in favour of assignations *à deux*. They would be the subject of gossip, certainly, but didn't young people fall in love all the time?

He rehearsed various speeches as he walked from Paradeplatz across Bahnhofstrasse, clutching a Sprüngli box he could ill afford. It would be worth the expense to prove his sincerity. Only a man in love would give his sweetheart the most expensive chocolates in the city. *Flora, I can no longer suppress my innermost feelings.* Züghusplatz was crowded with couples sitting outside the cafés or strolling hand in hand over the square. Fewer than half wore wedding rings. *You are everything I want in a woman. You occupy my thoughts night and day.* A breeze carrying scents of melted cheese reminded him of the night they first made love, when she seduced him, fed him cheese, gherkins and day-old bread, then seduced him again. *Inexperienced in some areas, yes, but never naïve. I know what I want.* He cut through a side street to Münsterhof, where the street lights on the wet cobblestones gave Bastian the impression he was walking through an artwork. *I want to hold your hand, kiss you, clasp my arm around your waist and announce to the world with the greatest of pride, 'She is mine!'* On passing Fraumünster, he averted his guilty gaze, having attended not a single church service since he took up with Flora.

April was a magician, taking citizens for fools by luring them outside with warm winds and blue skies, only to hurl a hailstorm at their heads. Preoccupied with his own grandiloquence, Bastian failed to note the turbulent clouds until needle-sharp sleet hit his cheeks. He debated running across the bridge and catching a tram a few stops, but didn't dare risk soaking his precious box of chocolates. He doubled back, sheltering under the eaves of the church and saw the lights of a café he'd never noticed before. Tucked in the corner of the square, as if it were hiding, stood Café de la Presse. His expression softened. A long time ago, in another city, in a previous life, he had courted a pretty girl in another Café de la Presse. It was a sign.

He tucked the box under his jacket and ran across the cobblestones towards the tiny bar. Prices were extortionate this side of the river, so he would drink an espresso, a beer at most, and leave when winter's final blast blew out. He brushed the icy residue from his shoulders, knocked his hat against the wall and reached for the door handle.

When one is in love, heightened awareness causes the object of one's affection to appear everywhere. Only to be dismissed as plainer, taller, thinner, more angular or with an entirely different gait. Flora was hard to mistake. One of the most diminutive women of his acquaintance, she had a towering presence. Her green-ribboned bonnet framed the face of an imp with a pointed chin, unruly hair, freckled cheeks she refused to powder, and wide grey eyes. Nobody looked like Flora. Therefore the woman sitting at the rear of the room, her gaze locked on her companion's, her hands clasped in his, could be no other than the woman he loved.

He stepped away from the door, his back pressed to the wall, and his foot sank into a puddle. Water seeped through the worn leather, soaking his sock. His breath came hard and ragged. She was indeed a dilettante! Who was his challenger? *Not Julius, please not Julius*, or he would lose his two closest friends in one fell swoop.

Replacing his hat low over his eyes, he leaned forward to peer through the windows fogged with condensation. The man was neither of his friends nor anyone else he recognised. Grey hair, a stiff collar and a familiar impertinence manifested by his fingers touching her cheek, chin and lip, even a caress of her knee. This was no avuncular protector but a bird of prey circling a blackbird.

"*Entschuldigung?*"

Bastian jumped and made way for three young apprentices, filled with self-importance. He feigned a mature detachment but ducked out of the light lest Flora and her beau should tear their gazes from each other. Sleet became icy rain as he jogged along Limmatquai, his jacket, hat and cardboard box growing wetter each step. He was almost at the Polybahn when someone stepped into his path.

"Are you avoiding me as well? Or can I invite you to a little bar where we are guaranteed to meet no one of our acquaintance?"

"Julius!" At the very sight of the man, order was restored. "Yes, I'd like that very much."

Over a glass of port, Bastian shared his grief and his chocolates. Julius pronounced the truffles as excellent and the emotional trough as pure invention.

"Betrayal, *mon brave*, is when good faith becomes bad. Two people come to an understanding, whether professional or personal. One party contravenes agreed terms. In such circumstances, the injured party can indeed claim betrayal. I wonder, indelicate as this may seem, if our mutual friend gave you any assurance the arrangement would continue at your convenience?"

"Julius, how can you ask that? Look at these chocolates! These were intended as a gesture to prove my devotion. I place my heart and soul at that woman's feet yet she toys with them like a cat with a shrew."

"I think I shall try a caramel. Did you know Walter has once again changed his metier? This week he wants to become a poet, influenced by that Irishman. It's not a success, I'm afraid. His early writings are derivative and dull. Moreover, he's handicapped by the inescapable fact he comes from Dietikon, not Dublin. I should advise him to spend more time with you, listening to your flights of fancy and colourful turns of phrase. Hmm, the caramels are good, but can't hold a candle to the truffles."

Bastian's foot was wet, his heart sore and he preferred wine to port, but had no idea of the prices in such a chic establishment. He took another sip from the tiny glass and pushed it away. "I'm a plebeian, unsophisticated and awkward. No wonder she prefers an older man."

"Bastian, my friend, my partner in discovery, you should appreciate that our happiness is our own responsibility. Blaming *Die Blume* for your misplaced affection is unreasonable and I believe you are sensible to that. She taught you all you need to know. Go forth and share your knowledge, or at least your chocolates, with the world!"

"Only a man blessed with your looks and charm would assume it's that easy. Zürich is full of cosmopolitan characters with whom I just can't compete. Perhaps I'd have better luck in the mountains."

Rather than laughing at Bastian's lugubrious tones, Julius cupped his chin and stared into the fireplace, his expression pensive. "By the mountains, I assume you mean the Alps of Valais, where you can speak your mother tongue?"

"The issue of language vexes me no longer. In truth, I'm a less articulate speaker in Swiss German than in French, but for all practical purposes, I'm at ease with both. My curiosity is piqued by the reason for your question."

"And rightly so. Our next and final year means all medical practitioners-to-be must undertake an apprenticeship, in a position secured by ourselves. Naturally this onerous obligation has sent every student into a frenzy of applications or judicious use of parental influence." On seeing Bastian's look of alarm, he shook his head with a chuckle. "At least those students not wholly possessed by lust, that is. Am I wrong in my assumption that you have not a single offer of an assistant role beginning after the summer? No, I thought not. Since the rain has stopped, let's pay our bill and take the air. An idea is germinating and I'm prepared to share it with no one but you."

Appenzell Ausserrhoden. Even the name seemed impenetrable. Nevertheless, he was thankful. Whereas many of his fellow trainees were fighting over the few remaining options of field work in the cities of Zürich, Luzern or Basel, Bastian had landed a plum position without lifting a finger. At the hospital of Herisau, 70 kilometres east of Zürich and out in the country, he would assist the chief physician. It was hardly fair, as many of his classmates had made Herculean efforts to secure a similar role, yet Bastian was unable to summon a guilty conscience. Gratitude, undoubtedly, but guilt, no. He leaned against the window of the train and watched the suburbs give way to countryside.

A gentleman never questions his luck. Only Julius could say something of that ilk. His cup overflowed while others bickered over the dregs. When a person with an abundance of good fortune was willing to share, no one but an idiot would refuse. Bastian might be many things, but he was no idiot. The nub of the issue concerned specialisation. Julius already knew in which field of medicine he wished to focus his considerable ability: ophthalmology, the study of the eye. Therefore it was unthinkable to squander his time trying out everything from podiatry to paediatrics. The University Hospital of Zürich was the obvious choice. The man could even reside in his own campus rooms.

Where Bastian would reside was yet to be seen. Of the many offers Julius had received, the one he passed on to Bastian was the least specific. The post of Assistant to the Chief Physician required a capable doctor competent in both general practice and administration. Accommodation would be provided along with a small stipend to cover expenses.

Bastian thought of Julius lounging on his sofa, sipping champagne, and laughed with genuine admiration. He was going to miss his friend. He would also miss Flora, now they had overcome the redefinition of their association. He would even miss Walter. The thought of the latter cast a shadow over his good humour and he paused in his pleasant reflections to consider why. The disparaging slur Walter wielded most often, other than 'bourgeois', was the word 'dilettante'. By which he meant a person who dabbled without commitment between professions, lovers or areas of study. The irony was that of everyone in their acquaintance, no one merited the term more deservedly than Walter himself.

Am I a dilettante? Bastian examined his own situation with clear eyes and found good reasons to agree. Instructed to leave Fribourg and resume his studies in Zürich, he obeyed orders without demur, as if he had no will of his own. In his lectures, social life and career path, he reacted, responding to stronger personalities. Rare was the occasion he voluntarily proposed a scheme. He fitted in, as a soldier, as a student and as a sexual partner, because he did as he was told. If ever there was a time in one's life to act, it was now, his first foray into the professional world.

The small town of Herisau was a blank slate on which Bastian Favre could make his mark. He was a man of the world, equally at home in military bunker or university hall, broad of mind and knowledge. Here was where he would mature and ripen, developing a mind of his own.

.   .   .

"Herr Doctor? Your new assistant, Herr Favre." The unsmiling nurse indicated Bastian should enter and stalked off down the corridor.

Eggenberger's brows rose, creating a relief map on his forehead. His appearance was youthful, his hair slick with oil, his moustache and beard neatly trimmed. He stood to attention and extended a hand.

"Herr Favre. What great good luck for our practice! A fresh scientific mind and a French speaker to boot. The timing is most fortuitous. Young man, you are my scout, my mountain guide, my expert in the field. My intention is to instruct you in your most urgent mission. Tell me, has the maid unpacked your trunk? You shall need formal attire this evening as you are invited to dine with my wife and family, along with some notables of the region. I confess I was disappointed that Julius chose Zürich over his local canton, but his choice of substitute happens to meet everyone's needs. Sit, sit. My duties cannot be ignored, and thus I beg your patience for every occasion I am called away. Interruptions notwithstanding, we embark on a voyage of discovery. What is your particular interest? What did they teach you at UZH?"

Bastian floundered for an answer. "I am yet to settle on a specialisation, sir. At university, I learned a little about everything."

Eggenberger clapped his palms together. "As it should be. Everything comes at the right time. Our time is today. Tell me, are you willing to travel on my behalf? There are some interesting experiments in other areas of the country I would like to know more about. I believe they can benefit all the people of Appenzell yet I am chained to my practice. You, on the other hand, can roam freely, seeking out knowledge and bringing it home to Herisau."

"I would be most amenable to travelling and learning more during my year here, sir."

"As I said, this is great good luck and I feel certain ..."

The nurse rapped on the surgery door.

"*Ich komme gleich!*" Eggenberger called and dropped his voice. "Oh dear, she's already in a bad mood. I can tell by the curt way she raps. A good woman, really, even if she is from Urnäsch. Just remember, her bark is worse than her bite. You are most welcome here, Herr Favre, and I look forward to our working together."

6

The Swiss could have been the most revolutionary of all because almost everybody has a gun at home.

— Vladimir Ilyich Ulyanov

DRAMATIC SCENES AT ZÜRICH MAIN STATION
Text by Walter Brunn

Zürich, 9 April 1917

Russian exile Vladimir Ilyich Ulyanov (nom de guerre Lenin), orator, agitator and political organiser of the European left wing, today boarded a train in Zürich Hauptbahnhof, the first step on a journey back to his homeland.

A party of thirty émigrés, including Lenin's wife Nadezhda Krupskaya, is guaranteed passage from Switzerland, through Germany, Sweden and Finland with the eventual destination of

Petrograd. Since the recent deposition of Czar Nicholas II, the Russian people are in open revolt. Control of the country is temporarily in the hands of the Soviet provisional government, largely comprised of the bourgeoisie, a state of affairs which has enraged the exiled radicals.

On return to his homeland, Ulyanov/Lenin intends to establish a 'dictatorship of the proletariat'. In other words, he plans to oversee a Russian revolution, an aim long held by the political firebrand. "Attention must be devoted *principally to raising* the workers to the level of revolutionaries. It is not at all our task to *descend* to the level of the working masses," he writes in a pamphlet published in 1902 entitled *What Is To Be Done?*

Police attended Zürich Hauptbahnhof after a crowd of over one hundred angry Russian sympathisers gathered to hurl insults at the departing exiles, calling them 'traitors, spies and provocateurs', claiming the transport was funded by the Kaiser. Since Russia and Germany are at war, some commentators cast doubt upon such an accusation, whilst others believe unleashing a disruptive influence into Petrograd's volatile situation will benefit its enemy.

One source close to the transport organisers said, "The Entente Powers have denied safe passage for revolutionary groups. Therefore, Lenin and his comrades must travel through territory controlled by the Central Powers. The unmistakeable conclusion one must draw is that Germany hopes the group will achieve their stated aims: Russia's withdrawal from the war."

The party's transportation and its route is chiefly due to the diplomatic efforts of Swiss Social Democrats Robert Grimm and Fritz Platten, the latter a close colleague of Lenin. These two men achieved the impossible feat of negotiating safe passage through German territory. Expert opinion, supported by Lenin's own missive to his Swiss supporters, indicates the vocal revolutionary sees his role as implementing a well-prepared plan. In his view, the situation in Russia as the first stage of an inevitable Europe-wide shift of power to the people.

The Marxist agitator, once exiled to Siberia for three years and a previous resident in European cities such as Prague, London and Bern, has been a resident of Zürich since 21 February 1916. Hard-working and productive, he spent many hours in the Zentralbibliothek, writing treatises and tracts exhorting the overthrow of governments. His current opus *Imperialism: the highest stage of capitalism* may well be ahead of its time.

Yet even amongst the left wing, he drew criticism from certain quarters for his uncompromising stance. At the infamous 1915 Zimmerwald peace conference, he and Leon Trotsky were dissatisfied with the final manifesto. The three main tenets: a peace without annexations, a peace without war contributions, and the self-determination of people, did not go far enough, in their opinion. They argued forcefully for replacing war between nations with an armed class struggle. Unsurprisingly, they were outvoted by the other socialist attendees.

Time has done little to dilute the Bolshevik rhetoric. On the train step with hat in hand, Lenin had a few words of farewell to Zürich. He expressed his disappointment at the fractured character of the Swiss left wing in the harshest terms, calling them 'social pacifists'. He quoted its reluctance to overthrow the government despite a sincere and radical group agitating for true socialism, while acknowledging its true core comprised fewer than twenty individuals.

With one final flourish, he called out to a friend, "Either we'll be swinging from the gallows in three months or we shall be in power!"

Railway personnel sealed the train as a security measure and the locomotive departed for the north. The journey could take weeks by rail over land, boat across the Baltic Sea and a convoluted path over Finland. All this through hostile territory towards an uncertain welcome.

What becomes of the Swiss radical left remains to be seen, but Lenin returns to his country with every intention of inciting another war. In this case, not disputing borders, but claiming ultimate power. The revolution he demands is in the balance.

7

My life closed twice before its close;
If Immortality unveil
A third event to me,
So huge, so hopeless to conceive,
As these that twice befell.
Parting is all we know of heaven,
And all we need of hell.

— Emily Dickinson

March 1918

The farm was a miserable place to be in the early months of 1918. Silent, dark and bitterly cold, the house was less a home than a tomb. Loss loomed larger than presence. Two deaths, that of Anton over a year ago and the baby Clothilde was carrying mid-February, left the two women with no common language to express their pain. Two absences, those of Henri and Josef, gave the farm a fallow air, with women doing one of the things women do best: waiting.

School began in January, enabling Seraphine to escape for a large part of the day. Her relief was mixed with guilt and determination. If she stayed home, her mother would do nothing but stare into the fire. Without her daughter, she was forced to feed and milk the goats, collect wood and maintain their home. One morning when collecting the eggs, Seraphine found the special salt she had forgotten all about. As a child, she had sometimes hurt or even killed creatures all because she wanted to help. The chick she believed was too weak to peck out of its shell died after her well-meaning assistance. The cat stuck in the tree ended up with a broken tail after she climbed up to 'rescue' it. But those instances were nothing compared to her ignorant and arrogant interference in her brother's diet, resulting in his early death. She scattered the salt across the snow and prayed to Anton for forgiveness.

Late February, some post arrived, the first in two months. The parcel was from Tante Margot. It contained a brand-new book for Seraphine and a long and enthusiastic account of Henri's life in the Bern Boys' Home. Clothilde read the letter once, handed it to Seraphine and said nothing more. On the second, the sender's address indicated Josef was in Graubünden, but that was all Seraphine could deduce as her mother tucked the letter into her apron without reading a word. The third was an official invitation. Dr Bayard from the St. Niklaus practice wished to address all residents on the subject of the valley's health. He intended to propose a potential treatment for the goitre via the consumption of iodised salt.

The subject caused a spasm of guilt in Seraphine. It was treated salt that killed Anton. But if the doctor recommended it, perhaps it was not poisonous. Her introversion went unnoticed because Clothilde dismissed the entire notion as fantasy.

"Salt?" scoffed Clothilde. "You think this is something new? Young people always know best, of course. That interfering witch Alice from Dijon sent me this 'magical' salt a year ago! The French cure, she said, the way to treat your goitres. I threw it away and forgot about it. An insult! What the devil would she know about raising children?" The kitchen fell silent, Seraphine's frustration building. Her mother took her yarn to the bench at the front door, Barry at her heels.

Seraphine followed and sat beside her in the weak winter sunshine. She gazed across the valley, recalling her furtive experiments with the contents of the hessian sack. Obviously she didn't know best, so what better reason to listen to the experts?

"Maman, that is why we should go and hear what he has to say. The doctor thinks he can help people like us. The meeting is to address what happened to Henri, Anton and all the others. All they ask is to take the properly treated salt. It is supposed to help the swellings and ... other problems. Nothing like an operation or medication, just salt."

"He'll convince the villagers, of course he will. Sheep, the whole stupid lot of them, all following whatever rumour whispers through the grass, not once using their heads. Well, I'm not going and neither are you."

Barry's tail beat once as Seraphine stroked his black and ginger ears.

"Doctors do not spread rumours. They want to help our people by using science. If the salt can reduce this," she pointed at her bulbous throat, "I want to learn how and why. You should care about what they have to say for the same reasons." She was about to invoke the latest failed pregnancy but held her tongue.

Clothilde threw down her knitting. "Listen to me, you head-strong little madam, go to the meeting if you think it is that important. Whatever idiocy they convince you to believe, you can test it yourself and leave me out of it. Those deluded medics would have us all poisoned in the name of research. Nothing can cure boys like Henri or Anton, no more than those physicians' hocus-pocus can reduce our lumps. This is our burden. The sooner you learn to live with it, the better for us all. How did I bear such a *naïf*?"

They said no more on the topic at home, although school was buzzing with third- or fourth-hand accounts of what the doctor would say and who would be chosen as his test specimens. The day of the meeting, Seraphine pulled on her boots, wrapped a scarf around her neck and heaved on her rucksack. Barry came at her whistle.

"You are sure you don't mind me taking the dog?"

"If you insist on staying on after school to hear this foolishness, you need him to make sure you come safely home. No dallying, just get on the bus as soon as it's over."

"Thank you. Don't worry, I am not callow and will not be browbeaten. All I want is to learn. *Bonne journée,* Maman."

Clothilde's needles clattered, her face glowing pink in the morning light. "Be careful, Seraphine, you are so young and trusting. Take everything with a pinch of salt."

"A pinch of salt?" Seraphine stopped and looked over her shoulder.

Clothilde screwed up her face in embarrassment. "You know what I mean." A rare chuckle echoed in her chest. "Take good care, *ma chérie*. I need you."

With twenty minutes before the biggest event since *Fasnacht*, Seraphine walked through the narrow streets to the Hotel Lochmatter, where the medical practice was located. She didn't dare go inside, but stopped to read the poster pinned to the board outside. One of the mountain guides came out of the door, placing his wide hat on his head to shadow his eyes.

"*Hoi, Meitli*," he said, his tone soft. These men impressed and intimidated everyone in the region with their superhuman achievements, so it was all Seraphine could manage to bob her head in acknowledgement. Barry wagged his tail.

"You're coming to the meeting? Clever girl. The doctor wants to help the valley because he is one of us. *Viel Vergnügen*." With that, he strode off in the direction of the train station.

Enjoy yourself? Not likely at a lecture from the doctor. The other thing the man said echoed in her ears. *He is one of us.* Yes, he lived among them, ate the same food, absorbed the sunshine and blue skies, or sheltered from the wind and snow just like everyone else. If the right amount of salt could help a single person, Seraphine had to learn how.

The village hall was too small to house all the people from various communities, so everyone crowded into the church, amid much muttering about time-wasting nonsense. Only Dr Bayard could have persuaded so many villagers to come out on a chilly spring evening. His practice had provided succour to every single family, or failing that, someone close. The atmosphere was uncertain, people torn between giddy delight at seeing their friends and neighbours and practised cynicism for fear of disappointment. When the doctor arrived with his wife, the jocular conversation hushed to respectful whispers.

Dr Bayard, a lean, wiry man, clean-shaven with a high fore-head and receding hairline, greeted many in the audience by name. His wife gave a general vague smile and allowed the priest to escort her to a chair in the nave. She was a handsome woman, as far as Seraphine could see around the edge of her hat. The moment she eased herself into the chair, facing the audience, a murmur rushed through the crowd. *Sie ist in guter Hoffnung*! There was no mistaking the careful lowering of her body, leaning heavily on the priest's arm, nor the way she folded her gloved hands over her belly. Pregnant, without a doubt.

The appropriate reaction to such a revelation was not always obvious. People sought clues as to whether to commiserate or rejoice. For instance, when Seraphine's own mother fell pregnant with Henri, it was cause for celebration. After all, was she not fortunate, a young, strong widow remarrying a decent farmer? With one healthy daughter, she was indeed blessed to conceive a second child. However, once Henri's condition became clear, her appearance in church two years later with another bulging stomach elicited more sympathetic looks than congratulations.

Frau Bayard, on the other hand, was different. The wife of a doctor, she was rich and had less to fear, particularly as she had already delivered a normal baby girl. Therefore, many of the women in the audience gave her approving nods. The doctor's wife gave a shy smile of acknowledgement and fixed her attention on her neatly laced boots, just visible beneath the hem of her skirt. Seraphine gazed at her with undisguised curiosity, marvelling at the rich colours and fabrics draped over her body. Like most of her neighbours, Seraphine wore sturdy garments in earth-tones, almost indistinguishable from the ground itself. In the candlelight of the church, Frau Bayard glowed like a precious jewel, beads on her coat reflecting purples and blues, while a brooch at her throat flashed silver every time she moved. Beneath her gloves, Seraphine guessed, must be rings set with rubies or diamonds.

Barry sat up and began kicking his back leg against his ear. The movement caused the little bell on his collar to tinkle and the room hushed, as if ordered into silence. Seraphine placed a hand on the dog's head, but the doctor was already moving toward the pulpit, taking advantage of the interruption. He cleared his throat and looked at them all through his circular glasses.

"Good evening, dear friends, and I thank you in all sincerity for attending this meeting. I will not keep you from your hearths for long. Everyone here has known me for a long time, not only as your neighbour but as your doctor, a man of medicine with an interest in the health of the Nikolai and Matterthal region. I dare venture that after many years of service in our community I have earned your trust." He paused and a chorus of grunted agreement echoed around the building.

"Thank you," he continued. "I live to serve you all. Now cast your eyes around this room."

His command resulted in confusion, all looking to one another for guidance.

"Look around this room, I say, and simply regard your friends and neighbours. Then identify any single family untouched by the afflictions which plague this valley. You know of what I speak even if you refuse to name it yourselves. My theme is this: goitre and cretinism. Can you count the unafflicted on one hand?" His voice had risen to a thunderous volume, making some cower in the pews.

His frank articulation of the burden they all carried shocked everyone into silence. It was an intrusion, an exposure, as if he had torn off their clothes. Frau Bayard did not lift her gaze from the ground.

The doctor's voice softened. "To tend to your soul, you place your faith in the priest, Pater Gratteau. To tend to your bodies and those of your children, you place your trust in me. Tonight, I ask you to take one step further. If some stranger rode into the village and promised a cure to your ills, you would be right to mistrust him. I am no stranger and promise no panacea. In fact, I promise nothing but an experiment which may or may not change our lives.

"There has been much discussion regarding the cause of these unfortunate conditions, ranging from heredity to poor hygiene. My colleagues and I, men of science from Europe and beyond, reject such assumptions, not least because they lay the blame at the feet of the ailing. We have learned the root cause of such defects is dietary. Here in this Alpine valley it would be easy to assume we are alone in our suffering. Not so, my friends, not so. Our French brothers and sisters report that entire regions demonstrate similar symptoms, as do remote areas of Austria and even as far as the Americas. The unifying link is a lack of iodine."

A rush of whispers and comments swelled and subsided, unpredictable like the river when the waterfalls thawed.

"Iodine is a key to our bodily function. A deficit forces the thyroid gland to swell and thicken, in an attempt to retain what little is available, creating a goitre. A woman with child cannot provide her unborn infant with sufficient nutrients to develop normally, hence the preponderance of underdevelopment in our community. One thing I need you to understand. None of this is your fault. None of it. You have made no errors of judgement or lapses in care. Not one of you is to blame. If anything, it is my profession deserving of censure."

Whispers ran through the congregation, peppered with a few groans. Yet no one challenged the medical man.

"News may have reached you of failed experiments due to incorrect dosages, but those are outdated and no longer a matter of concern. My proposition is this: I will treat half a dozen families for no longer than six months with carefully measured doses of iodised salt. There is no obligation to participate, but those who do will be recorded and examined on a regular basis, forming the bedrock of a scientific study which could benefit not only this valley, but the entire country of Switzerland."

His enthusiasm took effect and a spontaneous round of

agreement made Frau Bayard lift her head for the first time. The feather in her hat caught the doctor's attention and his face softened as he met his wife's eyes.

"To demonstrate my conviction, my wife is also committed to taking iodised salt throughout the duration of her pregnancy. I thank you for your attention and will release you to discuss and think about what I propose. Those interested in participating may apply in person at my practice in St. Niklaus. I wish you a good evening and a safe return to your homes."

8

Because your own strength is unequal to the task,
do not assume that it is beyond the powers of man;
but if anything is within the powers and province of man,
believe that it is within your own compass also.

— Marcus Aurelius, *Meditations*

June 1918

It took less than one calendar month for Bastian to awaken to the fact he was appreciably happier in the small town of Herisau than he had ever been in the city of Zürich. Each morning he awoke and opened the window of his room, filling his lungs with good clean air and anticipating the day ahead. He was never a minute late for work and often stayed late to help with administration. Dr Eggenberger allowed him to treat patients under the supervision of the senior nurse, Frau Neff. He was right to say her bark was worse than her bite. That said, her bark was truly terrifying.

In Herisau, doctors were men of the people, an example set by Eggenberger himself. No distance existed between the medic and his patient. Everyone was worthy of respect, from the farmhand to the surgeon. After a matter of weeks, people greeted Bastian by name when passing in the street. The greengrocer saved him some of his favourite apples when in danger of selling out. Two woodsmen invited him to sit at their table one Friday evening in a crowded restaurant. He was not a faceless greenhorn amid so many others, but a man worthy of regard. At the weekends, he studied, sometimes alone, sometimes with Eggenberger, and always went to church on Sundays.

Ten months passed in what seemed like a heartbeat. When the time came for him to return to Zürich for his final exams, he found himself reluctant to leave, but did so in the knowledge he had a position waiting for him on his return. Eggenberger was satisfied with his young assistant and had asked him to join his staff permanently. Bastian accepted without a second thought.

The first thing he did on arrival in Zürich was to buy a good quality wine and seek out Julius. If anything, his friend was more assured than ever, every inch the man about town. He welcomed Bastian with great enthusiasm and immediately reached for a corkscrew.

"I have mentioned nothing of your arrival to Flora and Walter, selfishly claiming you for myself this afternoon. However, we had plans to dine tonight at a cheap and nasty place close to Rosenhof. I am sorry to inform you Walter's infatuation with the sound of his own voice has developed into a full-blown love affair. Even more so since he has no exams, he can light his candle every night of the week while the rest of us must burn the midnight oil. Have you eaten? I can rustle up some dried meat and pickles."

"Frau Eggenberger packed a picnic for the journey, thank you. She sends you friendly greetings. Why has Walter no exams? And how is Flora?" He hitched up his trousers and sat at the open window, with its view over the city and up to Uetliberg.

"Our friend is no longer a student. Walter Brunn works as a freelance journalist, exercising his natural aptitude as a gossip and earning just enough to keep him in beer. For the first time in our acquaintance, I can see him sticking at something. Flora is an entirely different proposition. Single-minded as always, the woman intends to become Europe's best-known female architect. As far as I know, she has turned down two proposals of marriage. Therefore, unless she falls pregnant, and she's too clever for that, she will blaze a trail for all womankind. Tell me about your banishment to the north. *Prost*! This is rather young, but with a little air, it will develop."

"*Prost*!" They sipped from Art Deco glasses with green stems, drinking in one another's presence as much as the grape. "Hmm, not bad for something I grabbed from a shelf in a hurry. My sojourn in Herisau was hardly a banishment. Truth be told, I was loath to leave and am eager to return. A full-time job awaits me, presuming I pass my final examinations. I owe you the most sincere thanks for introducing me to Dr Eggenberger. To benefit from a mind both brilliant and kind is more than I might have hoped."

"Good gracious!" Julius exclaimed. "You're going back to Herisau? Three months in a backwater would bore me to death, but I see you and I are cut from quite different cloth."

Previously, with all the insecurities attached to comparisons with his peers, Bastian might have read a similar comment as a slight. No longer. "We are indeed. You thrive in this environment and I admire you for that. My sense of worth is far greater in a small town. That speaks to my ego as much as Zürich does to yours. Nevertheless, the principles we share rest on the same fundament. Our life's work is to improve the lives of others. For my part, I can conceive of no better time or place to be than at this moment in Herisau with the visionary mind of Dr Eggenberger."

Julius stared, a half-smile playing on his lips. "In that case, *chapeau*, my friend! To find your true vocation is something to celebrate. I regret the necessity of distance, as your companionship is a source of unfailing pleasure to me and I've missed your good sense. But let us toast, Herr Doctor Favre of Herisau!"

Bastian joined in, with a qualm regarding his lack of humility. He was confident he would gain his medical qualification, but prayed he was not tempting fate. "If I do become Herr Doctor Favre, my first professional position will be in the Alps, not Herisau. One of Eggenberger's colleagues, Dr Bayard of St. Niklaus in the Matterthal valley, is experimenting with a cure for the blight of goitre."

Julius looked blank, his eyes roaming over the contours of distant mountains.

"Not a subject to set hearts beating, I recognise that, but an important step forward in medical science," Bastian babbled. "I find it rather a thrill that a condition affecting many regions of the world could be eradicated due to the work of local Swiss doctors. Not surgeons from Bern or Geneva, but small practitioners in remote valleys."

Julius snapped his focus to Bastian, his eyes shining. "It is without a doubt a subject to set hearts beating, my modest friend. One cannot deny that the discoveries of Pasteur, Röntgen and Funk changed the international landscape of medicine. It all starts somewhere. You notice a problem, study the issue and identify cause and effect. Then under rigorous scientific methodology, you test treatments, refine, modify and report to the health commission. Bastian, you have stumbled across an enormous chance for betterment, not only for yourself, but for your countrymen. Another toast! May fortune, fortitude and friendship continue to bless us!"

. . .

B astian spent two weeks in the city, sitting theoretical tests, performing practical exams and anxiously awaiting his results. To no one's surprise, Julius surpassed all previous UZH records. Flora came third in her year, the highest ever placing for a woman in architecture. No such lofty achievements for Bastian, which did not affect him in the slightest. He passed with mediocre marks overall, but gained an exceptional rating for his final thesis on the subject of iodine deficiency, its symptoms and potential treatment. The good doctor's assessment of his final year in the field lifted him above the average. He sent a prayer of thanks to Dr Hans Eggenberger.

They celebrated with abandon, warding off the knowledge that real life was waiting in the wings. Walter joined them every night, despite having achieved no grades whatsoever.

"Meaningless values bestowed by a fossilised faculty hold no thrall for me. The only seal of approval I rate comes from the street. From real men and women whose causes I champion in the pages of a newspaper. Bastian, Julius, you consider your-selves experts on the nation's health, but I tell you this: only a journalist can take the true pulse of the people."

"Walter, you are an insufferable prig." Flora yawned. "Only a journalist has the gall to criticise his friends while drinking their champagne. Spare us your next column, for pity's sake. Unless you stump up for another bottle, take your 'street education' up a dark alley and leave us in peace."

"Well said, *La Belle Dame Sans Merci*." Julius raised his glass to hers. "She's right, my friend. Whether you respect our achievements or not, we are toasting one another's success. Take part or depart. Bastian, what say you?"

Bastian lifted his glass and raised his face to the sun. "The old adage says that a friend in need is a friend indeed. I can agree with that sentiment, as far as it goes. But a friend who cheers and revels in another's success is possibly an even greater friend. Julius, Flora and Walter, I am happier than I can say to see you blazing your trails through the world. To our futures!

Not even Walter could object to such a well-intentioned toast. But his bonhomie lasted mere seconds. "I applaud each of you. You jumped through all the hoops required by a rigid system and earned your rewards. Exemplary members of society! My point is that nothing will change for the working man."

Julius, generally louche and relaxed in posture, sat upright. "I cannot allow that to stand. Sorry, Walter, but you are completely ignorant of what scholars of medicine aim to achieve. Right in our midst, we have a man who plans to tackle this country's curse. Dr Favre, I may now address him thus, is pursuing a treatment which might cure the goitre. If his theory is correct, *everything* will change for the working man. And woman."

"It's not my theory," Bastian added. "Herr Hunziker of Adliswil was the first proponent. If you're looking for a story, Walter, I suggest you start by speaking to him."

Walter's nose twitched, like a sheepdog scenting the air.

Before he could speak, Flora kicked his ankle and turned her glass upside down. "I suggest you start by buying more champagne." While he was in conversation with a waiter, she added in English, "What a pompous ass."

B astian understood their camaraderie would never recover the ease or simplicity it enjoyed when they were undergraduates. He bade his friends farewell at the Hauptbahnhof, waving from the window of his carriage until they were no longer visible. Walter's words echoed in his ears, 'Keep in touch, especially if you have a story!' Flora waved and blew kisses, even shedding an un-Flora-like tear, because their future paths were unlikely to cross. Only Julius doffed his hat and said, '*Uf Wieder-luege*', or 'until we see each other again'. Their friendship was forged of lasting material, of that Bastian was sure. He opened the newspaper, seeing nothing of the words and relinquishing a phase of his life he would always recall as halcyon.

The journey to the little town of St. Niklaus, with changes at Bern and Visp, took nearly seven hours. It was already getting dark and cool when he heaved his trunk onto the platform, craning his neck to see the surrounding peaks. With a whistle, the steam engine lumbered on up the valley, heading for Zermatt and the foothills of the Matterhorn, leaving an eerie silence in its wake. He hired a carter to take him and his luggage to the Lochmatter Hotel. For the next few months, that address would be his residence and also his workplace since Dr Bayard's practice occupied rooms on the top floor. Afternoon sunshine lent the village a soft, golden air which rapidly evaporated the moment one entered the narrow streets below. Bastian gave an involuntary shiver as he tried to imagine winter in such a place.

Only when the carter set down his trunk on the hotel threshold did Bastian notice his leathery pouch of skin at the neck. The man's unfortunate deformity was a physiological phenomenon he had only studied in theory, so to confront it at close quarters came as a shock. He paid the fellow and wished him a good evening. The encounter was timely, acting as a jolt to his memory – the singular reason he had been sent to St. Niklaus was to prevent that very affliction.

"I am greatly beholden to Dr Eggenberger," said Otto Bayard, lifting the jug to fill their water glasses. "Not only does he loan me a fresh medical graduate to facilitate my research, but accompanies his generosity with a wheel of Appenzeller. My wife will be transported. Of all the cheeses in Switzerland, she professes to love Appenzeller the best. My palate tends to milder flavours, which means we are never in dispute over a cheese platter."

Something about the way Bayard's conversation flowed effortlessly between the mundane and the significant reminded Bastian of Julius, a man at ease wherever he found himself.

"Like you, sir, I prefer subtle to overpowering, in everything from cheese to music. As for gratitude, I count myself fortunate to have worked with Dr Eggenberger and look forward to learning a great deal from you. What can be achieved in a matter of months, I cannot say, but I will devote all my energy into your assistance."

Bayard watched him through his round black-framed glasses and Bastian had the strangest sensation of being under a microscope.

"What we can achieve in a single quarter will astound you, young man. If I am not mistaken, the possibilities are extraordinary. But documentation is vital. You are here to ensure the methodology and record-keeping are beyond rigorous. What happens in this valley between now and the spring of next year will form the basis of a letter to the Federal Health Office. By 1920, I hope to see many other villagers and medical practitioners adopting a similar approach. How do you like St. Niklaus? A far cry from Zürich, I'll warrant."

The lamp reflected on Bayard's pate. Although it was shortly after lunch, candles were essential as the practice's small windows overlooking the street admitted little daylight.

"In the few days since I arrived, I confess I have not ventured far. A city, in my limited experience, has a plethora of attractions. Nevertheless, I find myself more suited to a smaller community. Indeed, that is one of the reasons I feel quite at home in Herisau."

"A good answer. In Herisau, you likely know the people you treat. Changes you make to the lives of a small town are instantly visible. Here even more so. One family, a ten-hour hike from here, has four children, each one a cretin. Those are four hungry mouths which will never contribute to a couple already struggling to eke out a living."

Bastian recalled the sheer scale of the mountainside with little farmsteads perched on an outcrop, unable to imagine how their inhabitants survived. "Your research, sir, will help those people?"

The doctor pulled his napkin from his knees and folded it on his plate, his eyes sharp. "How exactly could it do so? Can you name one benefit of altering a dietary monoculture which might touch such a family?"

"Unless the wife becomes pregnant again, I assume not." Bastian took care over his reply. "Foetal underdevelopment happens in the womb and once the child is born, his condition is irreversible."

Bayard nodded. "I knew Hans Eggenberger would never have sent me an idealist. The goal of our intervention is to restore balance, delivering what the thyroid gland requires in order to treat the root cause. In my opinion, we can eliminate cretinism within a decade. Better still, we can eradicate the goitre in a matter of months. We will make it vanish, like magicians." He waved a hand in a theatrical gesture favoured by conjurors. "I see your doubt, Herr Favre, and respect you for it. That is why I need someone like you. You will challenge me, hold me to account and painstakingly record every dose I administer while detailing its results. Magic is sleight of hand combined with willing belief in deception. Not so with medicine. Medicine must expose its methods, combating unwilling participation and mistrust. We are scientists and therefore must prove ourselves at every step. Together, we have a mountain to climb."

I f the doctor's words had not already convinced Bastian, visual evidence of the malaise affecting large areas of the valley would have persuaded the most hardened sceptic. Unlike Eggenberger, who kept his assistant busy at the practice dealing with minor ailments, Bayard believed in field work. With nothing more than his medical kit and a mule, Bastian trekked along rough trails visiting tiny communities to provide basic healthcare. In many of these remote hamlets, more than half the inhabitants had severe goitres and a significant proportion of the children were mentally impaired. In Bastian's view, a country which boasted feats of engineering like the Simplon tunnel or the Zermatt railway should be ashamed of failing its people in the sphere of health.

He threw his loyalty behind Bayard, working long hours by candlelight to register detailed measurements, accurate dosage, and significant changes in physiology, and searching for alternative explanations when a child's throat shrank to normality after mere weeks. After all, had not the doctor stated the role of an assistant should include challenging every assumption?

The 1st of August was Swiss National Day, marking two months into Bastian's tenure at St. Niklaus. The village celebrated in style, with a bonfire, flags draped between trees, lanterns, sausages, beer and music. The school became a *Bierkeller* and the yard a dance floor, where children squealed and chased one another, giddy with the break from routine. Dr Bayard gave his practice staff the afternoon off and wished them happy festivities. Unused to more than an hour of leisure, Bastian sat at his desk to catch up with correspondence, until the lure of sunlight and promise of society drew him outside, aimless yet content. He bought a beer and sat on a bench, watching a succession of musicians perform folk songs with varying degrees of talent. Dr Bayard strolled around the village stalls with his wife, dallying for a purchase here or a conversation there. How embedded the man appeared. As fundamental to society as the priest, Pater Gratteau, and a great deal more effective, to Bastian's mind.

The baker's wife clapped him on the back and demanded he dance with one of the many eligible young ladies. It was a long while since he had taken to the floor, as public dancing had been forbidden in the cantons of Appenzell and St. Gallen since the outbreak of the war. Nevertheless, he did his best, stomping up and down with half a dozen forgettable faces, finally pleading thirst and hunger. He drank another beer and ate a cervelat with mustard and crusty bread, leaning against the doorway of the school.

"Good evening, Herr Doctor Favre. How do our rural revelries compare to those of the city?" Frau Bayard tilted her face to his, with an innocent smile. "Am I too late to add myself to your dance card?"

By now he knew the lady well enough to respond with his own teasing. "Madame, I would enjoy nothing more than trampling on your dainty boots with my clumsy great hooves. However, my mother always told me it was bad for the digestion to exert oneself immediately after eating. As for city revelries, there's always something to celebrate. I prefer the atmosphere here because it feels like something special."

"You and my husband have so much in common. Of all the places he has lived or visited, whether Switzerland, Germany, Ireland or the Far East, he swears he is happiest here. Since we cannot dance, shall we stroll? My husband has returned to his work and I have an afternoon to myself. I should like to fill it with nothing more than idle entertainment and serious conversation."

He held out an arm and she rested a hand in the crook of his elbow. "Your husband is a fortunate man with much to envy. Why would he desire to be anywhere else than by your side?"

"Small wonder the young ladies were queuing for a dance, you silver-tongued charmer. Did anyone in particular make an impression?"

He hesitated, searching for a way to express his indifference without causing offence.

She guided him away from the noise of the band. "Or perhaps you left your heart in the city? Is a pretty girl with sad grey eyes pining by the lake of Zürich?"

Bastian forced a laugh, covering his embarrassment. "If there is, she is not pining for me. No, I refuse to be derailed by pretty eyes or feminine wiles. My passion is for medicine and science." He continued before she opened her mouth to reply. "Am I imposing my own perceptions or is there some wistfulness in your tone when you say Dr Bayard is happiest here? For me, it is no leap of imagination to picture you in a fashionable *quartier* of Paris, taking tea at Ladurée."

She gave a little laugh and a sigh. "We can but dream, especially now. Tell me, do you think the end of the war will be hastened or delayed by the ghastly events in Russia? I pray it is the former. You were called to serve, I understand, which means your assessment of the situation is better informed than the gossipy clientele of the *Metzgerei*."

Contrary to his earlier assertion, Bastian did take an interest in more than medicine and science. Each evening after his meal, he read the newspaper, scrutinising military details and questioning political assumptions. It was his duty to remain informed, even if that information was contradictory and confusing. On many an occasion he longed for the company of Julius, who unerringly punctured blatant propaganda.

"The butcher's customers may well have a broader perspective, Frau Bayard. My short turns of duty in military service deliberately reduced my capability of assessing the war. A soldier's role is operational. We perform our own small tasks, trusting our generals with tactical manoeuvres supporting a strategy. We obey orders without question, otherwise moral, practical or selfish dilemmas would paralyse us into inaction. I'd rather die fighting in a trench than crippled by doubt in a bland bureau. To make a pronouncement on the role of any country's role in this conflict would be rank ignorance.

"In contrast, launching an attack on a scientific front is both strategic and direct action. One devises a plan to outwit the enemy, tests its efficiency and walks onto the battlefield armed with the most accurate weapons known to man. Dr Bayard and Dr Eggenberger stand on the front line. Fighting beside them is an honour."

Frau Bayard stepped away to regard him with a mixture of admiration and amusement. He blushed, recognising a touch of Walter's verbosity in his declamation. She applauded and caught his arm once more.

"Bastian Favre, I find you most intriguing company. Look, the schoolchildren are in charge of the Weisshornstube this evening. We should patronise the establishment and encourage their enterprise, don't you think?"

He allowed her to guide him up the steps and into the dark and smoky little room. As she said, the servers were between the ages of fourteen to sixteen and welcomed them with giddy politesse. The difference to the usual apathetic reception made him smile.

"What will you have, Bastian? For my part, I will drink a wine and sample a slice of *Cholera*."

"An elegant pairing befits a lady like yourself. My choice is sausage and beer, perhaps not as sophisticated a combination but equally true to character."

A young girl came to take their order, greeting them politely.

"Good evening, Seraphine," said Frau Bayard. "Is the evening a success so far?"

"I think so," the girl answered, with a shy smile. "We made a few mistakes at first, but now everything runs like a Swiss clock."

"Well done to you all! I would like a piece of *Cholera* and a small glass of Dôle. Herr Favre wants beer and a Bratwurst."

"What size of beer would you like, sir? We have small or large."

Bastian looked up at her face. She was a pretty little creature with striking blue eyes, rather incongruously dressed in a high-necked matronly blouse, most likely borrowed for the occasion.

"Small is safest, I think. Thank you."

She bobbed her head and went behind the bar.

Frau Bayard continued. "As I was saying, your conversation is a tonic. Like my husband, you do not talk down to women, instead treating everyone with respect and crediting them with intelligence. It is an uncommon trait."

"In an all-female household, I had no choice. My mother raised me and my four older sisters on her own for the most part, as my father travelled a great deal for business. If I ever attempted to claim superiority based on my sex, she soon slapped me down."

Frau Bayard laughed, her expression one of genuine delight. "Then we shall toast your mother, for raising a well-mannered young man. You are a credit to her."

The waitress approached, her concentration on the tray she carried. She rested it on the table with some relief. "A glass of wine, a small beer, one slice of homemade *Cholera* and a cervelat with a bread roll for the gentleman. Oh!" Her face flushed pink.

"You wanted a Bratwurst. I'm so sorry, I will change it immediately."

"That's not necessary. A sausage is a sausage. But I would be very grateful if you could bring me some mustard."

"Are you sure, sir?"

"Absolutely. What was your name again?"

"Seraphine, Herr Doctor."

He smiled. "Thank you, Seraphine. My compliments. You and your colleagues are doing a very good job."

She bobbed her head and hurried to get the mustard.

"All these poor girls of St. Niklaus will soon be hopelessly smitten with the handsome, charming young doctor. So let us raise our glasses and toast your mother. To Madame Favre and her achievements!"

"To Madame Favre!" Bastian echoed, imagining his mother's dismissive shake of her head at such nonsense while trying to hide her smile.

9

EIGHT DAYS IN NOVEMBER
Text by Walter Brunn

November 1918

The working class of Switzerland has borne the brunt of
wartime deprivation. Conscripted and paid far less than
their wages, while prices of bread and milk doubled, workers
live a miserable existence. Poverty is rife, hunger constant and
the resentment of war profiteering by businesses and farmers
has fermented to boiling point. When even bank employees
walk out in protest, as they did at the beginning of October,
trouble is brewing.

On top of all this, the government proposes the introduction
of compulsory civil service, a move seen by many as overstep-
ping its powers. Unions and trade organisations have appealed
to the Swiss Social Democrats (SP) to organise the might of the
workforce. The Oltener Aktionskomitee (OAK), an executive
committee representing a loose coalition of unions and the left

wing, is prepared for exactly such circumstances. Leading socialist lights include Robert Grimm, Friedrich Schneider and the only female on the committee, Rosa Bloch.

The combination of a disaffected workforce, well-organised political left and an overbearing government fearful of a repetition of civil unrest in Germany or Russia is to bring Switzerland perilously close to civil war.

Timeline of key events

Thursday 7 November 1918

Troops marched into Zürich at the order of the government, ostensibly with the aim of maintaining order. The fuse was lit, inflaming tensions and giving rise to accusations of dictatorial repression. The members of OAK implemented its plan by calling for a one-day protest strike in nineteen cities.

Saturday 9 November 1918

Not all the nineteen cities were able to mobilise at such short notice and the level of commitment to the cause varied. In Zürich, however, protestors vowed to continue their industrial action until the government ordered the military to withdraw. This forced the hand of the executive committee to consider the idea of a national strike.

At the same time, rebellions in Germany led to the ousting of the imperial monarchy and the establishment of a democratic republic. The time was ripe for workers to make themselves heard.

Sunday 10 November 1918

Labour unions in Zürich planned celebrations and demonstrations for the first anniversary of the Russian Revolution. Under the febrile circumstances, the military forbade any such public gatherings. When a large group clashed with soldiers, resulting in injuries and the death of a serviceman, passions ran high. Cavalrymen charged protestors with sabres, deepening the rift between civilians and the army.

Meanwhile OAK finalised their nine demands to the government. These comprised:

- national council elections with proportional representation
- women's suffrage and women's right to hold office
- a general obligation to work
- a 48-hour working week
- changing the military into a people's army
- improving the food supply
- old age and disability insurance
- a state monopoly on foreign trade
- paying off the country's sovereign debt by taxing the wealthy

Otherwise, the whole country would go on strike.

Monday 11 November, 1918

Waffenstillstand von Compiègne. Armistice de Compiègne. Armistice of Compiègne.

French Marshall Ferdinand Foch, Allied Supreme Commander, today signed an accord with Germany, agreeing a cessation of hostilities of all fronts. This follows similar agreements with Austro-Hungary, the

Ottoman Empire and Bulgaria. Fighting is to halt with immediate effect.

The Great War is over.

Weeks of negotiations with Entente Powers following a German rebellion and the abdication of Kaiser Wilhelm II resulted in a cease-fire and the aim of a permanent peace treaty. For four bloody years, the Great War has claimed millions of lives, both military and civilian.

This day marks an historic end to the bloodshed. Our world will bear the scars of this conflict for generations.

Now we mourn our losses, celebrate peace and make a solemn promise: Never Again.

Tuesday 12 November 1918

In light of the government's rejection of all OAK's requirements, the General Strike went ahead. Peaceful in the main, and more enthusiastically welcomed in the German-speaking areas than the south and west, some 250,000 people stopped work. These included women. Rosa Bloch, chairwoman of the Social Democratic Women's Agitation Committee, had previously led thousands of women to protest against inflation at the cantonal council. Side by side with their menfolk, both working and middle-class women supported the strike.

Wednesday 13 November 1918

After a majority vote, the Swiss government offered OAK an ultimatum: call off the strike by 17.00 and reforms would be managed through legal means. Since military law was imposed on federal employees, the strikers were left with few options. The committee debated long into the night but finally agreed to the request at 02.00 on 14 November.

Thursday 14 November 1918

The strike was over, bar a few dissenting groups in Basel and Zürich. In Grenchen, Canton Solothurn, some protestors were shot at while tearing up railway tracks. Three were killed and others injured when the military opened fire.

These eight days will shape the future of Swiss society. Credit is due to both governmental bodies and representatives of the working class in striving to avoid bloodshed and violence. Yet the seething undercurrents of resentment and injustice still roil beneath the surface. The leaders of this country should heed the concerns of the electorate or confront a far more serious rebellion on the next occasion. Switzerland maintaining neutrality in the face of a world war necessitated a complex diplomatic dance. Switzerland remaining neutral in the face of civil war is an impossibility.

Our government's obligation is to serve *all* its people.

10

The happiest of all things is when an old friend comes and greets us as in former times; the heart is comforted with the assurance that some day everything that we have loved will be given back to us.

— Johanna Spyri, *Heidi*

April 1919

The encounter with the new doctor and Frau Bayard affected Seraphine more deeply than such a brief interaction deserved. At first, she was merely grateful that the smart city gentleman had not made a fuss about receiving the wrong meal. But something drew her eyes repeatedly to the couple, conversing easily as they ate, laughing together like old friends. In Seraphine's eyes, Frau Bayard's beauty was due to much more than her stylish dress. Her pale fingers clasped the stem of her wine glass and her teeth flashed white when she smiled.

Most of all, she had an exceptionally elegant throat. The

colour of fresh snow, it rose from her lacy collar like that of a swan, without a blemish. She wore her hair in a roll so that one could appreciate her slender neck from all angles. The new doctor seemed quite hypnotised by his companion and rightly so.

Long after they had paid their bill and gone, Seraphine continued to think of them, and not only because of their generous tip. Her mind returned to the question of the salt. Her mother had forbidden her to join the villagers applying to be a part of Dr Bayard's experiment. Seraphine's resentment lessened when she discovered that the doctor was only interested in large families as his target group. If his trials were successful, he would offer it to more local people and she would be first in line. Her guilt at poisoning baby Anton still weighed on her conscience, but if the doctor prescribed the exact amount, the only life at risk was her own.

Even more important was her mother's condition. Josef's returns were unpredictable in frequency but only too predictable in content. Seraphine was banished from the bedroom so they could do what married couples do. She didn't resent sleeping on the kitchen floor. Her main concern was the chance of her mother conceiving another baby. A girl didn't grow up on a farm ignorant of where babies came from. Clothilde refused to entertain any discussion on the subject of medicine, muttering gnomic phrases about female wisdom and ancient knowledge, none of which held any sway with her daughter. Nevertheless, after three visits from her husband, Clothilde only carried one swelling; the one at her neck.

Rumours ran around the school, as they always did once or twice a year. This time it was yet another myth about the origin of the goitre. Not voicing one's anger caused a build-up of bile, quite literally sticking in one's craw. Seraphine dismissed such baseless talk with an arch of her eyebrow. After all, her own mother did nothing but complain and rage against the injustice of her situation. No amount of spilled venom reduced the lump at her throat.

Spring was approaching and Seraphine gathered her courage. She waited until Clothilde was comfortably full after a meal of *Spätzli* to raise the subject. They sat on the bench in front of the house, one repairing clothes and the other fashioning new ones, watching late February sun play on the waterfalls as they tumbled down the opposite side of the mountain. Barry lay at their feet, soaking up the warmth just as Henri used to do.

"Look, Seraphine, over there! A rainbow!" The arc of colours crossed the gorge, so vibrant you could almost believe it solid. Clothilde clasped her knitting to her chin, gazing in wonder.

In that instant, Seraphine saw the light in her eyes and knew now was the time to speak her mind. "This valley," she breathed. "There is nowhere more beautiful."

Clothilde sighed. "It has its moments."

"Maman, I have a question."

"I thought you might. Always restless." She resumed the clattering of her needles. "Spit it out, girl."

"A person can leave school at seventeen if she has good reason. The Weisshornstube in St. Niklaus, you remember our class took it over last National Day? They offered me an apprenticeship as a waitress. I can earn money, learn a trade and contribute a little something to the farm. That does not mean I will neglect my duties or my studies. I can do both. With your permission, I would like to leave school after my birthday and start work."

With a snort, Clothilde set down her knitting. "Why bother asking me? Sounds like you have it all worked out and even if I say no, you will do whatever you want regardless of your mother's wishes."

The rainbow faded but light refracted from the water droplets, hinting at sprites and magic.

Seraphine sidestepped the comment. "I would prefer to have your blessing, and if you are willing, your advice. There is something else." While she had her mother's attention, it was imperative to press every point. "Josef will be home at Easter, no?"

"You mean Papa?"

"Papa, yes, of course. It seems a good time for me to make myself scarce, give you some privacy to be together." A glance at her mother's brow indicated the clouds were gathering. "That is why I would like to visit Tante Margot in Montreux. I want to see Henri, Maman, and I cannot be sure how much time I have left. Please give me two weeks to see my brother. Then I will return to my job and bring home a regular wage. What do you think?"

"Go inside and boil the kettle. I want to drink a cup of tea and have a few moments of stillness. We will talk of this tomorrow."

Seraphine gathered her darned stockings, stepped over Barry's furry form and did her mother's bidding. At least Maman had not refused outright. Seraphine had managed to mention several advantages for Clothilde; a new if meagre income, an opportunity to lecture her daughter and two weeks of privacy to enjoy her husband. Any or all of those were easily outweighed by uttering the name of her detested sister.

The kettle bubbled on the stove and she tipped hot water into the teapot. While the flavours of Alpine herbs developed, Seraphine waited for her mother's mood to steep and settle. With fifteen years' experience of her intractable parent, she was an expert at biding her time. But her determination was unwavering; after her next birthday, she wanted to be more than an unpaid goatherd and a repository for her mother's disappointments. One way or another, she would make it happen. From her mother, she had inherited more than blue eyes.

In the event, disobedience was not necessary. Clothilde gave her permission as if the whole idea had been hers. It was indeed time Seraphine earned her keep, and working at the restaurant would be a good way to learn practical skills. School was superfluous to requirements now she had the basics. After her birthday on the 1st of March, there would be no need to go back. Seraphine's duties around the house remained her responsibility, but she could do those before going to the restaurant.

"Thank you, Maman. I am grateful to you. As for travelling to Montreux over Easter, is that acceptable to you?"

"You will be seventeen years old next month. Papa and I planned to give you something for your birthday. Instead of trying to choose something I think you might like, I will give you money. You can spend it on whatever makes you happy. That might be more of your wretched books or a train ticket, it's up to you."

Seraphine couldn't hide her smile. "How kind and thoughtful of you and Papa! I am fortunate to have you as my parents." She kissed her mother's cheek.

"That is true. Are you watching that pan? Because I cannot abide burnt oats."

Seraphine tended to their breakfast, elated by her success. Two out of three. She had permission to leave school and start work. With her own money, she could take the train to Montreux, stay with her aunt for two whole weeks and visit Henri. Her third request remained unvoiced for fear of losing all she had gained. Any attempt to raise the subject of treated salt and her mother would change her mind about everything. She reasoned with herself. If she did not ask permission, her mother could not forbid it. If salt was not forbidden, taking it was hardly an act of disobedience. She drank her milk, ate her oats and gazed out at the crocuses, snowdrops and primroses, their tiny bursts of colour heralding the return of life.

. . .

Her trip to Montreux soon seemed at risk of postponement due to the lack of a chaperone. Plenty of people were travelling down the valley to Visp, but no appropriate ladies could be prevailed upon to guarantee a seventeen-year-old girl's safety all the way to Montreux. The arrival of a telegram put Seraphine out of her agony. Tante Margot would travel to Visp to collect her niece in person.

The girl floated on air for the following week. Customers at the Weisshornstube received an unprecedented amount of smiles, the bus driver complimented her radiance, and never before had the goats enjoyed more singing. She was careful to subdue her high spirits at home because Clothilde had an allergy to other people's happiness. It was not a demanding challenge, as Seraphine was usually exhausted after waiting tables from nine in the morning till three in the afternoon, followed by all her domestic chores.

The day she was due to leave the valley, three peculiar things occurred. Firstly, in the kitchen, her mother handed her a knitted object the size of a rabbit. It was black with touches of white and brown on its appendages, with a pair of brass buttons at one end. In an instant, she understood what it was meant to be and her eyes flooded with tears. Clothilde despised crying, so Seraphine dropped to a crouch to hide her emotions.

"Look, Barry! It's you! Your ears, your tail, your eyes." The dog sniffed the object and on finding it was nothing to eat, wandered off into the barn.

"It's for Henri. He always loved that animal. Maybe he remembers, who knows?" Clothilde shrugged, her jaw set. "Get up now, girl, and ready yourself. Have you everything you need?"

"Yes, I checked last night and again this morning. I am ready.

Give my love to Papa and I will see you in two weeks." She kissed her mother on each cheek and clasped her hands. "I promise to be good and careful and always to mind my manners."

"You can be bad and careless and behave like a lumpen oaf for all I care. Just come home."

"I will, Maman. I promise I will."

Clothilde moved away with a sniff. "Hurry now. The bus leaves on time whether you're on it or not."

The second unexpected event occurred in St. Niklaus. She had forty minutes to wait for the train so she naturally dropped into the familiar and friendly Weisshornstube. Only Hermann, the oldest son of the owner, was behind the bar, while most of the tables were filled with working people having their morning break. Seraphine left her bag in the alcove by the door and walked towards the kitchen.

"Where are *you* going?" barked Hermann. The spite in his voice turned heads.

Seraphine halted. "I was going to say hello to Romy."

"You aren't working today. Why are you here?"

She struggled to find a response, her face aflame.

"If you're working, put on an apron and serve the guests. If you're a paying customer, have a seat and I'll take your money."

"I'm not working today," she managed.

"No, not today and not for the whole of Easter! Just when we need staff the most."

"But I asked for the time off weeks ago."

"*Weeeeks agooo*," he sneered, mimicking her voice. "Well, enjoy your holiday, Little Miss Seraphine, because you no longer have a job. We need loyalty from our workers. Unless you're going to order a coffee, you can get out."

She backed away, horrified by his aggression, and fumbled for her bag. A bass voice spoke at her shoulder.

"What a coincidence. We are looking for bright young

people to fill positions at our hotel. My name is Lochmatter. And you?"

Her throat was swollen with unshed tears. "Widmer, sir. Seraphine Widmer."

"I am pleased to make your acquaintance, Miss Widmer. After Easter, come to reception and ask for me. If you are prepared to work hard and meet high standards, you will be a welcome addition to our little family."

"Thank you, sir. I appreciate your kindness." She dropped her head and hurried out of the door, confused, mortified and incredulous. To be sacked and offered a new job in a matter of minutes was more than she could comprehend. Why would Hermann throw her out in front of the morning crowd? Was Herr Lochmatter serious? Working at the hotel was an unattainable ambition and she did not dare to believe it was a possibility.

Occupied with her thoughts, she shouldered her bag and trudged up the hill towards the wooden station building. It was still early but she was prepared to wait in the sunshine until her chaperone appeared and the train whistled down the tracks.

"Can I carry that for you, Fräulein?" The voice was male with a cultured accent.

Seraphine started with a gasp, already unsettled by the events of the morning.

Dr Bayard's assistant extended a hand. "It looks heavy and I am stronger than I look."

"Thank you. I'm only going as far as the railway station." She relinquished her hold on her weighty bag. "This is very kind of you."

"Not at all. My sisters, if they could see me, would berate me for ungentlemanly behaviour had I not offered to lighten a lady's load. My name is Bastian Favre and your face seems familiar."

"Seraphine Widmer. Yes, I served you and Frau Bayard at the Weisshornstube last Swiss National Day. I have not seen you in

St. Niklaus or thereabouts since then. I understood you had returned to your employer."

"That is correct. I am the assistant to a chief physician in Appenzell, a long journey from this valley. During the winter, I conveyed all my learning to my patron and am now returned to see the results of Dr Bayard's work."

Seraphine slowed her steps. The second the priest's wife saw her in conversation with a young man, she would rush at him like a goose, hissing and flapping in alarm. "My knowledge of the doctor's work is limited, I confess. All I understand from hearing him speak is that he suggests a remedy for our ailments. In your opinion, do you believe that a possibility?"

Herr Favre matched her pace and gave her a searching look. Without conscious thought, she pulled her scarf a little tighter.

"Fräulein Widmer, it is my belief that Dr Bayard can alleviate much of what ails this valley and ensure other issues never recur. The results since the winter are quite remarkable. His test patients are already transformed. Had I not seen it with my own eyes, I would have guessed at subterfuge."

She liked the sound of his voice, the strange sharp accent softened by his passion for his subject.

"May I ask you a question, Herr Favre?"

"Please do." He switched her bag to his other hand.

"The test patients, as you call them, are all children, no?"

"Not all, no. We selected half a dozen families to treat and study the effects. The most dramatic results were visible in children, that much is true. But the benefits can be seen at every age. The fact is that children's bodies are still developing and the tissues are softer, making them more responsive to ..."

"Doctor Favre. What a pleasant surprise." The priest's wife had appeared from behind the train station. The tone of her voice belied her words. "I am to chaperone Seraphine as far as Visp, where I shall deliver her safely to her aunt."

He doffed his hat. "Good morning, Frau Gratteau. The weather is ideal for making the journey down the valley. Miss Widmer, your bag. I hope I answered your question. If you wish to know more, why not come into the surgery? Have a wonderful trip, ladies. Good day to you." With a bow of his head, he replaced his hat.

"Thank you for your help," said Seraphine. The priest's wife shot her a look but did not speak until Herr Favre had disappeared around the wood merchant's wall.

"When a young lady is alone, she must do all in her power to avoid compromising situations. Your mother entrusted you to my care for that precise reason. Remember your position, Seraphine. It is bad enough that your father is absent for months at a time and you, barely seventeen years of age, are waiting tables in an establishment where drink is taken."

Seraphine picked up her bag with a little grunt. "The doctor, out of gentlemanly good manners, offered to carry my bag. Hardly a compromising situation. My stepfather works for the military, playing his part in keeping our country safe. And for your information, I am no longer waiting tables at the Weisshornstube." The moment she said the words, she wanted to kick herself. Now word would get back to her mother that she was unemployed and the whole strategy of attaining independence would shatter and collapse.

"I hope it was not some kind of misconduct that caused you to lose your job." For someone who preached purity of thought at Sunday school, Frau Gratteau was remarkably quick to assume the worst.

"I did not lose my job," Seraphine replied. "It is merely that I have a better offer of employment."

"Ah ha, now I see the purpose behind your trip to Montreux. Your aunt has secured you a position, I assume. Well, good luck to you. All I can say is that I hope it is with a respectable family."

"The family is very well respected," said Seraphine, thinking of the Lochmatters. "Its members are regarded as pillars of society."

"I should hope they are. Oh dear, let us move a little further down the platform. A party of climbers is going to join the train and I find them most unpleasant with their loud voices and cumbersome equipment. The railway has brought us a myriad of benefits, I cannot deny. That said, endless waves of pleasure-seekers is not one I welcome. Even the way they speak in terms of 'conquering', 'mastering' and so on. My husband and I share the opinion that God created nature and man to live in harmony. This landscape does not exist to be subjugated. To think otherwise is arrogance."

For once, Seraphine found herself partly in accord with the priest's wife. She too believed in peaceful co-existence with the natural world. Where they differed in outlook was what the climbers, wanderers and visitors brought to the valley. They spent money, yes, but their foreignness suggested a much wider view. One she could learn more about if she took a position at Hotel Lochmatter. Guests from France, Germany and Italy, perhaps even from England and America, could tell tales of worlds she could scarcely imagine.

The train pulled into the station, a fearsome and impressive sight. Passengers clambered aboard and to Seraphine's delight, Frau Gratteau recognised a couple from the church in Zermatt. They sat together, conversing with great animation, allowing Seraphine to take out one of her books. She chose a nature story with illustrations, lest Frau Gratteau object. Then she rested her head against the window and puzzled over the day so far. *Nothing happens for months and then it all comes at once.* She thought about the doctor's words and made a firm resolution. When she returned to the Matterthal, she would seek him out and beg his permission to be a test patient.

In Visp, Tante Margot bought Frau Gratteau a cup of coffee and a cake to thank her for her efforts. It was an uncomfortable encounter. While Margot Dechet's appearance and manners were beyond reproach, she was a progressive woman and a Protestant to boot. After a frosty farewell to the priest's wife, Margot treated her niece to lunch at a hotel since they had an hour to wait for the train to Montreux. Seraphine paid particular attention to the serving staff; the way the women wore their hair, the polite phrases they used and how they moved around the room. They were present, but not obtrusive. She admired the way they hopped from German to Italian to English, according to the needs of the guest. Preoccupied with how ill-equipped she was for a similar role and intimidated by her surroundings, she said little, responding to her aunt's queries with brief responses and polite nods.

The train chugged past spectacular scenes of lake, forest, mountain and river, drawing comments from awestruck passengers. Seraphine and her aunt rode in silence, communicating via a smile or the touch of their shoulders as they sat side by side. It was only when her aunt patted her arm that she realised she had dozed off and slept for the best part of the journey.

What an ungrateful guest! She sat up and apologised to Margot, embarrassed by her withdrawn attitude and lack of grace.

"My dear sweet girl, it matters not a jot. You are weary and in need of a rest. If I had to spend an entire morning with the pious Frau Gratteau, I would sleep for a week. The woman makes a hobby of judging others and hence has a face like a lemon. *Tant pis*. We have an entire fortnight to amuse ourselves with conversation, relaxation and beautiful things of which she would disapprove."

"A face like a lemon?" Seraphine giggled. "I always think of her as a goose."

Margot pressed her hands over her mouth and creased into laughter. "What a keen eye you have! Let us gather our belongings, the next stop is ours."

After two days in the company of her aunt, Seraphine uncoiled like a cat in the sun. She had no duties, only indulgences. A walk along the lake, hot chocolate and pastries in an Art Deco café, a musical interlude in someone's drawing room, reading in the winter garden and the eagerly awaited visit to Anton's grave made her heart fuller than she could remember. The little plot with the boy's headstone was clean, the surrounding grass neatly trimmed, and a display of daffodils and irises threw yellow and purple reflections on a white slab, two thirds smaller than all the others.

Margot left her alone to say a prayer. On her knees, Seraphine prayed for his soul and asked forgiveness. She retrieved every single memory of the little boy; his starfish hands and sapphire eyes, his bumpy head and snub nose. Her words, little more than a whisper, were meant for no other ears than his.

"Anton, you were never much of a size. A grub, a maggot, just an unproven lump of dough, yet to become bread. When you left, your absence cracked open a chasm as deep as the Matterthal. Do you know how often I think of you? Imagining you by my side as we walk to school, frowning your fierce little frown. Sitting opposite as we milk the goats, singing the songs I would have taught you. Combing burrs from Barry's coat and trying to twitter along with Henri. We never did those simple things and that is my fault. I wanted to make you better but you were already perfect. My love for you burns with the heat of a furnace, *mon petit frère*, and that will never change."

She left some stones gathered from the farm in a pattern

around his name, each a reminder of the place he was born. Then she wiped her face and joined her aunt.

A spring shower scattered raindrops on the path and Tante Margot opened an umbrella. "Come, let's return to the house. Can I do anything?" Her eyes were reddened and swollen.

Seraphine did not care to examine her own face and shook her head. "Thank you, no. When can I see Henri?"

"The day after tomorrow. Your uncle will escort us, as one of the hospital's benefactors. He visits regularly, as you know from my letters, and has nothing but praise for the institution."

"Maman never lets me read your letters. She passes on news but never mentions Henri. I wasn't sure if he ..."

Margot drew her into an embrace. "Seraphine, you are so strong, so very brave. Henri, I promise you, is alive and as well as can be expected. You will see for yourself. What you need to comprehend is the significance of his age. Henri is relatively old for someone with his condition."

"There is a remedy." Seraphine choked out the words. "A doctor has made enormous changes in St. Niklaus. Couldn't he help Henri?" Her sobs overcame her, rendering speech impossible.

They splashed through puddles, running awkwardly under the umbrella to the house overlooking the lake. The maid hurried to open the door and at least three members of staff fussed and fluttered until the ladies were divested of their wet clothes. Seraphine soaked in the bath, softened and warmed, her hair floating around her head like river weeds.

At dinner, her uncle complimented both ladies' coiffures. "Margot, tomorrow you should take this lovely young lady shopping. She deserves to look her best. Half the bachelors of Montreux will cast their capes at her feet."

"Thank you, Uncle Thierry, but I am not here to seek admiration or potential husbands. Could we broach the topic of

Henri's health?" She cut up a spear of asparagus. "You visited the home recently, I believe."

Thierry nodded, with a glance at his sister. "For a boy with cretinism, he is stout and hearty. His mental aptitude and physical stature have changed little since you last saw him. He is content and well served by the institution, but any hope of longevity is futile. Henri's body and mind are underdeveloped and nothing can reverse that, I'm afraid."

The maid filled Seraphine's water glass and she took a large gulp. "Your candour is welcome. I know both my brothers were born with a defect, perhaps several. To my eternal regret, Anton died before a medical solution could be found. There is a doctor in my valley who claims he can cure these deficiencies. If I can entreat the man to share his wisdom with the home in Bern, there might yet be hope for Henri."

Uncle Thierry laid down his cutlery. "As a devoted sister, it is natural you reach for every straw. Searching high and low for a way to help your brother is admirable. Two things, Seraphine, and neither are intended to dampen your enquiring mind. Firstly, scientific advances rarely come from tiny communities in a remote valley. Switzerland is at the forefront of medical progress, particularly in the universities of Bern, Zürich and Fribourg. Your doctor may have some novel ideas to treat your community, for which he must be commended. However, I advise you not to place an excess of faith in a country practitioner with a theory to prove.

"My second point rests on a biological fact. Both your brothers inherited certain traits, whether from deficiencies in the womb or hereditary genetic disorders, we cannot say. These problems are irreversible. When a child is born malformed, there is no feasible way of curing him. It is not like a potter throwing some clay. Should he lose the shape, he can scoop up his raw material and try again. Unfortunately the same is not true of human beings. No medicine or prayer can alter the truth. I am sad to say Henri's life will be short. All we can do is to fill his brief time on earth with joy. When he sees you, his wells will overflow. I cannot deny, so will my own."

His words rang in Seraphine's ears when shopping with her aunt, while travelling to Bern and on approaching the children's home which housed Henri. A doctor welcomed them at the entrance and took them on a tour of the facility. It was light and colourful, with large communal rooms for eating and playing. The smell of disinfectant testified to the cleanliness of the dormitories. The only thing missing were the inhabitants.

"In good weather, we encourage the children to go outside. We have an extensive playground and thanks to the building's south-facing aspect, we enjoy a good deal of sunshine. Henri will be on the swing, if I'm not mistaken, along with Aramis and Porthos."

Thierry and Margot laughed, but Seraphine did not understand. She looked to her uncle for clarification.

"Have you not read *The Three Musketeers*, Seraphine? A novel by Dumas, it describes a group of inseparable friends, fiercely loyal to one another. Henri and two other boys are never apart. The staff members refer to them by the same names. A likeable pack of rogues they make, as you shall see."

The boys were, as the doctor rightly guessed, sitting in a row on a garden swing. The route towards them was not a smooth stroll across the lawn, but an obstacle course. The doctor with three well-dressed strangers attracted the attention of many groups of children, who came running to catch their hands and touch their clothes. The doctor addressed each by name and gently directed them back to the activity they had abandoned. Nurses took charge of the most persistent. With a cry, the three boys on the swing seat rushed towards them. Any hope that Henri had recognised his sister was soon dashed when all three made a bee-line for Uncle Thierry. He produced dried apricots from his pocket and greeted them with an easy familiarity.

Margot bent to pat Henri's shoulder and indicated Seraphine. His face had aged, as wrinkled as that of an old man. But he smiled, walked towards her and bowed, one hand to his chest and the other behind his back. It was a charming gesture, but lacked any form of recognition. Seraphine crouched to his eye line and blew him a kiss. He giggled and blew one to her in return then held out a hand. Obviously he knew that good behaviour earned a reward. She had no raisins or apricots, but reached into her handbag for the knitted version of Barry.

For a second, he seemed bewildered, staring at the object in confusion. Grateful to her aunt and uncle for keeping the other boys distracted, she twitched the toy's tail and made it lick Henri's cheek. He cackled in delight and took it from her, holding it to his chest. He ran in a wide circle, showing the woollen animal to everyone who would look, and finally returned to his swing seat, rocking back and forth like a mother soothing an infant.

The doctor and Uncle Thierry walked in the direction of the main building, each holding the hand of one of Henri's friends. Seraphine sat beside her brother, pointed at the toy dog and widened her eyes. He grinned, his mouth almost absent of teeth, and raised the toy to her face. She pressed his hand to her sternum so he could feel the vibrations and said, "Good dog, Barry, good dog," while stroking the dog's head,

Henri copied her gesture, burbling something in his own chirruping style. The seat sank a little as Margot sat the other side of her nephew with a smile.

"He doesn't remember. He doesn't know who I am," said Seraphine.

Margot reached an arm behind Henri to touch Seraphine's shoulder. "He knows you're someone who gave him a present and made him happy."

"Brr, brr, chack, brr brrreeeerrr," said Henri.

They swung to and fro, Seraphine trying to appreciate the beauty of the gardens, the unaffected laughter of little boys playing in the sun. It was a good place. She covered her nose and mouth with her hands, blinking away tears.

Little fingers patted her wrist and hot breath blew on her cheek. She turned to her brother. He pointed to her nose and curled over as if in pain. Then he looked up, expecting an answer.

She shook her head. "No. It doesn't hurt. Not really."

Still clutching his toy, he opened his arms and she clasped him close. Some things he did remember.

11

She walks in beauty like the night
Of cloudless climes and starry skies
And all that's best of dark and bright
Meet in her aspect and her eyes;
Thus mellowed to the tender light
Which heaven to gaudy day denies.

— Lord Byron, *She Walks In Beauty*

April 1919

B astian would be lying if he said Seraphine Widmer did not cross his mind. The truth was he remembered her only too well from last year's Swiss National Day. Her blush as she apologised for making a mistake with his order, her glacier-lake eyes of brilliant turquoise, her peculiar old-fashioned blouse at odds with her evident youth. *Pretty girl*, he had thought at the time. *Or will be when she grows up.* He had assumed her to be fourteen or fifteen, so was surprised and impressed to encounter the same young woman the very next year.

When he saw her come out of the Weisshornstube, he picked up his pace and offered to carry her bag. She started at his voice and he saw she had indeed grown into a beauty. She enquired about his work, with more than passing curiosity. He just began an explanation when that nosy old crow Frau Gratteau appeared. Had she not, Bastian could have explained further and offered to elaborate. Flustered by the priest's wife and her obvious disapproval, he handed over the girl's bag and said farewell. He had no idea where she was going or how to find her again. Even the most casual enquiry would alert the gossips.

Seraphine Widmer. He looked her up in the surgery's medical records and saw she lived a bus ride and long walk further up the mountainside. She was not a regular visitor to the practice. The last time she received treatment was several years ago for a scald on her leg. His only hope of meeting her by accident was at the Weisshornstube. Thus he took his *Znüni* or lunch there every other day. The man behind the bar was surly and uncouth, the food was unimaginative and the smoky air penetrated his clothes. In vain he waited for her appearance. After two full weeks, he resigned himself to the fact he might never see her again and returned to dining at the far superior Hotel Lochmatter for the remaining fortnight of his stay.

He was browsing the paper in the dining room one morning, reading reports of the Paris Peace Conference, when something made him look up. A slight figure in a maid's uniform passed the doorway, with the briefest glance inside. Their eyes met for less than a second but her gaze hit him like a lightning bolt. With unseemly haste, he emptied his coffee cup, folded the paper and hurried after the girl. He climbed the stairs and checked every floor, but found no sign of her. She had to be inside one of the rooms. Other than knocking and demanding entrance, he had no way of knowing which.

The church bells rang eight times and he took the final flight to the surgery two steps at a time, ready to report for work. There she stood with her back to the door, wide-eyed and apparently waiting for him.

"Fräulein Widmer! My apologies for startling you. It is a pleasure to see you again."

"Good morning, Dr Favre. I came because you said if I wished to learn more, you know, about the salt and the tests, I should come to the surgery."

"I see. Of course." He was out of breath from leaping up stairs. "You work here?"

"I do now, yes. Herr Lochmatter has given me employment as a chambermaid. It is my first day today but I wanted to speak to you and I did not wish to approach you in the dining room."

"Quite right. Can you come back after surgery hours? I will be happy to explain in detail."

"Yes, sir. Only, the last bus leaves at seven-fifteen."

"In that case, I will see you here at six o'clock."

"Thank you very much. Have a good day."

"I wish the same to you."

She smiled and trotted off down the stairs.

He stood there a moment, shaking his head in disbelief. Six o'clock could not come soon enough.

That day, of all days, Dr Bayard returned late from a visit to a patient at the other end of a valley. He was still writing up his paperwork at twenty minutes after six. Bastian paced the surgery, both dreading the knock on the door and awaiting it with keen anticipation. Eventually, Bayard pulled on his coat and suggested Bastian should finish for the evening.

"I shall just complete the last few reports and do exactly that, Herr Bayard. Give my regards to your wife. *Bis morgen!*"

"*Bis morgen.*" Bayard's footsteps creaked down the stairs and in a few seconds, his black hat appeared in the street below. Just then, a light tap came at the door.

Bastian opened it to see Seraphine, still in her uniform, standing beneath a wall sconce. "I am sorry to be late, sir, but I thought it best to let Dr Bayard depart before knocking."

"A wise decision. Come in and take a seat. Your bus leaves at seven-thirty, I believe, so I will get straight to the point. You are interested in Dr Bayard's experiments with treated salt, no?"

"Yes, that's correct."

"Can I ask why?"

She cast her eyes down and her mouth twisted into a moue of embarrassment and unhappiness. "I have two brothers. No, that's not correct. I had two half-brothers. One died of the White Plague and the other is in a home in Bern. They were both born cretins, sir. As for myself, I fear I am following my mother and developing the same thick neck." She put a hand to her throat. "I know it is too late to help my brothers, but if the salt can help me, I would like to volunteer as a test subject."

The speech was well rehearsed, Bastian could see that. The girl barely had her emotions in check and that was probably the only way she could explain without weeping. He had to proceed very gently. "As a young woman who is still growing, you might make a very good test subject. Before we go any further, may I examine your neck?"

She looked startled but gave a little nod and reached behind her head to unbutton her high-collared blouse. When it was partially loosened, she pulled the neckline down to the level of her sternum and lifted her chin to the air. Her courage touched him.

He picked up the lamp and pulled his stool closer so that he might sit opposite, their knees almost brushing. A significant bulge protruded from the centre of her throat, prominent but far from the worst he'd seen.

"I see. Now I must feel the thing to determine its texture. Excuse me." The heat of her skin under his fingers and proximity of her lovely face unnerved him despite his concentration on being professional. The tissue was soft and malleable, with none of the hardening he often saw in adults. His nerves abated as he moved away, slipping behind a screen of medical jargon.

"There is every chance your goitre will respond to the treatment Dr Bayard recommends. If you are willing to become a test patient, Fräulein Widmer, you must follow instructions to the letter, submit to regular examinations and agree to your being an exemplar. That means a photograph of you now and again in three months."

She buttoned up her clothes. "Yes, I can do all those things. I am very glad you think my condition can be improved and I thank you for your patience, sir. Doctor Favre? What I would like to know is why. For what reason do I have this lump, why is my mother's swelling three times the size of mine and how did it happen that my brothers were born that way? I know we are short of time, but you did say you would go into detail."

Astonished, he stared into her face, lamplight dancing in those luminous eyes, and noted the determined set of her jaw. "Indeed I did. Very well. In your throat, right where that lump is situated, is a gland called the thyroid. It is shaped like a butterfly and normally so thin you cannot feel it. This butterfly gland may seem unimportant in comparison to other organs such as the brain or lungs, but it performs an essential role. It regulates practically every bodily process. Growth, temperature, development of other organs and heart rate require those hormones, or perhaps I should say physiological messages, supplied by the thyroid. Without them, one's body becomes sluggish, weary, always cold and lacking in enthusiasm for life."

"You are describing my mother," said Seraphine, clasping her hands to her chest.

Bastian hesitated, but aware of the ticking clock, pressed on. "For natural functioning, the thyroid requires a small, but frequent amount of iodine. People who live near the ocean have no difficulty maintaining their supply from a diet of fish and so on. Here in the Alps, it seems our soil is deficient. When the thyroid cannot source sufficient iodine, it swells, trying to absorb every last particle in the body. Hence the goitre. This is why Dr Bayard wants to give everyone a tiny bit of iodine in their salt. Because that is all one needs, a tiny bit."

Seraphine's head cocked at the sound of seven o'clock bells. "Very soon I should go and stop trespassing on your *Feierabend*. One last question, sir, if I may?"

"You most certainly may."

"Every bodily process, you said. Every bodily process of our own bodies and those we carry within us, surely? If a mother's body is missing iodine, the baby she carries must have the same lack. Is this what happened to my brothers?"

Bastian released a sigh of sympathy. He could only guess at the toll it took on women struggling to survive who bore a defective child. Now he had a glimpse of the weight piled onto existing siblings. "Your brothers had no real chance of normal development, I am sad to say. Plant a seed in barren land and it is unlikely to grow. If it does, it is often stunted or deformed. I am sorry, Seraphine, this misfortune is cruel and unfair on everyone."

Her head snapped up, her eyes glistening with tears. He realised what he had said and could have bitten his tongue. To call her by her first name was a presumption of seniority, a patronising doctor rather than a potential suitor.

"My sympathy for your familial situation made me careless and I apologise, Fräulein Widmer. Perhaps I can walk you to the Postauto stop to ensure you catch your bus and to answer any further questions?"

"That is not necessary, thank you. When can I start taking the salt?"

"It is important that you understand this is a lifetime commitment. Your thyroid, the butterfly in your throat, needs this like a flower needs water or sunshine. Unless you want this lump to grow again, you must take the salt forever. Can you visit me tomorrow evening at the same time? I will arrange to borrow Dr Bayard's photo apparatus and record the current condition of your goitre."

"No, I cannot stay past three o'clock the rest of this week. Next Monday, I have permission to stay until the evening. Is that convenient for you, sir?" She gathered her bag and got to her feet.

"A week from now? Certainly. I shall see you here, take your measurements and prescribe the appropriate dose of salt. I hope I have not offended or upset you?"

"No." She looked directly at him and smiled. "Nor do I object to your calling me Seraphine. You say it with a French accent. I like that. Herr Doctor, you have been most patient and kind, for which I thank you. Goodnight."

She was out of the door before he'd finished saying goodbye. The echoes of her footsteps tapped downstairs like raindrops and he ached to call her back. Instead, he rushed to the window to watch her leave. Only when her figure turned the corner out of sight did he bend to blow out the lamps. He took a deep breath and stopped, his lungs filled with air. Across the street, his face also lit by lamplight, a man was watching him.

Bastian released his breath in a steady deflation, curious as to who would be spying from the *Meierturm*. The two men's eyes met. It was that harmless fool who spent most of his day snoring in the dining room. The old man raised a hand in a salute and Bastian returned the gesture, despite his irritation, then blew out the candles and closed the curtains. Next time he met Seraphine, he would use the examination room at the back.

Next time. Seven days until they sat so closely their breath mingled and he inhaled the scent of summer in her hair. Seven days until he ran his fingers across her skin. Seven days.

12

4 May 1919

My most respected colleague, Herr Doctor Hunziker
Once again, please accept my apologies for this hasty missive bare of the usual niceties. The pressing nature of my communication on this occasion is driven by far greater optimism than my last hurried scrawl. My fear at that time was that the conflict might drag Switzerland into its hungry maw and scientific exchange would be one of its many casualties. I am most grateful for our good fortune.

When we last had leisure to correspond before the outbreak of hostilities, we found ourselves in accord with the principles espoused by Chatin, Coindet et al. Since your informative and erudite contributions to Swiss medicine, many eventful months passed and other battles drew our attention. Nonetheless, I dare wait no longer.

Having read your theory in painstaking detail, I have no wish to misrepresent your words nor indeed deliver an inaccurate rendering of my own. Thus I beg your indulgence in noting the chief features of our discourse as an aide-mémoire.

Our above-mentioned predecessors take issue with the current obsession around bacteria: the goitre is not a manifestation of an infectious disease, poor hygiene or consanguinity. Fellow physicians support the theory that measured doses of iodine have a beneficial effect on a goitrous individual, yet the precise dosage remains contentious. While Chatin and Coindet were veritable pioneers in the field, the unfortunate reaction to inexact amounts of dietary iodine contributed to a mass poisoning and the French discrediting the project.

Moreover, the medical profession has a powerful body of evidence to show the importance of the thyroid gland on foetal growth. Congenital defects in a goitrous region are commonplace. Cretinism and myxedema, both effects of underdevelopment in utero, are irreversible.

I thank you for your patience thus far and hence to my point:

Having returned from my mission with the Red Cross, I am now the resident doctor in St. Niklaus (VS), a married man and a local practitioner. Herr Hunziker, I travelled the world as a ship's doctor and nowhere have I seen such fatalism and hopelessness than this region. Looking no further than my own valley, goitre is endemic, deafness is far in excess of typical occurrences and over half the offspring in some villages are unable to function as members of society. NB: _These are only the ones we see_.

My belief, based on your theory, is that treating a thyroid imbalance is a question of dosage. The only way of proving that is by a simple dose-response trial. Last winter, in one of the worst afflicted communities in the Matterthal, I persuaded a small group of residents to submit to a trial. The results are the most uplifting I have encountered in all my years of medicine.

In a tiny commune an hour and a half's walk from my practice, I delivered iodised salt for the inhabitants to last them the season. The populace, divided into three parts, consumed doses of salt iodised at different strengths: namely 3mg/kg, 6mg/kg and 15mg/kg. When I returned in spring, the difference was undeniable. Diffuse goitre in children below the age of puberty softens and retreats in under three months. Adult throats are reduced to half if not a quarter of the size, enabling normal breathing. Entire families are transformed.

Whilst we must adhere to documentary precision in medical trials, there is a place for non-clinical observation. As a man of poetry, I know you appreciate that. A fog has lifted. Optimism, laughter, energy and light are tangible in every home.

Encouraged by such results and determined to record with scientific rigour, I shall embark upon a wider dose and response experiment over the coming winter. My intention is to work with the same community of Grachen and a second remote region called Törbel. It is barely accessible other than by a stone-strewn track, rural in habits and insular in attitude. Rather than five families, I am determined to treat over one thousand people in this valley.

As I write the last, I can almost see your brows rise. Had I more time, I would write at great length to explain my reasoning, as I believe it to be sound. However, due to the aforementioned haste, I beg you to trust my judgement until I can send you definitive results.

My valued colleague and fellow scientist, by gathering your theory and my practical proof, we are on the brink of something so simple, yet mighty and profound. Our work could change not only the lives of our countrymen and women, but human lives the world over.

As you will doubtless read between my lines, I am in a state of high anticipation. The cause is at one and the same time professional and personal. My wife and I are expecting another child next year, a blessing we welcome. Therefore, with faith in my own methodology, I will treat my spouse and future son or daughter exactly as I do the villagers.

With my warmest and most convivial wishes towards you and your family, I bid you my leave.

Dr. med. Otto Bayard

4 May 1919

3925 St. Niklaus

13

I love you as fresh meat loves salt.

— Anna Walter Thomas, *Cap O'Rushes*

June 1919

The war was over. When she awoke, it was the first thought in Seraphine's mind. Every day, she closed her eyes again for a second to give thanks.

Along with the rest of the world, St. Niklaus and the surrounding communities rejoiced in the prospect of peace. The traditional toast for Silvester, or 31st December, was for health, wealth and happiness. Wealth was going to take a long time to rebuild, but seeing recent physical changes and families reunited, people dared to hope their luck had changed. All through the winter months, the tenor of conversation was one of optimism.

Unless, that is, one lived with the Widmer family. Released from his position in the military, Josef returned home to his farm, as bitter and resentful at the armistice as if he was the defeated party. He ranted for hours over dinner, lecturing his wife and stepdaughter on the political missteps of the Swiss government and the lunacy of the leftists. Three months of being trapped with him induced a feeling of panic in Seraphine's chest. Only this made her brave enough to accost the housekeeper of Hotel Lochmatter.

"Frau Hediger, can I wash those glasses for you? I have another forty minutes until my bus and I'd rather make myself useful than sit around daydreaming."

"Thank you, Seraphine. Although a girl of your age has plenty to daydream about, I will not refuse. On my poor feet all day, it takes its toll."

"Sit by the window and I'll bring you some tea. Do you think we can expect to see more tourists next year? Sorry, I mean this year."

The older woman sat with a moan of relief. "I know what you mean. Only this morning I dated an invoice with the year 1918 and had to write it all over again. Am I getting older and slow to change or did the year 1918 last for a decade?"

"The last three years seem a lifetime to me, if I am honest." She placed the cup and strainer beside the little pot, as if Frau Hediger was a hotel guest.

"Three years *is* a lifetime for one so young. It was hard for the whole country, but your generation suffered the most. You must be overjoyed to have your papa return unharmed."

For a moment, Seraphine was unable to respond. She soaped and rinsed the glasses, holding each to the lamp as she polished them dry. "Yes, thank you, it is a great blessing for my mother and for the farm. For myself, I hope to continue learning the hospitality trade. That is problematic when I have to catch the Postauto through the valley each day. When Hanna worked here, she lived in a maid's room, no?"

Frau Hediger's expression was guarded. "Yes. But Hanna was a married woman."

"With you to ensure I am suitably quartered and observing propriety, what is the difference? I could work longer hours, assist with breakfasts, take over reception when you need a rest and learn every skill you are willing to teach me. Frau Hediger, a girl in my position has limited chances and fewer than ever after the war. I am a hard worker, I swear."

The housekeeper stirred her tea, wagging her head from side to side in thought. "You do not need to tell me how hard you work. Answer me honestly, Seraphine. Do you want a job or a husband?"

Seraphine recoiled, shocked. "The last thing on earth I want is a husband! My mother put great store by marriage and look what happened to her. Neither of her men made her content. Josef is unhappy, she is disappointed and I am surrounded by misery. The sooner I leave the farm, the better. If necessary, I will go to my aunt in Montreux and seek employment as a nanny or lady's maid."

"If that is an option, why not?"

"Because all I desire is to stay in St. Niklaus with a roof over my head and the means to keep myself. I apologise for talking so much. My mouth sometimes runs away with me. I'll finish these glasses and let you rest."

"Thank you. You are a good girl. Let me talk to Herr Lochmatter and we shall see."

When Seraphine broke the news to her mother, she expected resistance. What she didn't expect was a look of abject fear.

"You're leaving me? Now?" Clothilde steadied herself against the rough wooden table as if she might faint.

Seraphine took a step forward. "Maman, what is it? Sit down, you look quite pale." She eased her mother onto a chair and sat opposite, unable to resist a glance at the barn door. Josef had gone up the mountain to repair some fences, leaving Barry to watch over the goats, and with any luck, her stepfather would be gone for hours.

"Why do you want to live at the hotel when your home is here?" Clothilde's voice was soft, almost plaintive, a complete contrast to her usual scolding pitch. "How will I manage alone?"

"Alone? Your husband is here to provide you with all you need. I turned eighteen three months ago and it is time for me to lead my own life. At eighteen, you were already carrying me."

"Yes. Now I'm thirty-four and carrying your little brother."

The room fell silent, other than the ticking of the clock on the wall.

"Again?" whispered Seraphine.

"Again. Josef is beside himself with happiness." She tried to raise the corners of her mouth.

"But what if the baby ...?"

"It won't be. I have a feeling. You know what they say, third time lucky."

Images flashed through Seraphine's mind: Anton's tiny white gravestone, the 'special' children in the school playground, Henri wailing after a blow from Josef's hand, the boys' home in Bern. Anger at her mother's stubbornness sparked into an uncontrollable conflagration.

"How can you be so selfish?" she spat. "You have no idea whether or not this child will suffer like Anton and Henri did. You refuse to listen to me when I tell you of the wonders the doctor has worked on the children and grown-ups in St. Niklaus, in Grachen and in other communities. Most of all, you cannot see, as I have, the differences in the new babies. All the mothers who take the salt have delivered healthy infants. Those who refuse run a far greater risk of their offspring having serious defects which require full-time care. That's why you don't want me to leave. You want a permanent nurse for the children you cannot love." She stood up and opened the front door, craving a cold breeze on her flaming cheeks.

"Seraphine! Don't go!"

"I'm not going anywhere. I just needed some air."

Clothilde came to stand beside her. "I thought you cared for your brothers."

"I did! I do! It's because I loved my brothers that I would do anything in my power to prevent another child suffering the same way. It's cruel and unfair, especially when you know it can be prevented. You cannot rely on female intuition or any other folkloric nonsense when it comes to bearing a child." She whirled to face her mother, pulled away her scarf and pointed to her neck.

"See this? No, because it's no longer there. My lump is gone. Because I listened to the doctors and saw the results of their studies and took their advice. I added special salt to my food."

"You took their medicine without my permission?" She was trying hard to muster outrage but could not take her eyes from Seraphine's throat.

From around the corner, Barry appeared, evidently curious about the shouting.

"Watch the goats, Barry, good dog." He sniffed Seraphine's hand and loped off in the direction he had come. "Yes, I did and now it's gone. As long as I keep adding a little salt to my food, it won't come back. Maman, you must give your unborn child the best possible chance at life. Your goitre," she paused, aware it was the first time they had ever spoken of her mother's affliction, "is a sign something is wrong. It is simple logic – if your body lacks something it needs, so will any child you carry."

Clothilde snorted and walked past Seraphine to sit on the

bench. "And this magic remedy is salt? Don't be ridiculous. I've eaten salt every day of my life."

She had not yet walked away, which meant the discussion could continue. Seraphine sat beside her, also facing forward and she proceeded as delicately as she was able. "Not ordinary salt. *Jodsalz. Le sel iodé.* Small amounts of iodine in our food, the doctors know how much, reduce the neck swellings and often make them disappear completely in young people. Pregnant women need a little extra for themselves and the baby, so they can deliver a healthy child. Nobody in this valley got sick from the salt because it's only a little bit. But the difference is enormous."

She waited, listening to the goats' bells and bleats from across the valley, the most reassuring sounds she knew.

"Bayard told you all this?" Clothilde's voice indicated curiosity.

"Herr Favre, Bayard's assistant. When I returned from Montreux, I persuaded him to let me try. It's not officially part of the trial, but he is impressed by the change in me."

"I'm sure he is! You think he is doing this out of the goodness of his heart? These men think nothing of having their way with silly country girls and abandoning them for someone with connections. You are as easily led as a lamb, trusting everyone and believing anything."

Seraphine clenched her teeth. "Less than you think, Maman. For example, I know my father did not die in an accident and you were never a widow. Before you blame Margot or Thierry, I can tell you I learned the truth from Josef. That night he was drunk on Kirsch and shouting, 'Why must I pay for another man's child? He earns plenty and contributes not a franc for the girl!' That is how I know my father is still alive and I was illegitimate. You want to protect me from making the same mistake as you did."

Clothilde said nothing, her face blank.

"Thank you for your concern. I know you want the best for me. So do I. The difference is we have opposing ideas of how to scale that mountain. I must do everything in my power to change my life. Otherwise I sit here and stagnate until Niederer the bus driver asks me to marry him. No. Never. I want more than that. My decisions are my responsibility. As are yours."

Every year in early summer, Clothilde and Seraphine hung the rugs over the balcony, covered their faces with scarves and beat the dust out. Motes flew in clouds, billowing in unpredictable patterns until finally settling into invisibility on the ground. In the last twenty minutes, mother and daughter had aired decades of dust which took its time to settle.

"I cannot take the salt," said Clothilde, staring across the valley, her voice flat. "Josef won't hear of it."

They watched the black-feathered *Dohlen* swirling in the sky, sometimes soaring, sometimes tumbling as if they had been shot, only to swoop upwards again, chirping as if asking for applause.

"Josef doesn't need to know," murmured Seraphine.

They sat there for another few minutes, deep in thought. Then Clothilde reached over, patted her daughter's hand and went inside.

The room was under the eaves and thus, warned Frau Hediger, sweltering by late summer and frigid in winter. In June, however, it was quite perfect. Seraphine walked around the space, ducking under beams to explore her new home. The attic floor was very large in terms of square metres, but only a third of it was high enough for her to stand upright. The roof sloped to a point both east and west, with two south-facing windows opposite the door. Her furniture was basic – a bed, wardrobe, chair, chest of drawers and wash basin with an enamel ewer. It was musty, dusty and cobwebbed but the most beautiful room Seraphine could imagine.

She opened the windows, swept, dusted, aired and cleaned as if it was one of the guest rooms and she was once again a chambermaid. She emptied her trunk, stowed it under her bed and spent an hour arranging her collection of books on the chest of drawers. Other than her uniform and the coat Tante Margot had sent her for Christmas, she owned precious little to hang in the wardrobe. But she had the greatest treasure of all – a door with a lock and key.

When everything was rearranged to her satisfaction, she sat on the chair and watched the sun sink below the mountain peak, giving thanks for a room of her own. Twenty-five minutes later, face washed, hair combed and uniform buttoned up, she locked her door. The weight of that key in her apron would have lifted her spirits all evening, but the arrival of a particular guest thrilled her to her bones.

"Good evening, Herr Favre. What a pleasure to see you again." She gave a demure bob of her head. He looked taller and broader than last time she had seen him, which rendered him more intimidating.

"Seraphine! The pleasure is mine. When one returns to a previous locale, nothing is as reassuring as a friendly face." He bowed, his hat and gloves still in his hand. "Are you well?"

"Thank you, sir, very much so. Are you just arrived? Do you require any assistance?"

"None whatsoever. The porter can manage my trunk. What I do require is a restorative glass of red wine beside the fire. That journey never gets any shorter and the minute the sun drops, so do the temperatures. Do I have icicles in my moustache?"

Seraphine smiled, surprised and elated by the man's imme-diate familiarity. "Take a seat in the parlour, sir. It is yet early and you can have an armchair by the fire. I will bring you some wine directly."

She turned towards the bar and saw Frau Hediger watching from the kitchen. Seraphine dropped her eyes.

"How do you find your quarters?" asked the housekeeper. "Does that room suffice?"

The delight Seraphine tried to contain would not be denied and spread over her face like a sunburst. "It is perfect. I cannot believe it is mine and keep checking my apron for the key. Thank you so much for giving me this chance. You will not regret it."

"I'm glad to hear that. Attend to your guests now because that's why you are here."

Seraphine poured the wine and carried it on a tray to the parlour. The room admitted little light during the day but in the evenings, firelight and the glow of lamps flickered over the wood panels, making the engravings dance. Herr Favre was one of only two people in the room and certainly the only one awake. Alois, once famous for his Alpenstock walking sticks, spent his days dozing in a leather armchair near the window. According to St. Niklaus legend, he was just resting until someone from the *Meierturm*, or mayor's tower, alerted him to a potential customer. Then he would leap into action and convince the amateur mountaineer that nothing could be achieved without a trusty Alpenstock. Seraphine had only ever seen him leap once and that was when a drunk trod on his foot.

"Herr Favre?" she said. "Your wine." She placed the glass on the side table with a little curtsey.

His eyes gazed up at her as if she had wings. "The journey was worth it, if only for this."

She tilted her head in a gesture of modesty and lifted her chin, willing him to look at her neck. "The end of a journey is always welcome. Am I to understand you are dining with us this evening?"

"Unfortunately not. Doctor Bayard and his wife have extended an invitation to dine at their home. Why are you here this evening? You only used to work daytime hours or am I mistaken?"

She brushed away a stray hair. "I have recently become a live-in member of staff, sir. Frau Hediger and Herr Lochmatter have entrusted me with more responsibility. Enjoy your wine and welcome back to St. Niklaus." She made to leave but his voice halted her progress.

"Seraphine, for the first time since we met, you are not wearing a scarf or prim blouse. May I make so bold to ask ...?"

She looked at the ceiling, giving him a clear view of her smooth throat, then dropped her chin with a conspiratorial smile. "Gone. Vanished without a trace. Herr Favre, I am truly grateful for your kindness. Our agreement was that I am measured at regular intervals in return. At your convenience, sir, I will attend the surgery."

The man shook his head, incredulous. "It's as if it was never there. Yes, we need to measure and record the changes in meticulous detail. Surgery ends at six. Do you have time tomorrow before you begin your evening duties?"

"Most certainly. Thank you, sir."

She looked across at Alois, but his steady even snores told her he had not heard a thing.

S eraphine knew, and suspected Favre knew she knew, she was not part of the official trials. Her wide-eyed plea to the young doctor had hit its target and he was only too happy to provide her with iodised salt in return for regular checks on the results. Why those checks always occurred out of surgery hours, Seraphine was astute enough never to ask.

Before she attended the surgery the following evening, she took it into her head to make the most of herself. She had never previously used any artifice to enhance her features, but she admired the adornments worn by Frau Bayard and the rouged cheeks or reddened lips of hotel guests. The problem was that she could afford neither jewellery nor cosmetics. There was only one person she could ask. When her morning shift was complete, she asked Frau Hediger's permission to take the air and scurried up the lane to the Weisshornstube. Instead of going through the front door, she ducked into the alleyway at the rear. As she had expected, Romy was sitting in the sunshine, her booted feet stretched out in front of her.

"Seraphine! Come sit with me."

"Is it safe?"

"Yes, Hermann is gone to one of the farms to demand some replacement flour. The last lot had weevils. He won't be back for hours. That uniform looks well on you."

"Thanks, Romy. Your hair is pretty today. How do you get it to curl so?"

"Rags. Twist and bind each hank tightly after washing and let it dry overnight. The next morning, it bounces. I can show you if you like. My sisters taught me how."

"You're lucky to have sisters. My mother never showed any interest in making me beautiful."

Romy bunted her shoulder against Seraphine's. "That's because you don't need it. Girls like me have to curl and colour and add all kinds of frills to turn heads. You need nothing more than nature gave you."

"Oh, but I do! The women at the hotel are all so sophisticated, with artfully painted faces and fashionable attire. I'm a sparrow amongst peacocks. Could you at least show me how to apply lip rouge?"

Romy gave her a critical look. "Yes. But only lip stains, no more. A little colour on your pale face will benefit your complexion. No powder, no cheek rouge and no colour around the eyes, for that would be placing a gaudy curtain over a fine picture window." She opened her little beaded bag and withdrew a small pot. "Come closer and open your mouth. No, much wider. Think of an artist stretching a canvas. Better. Now cover your teeth with your lips. Exactly. Stay like that."

While Seraphine sat like a frog, Romy dabbed her ring finger into the pot and smeared it over Seraphine's lips. Once finished, she used her index finger to tidy the edges.

"Now you can relax. Smile. Blow a kiss. Hmm, probably a bit too scarlet for your skin, but you can see the effect." She pulled out a compact, flicked open the brass clasp and showed Seraphine her face.

She looked horrible, as if her lips were crusted with dried blood, but she remembered her manners. "You are very kind to show me how it's done. It suits you far better, but maybe I need to get used to it."

Romy switched the compact around to check her own face. The little object had a black and cream pattern like the floor of a French café. It seemed strangely familiar.

"True, deep red really goes with my colouring. You're a blonde so I think we should start with a pink. I don't have any with me today, but I'll bring some tomorrow."

"Yes, I like pink. That compact is lovely. A gift from one of your sisters?"

"No, a gift from one of my suitors." She laughed, tossing her ringlets over her shoulder. "Each one swears he adores me but only Philipp proves it with trinkets." The church bells began to ring. "Eleven already? I have to go. Thanks for keeping me company and I'll see what I have in pink. *Tschüss.*"

D r Favre treated her like any other patient, formal and polite, without a hint of impropriety. Except for the fact they were alone together in a small room, his fingertips on her jaw, moving her head this way and that. She cast her eyes down or if she could not avoid his gaze, closed them altogether. His demeanour had always been kindly and helpful to the extent she thought nothing of visiting the practice alone.

On this occasion, something shifted. A darkening of his pupils as he opened the door. The warmth of his hands when he touched her throat. The slightest catch of his breath on eye contact charged the air like the presage of a storm. Seraphine understood. Whereas previously she had attracted no more attention than any other child, men now noticed her, making uncouth comments in the Weisshornstube or watching her movements at Hotel Lochmatter. Perhaps sitting in his surgery to undergo an examination was reckless. Nevertheless, she needed something and was determined to get it.

"Every morning I look in the mirror and tell myself I'm dreaming. But it's true, is it not, Herr Doctor Favre? The salt has made that lump disappear. I'm cured, yes?"

He moved away to make some notes at his desk, clearing his throat several times.

"You're not dreaming. The swelling has gone down but I cannot say cured. Remember what I explained to you at our first meeting? The treated salt compensates for an absence in your nutrition. That absence remains. Without it, your body will develop the same symptoms as before. You must keep taking the salt, Seraphine, especially while you are still growing. I can give you a larger amount this time."

"That would be much appreciated, thank you." With a double dose, she could easily share it with her mother.

"The one thing you must promise me is to consume only the amounts I prescribe. Dr Bayard and I have been meticulous in administering the correct dosage. The salt I give you is exactly right for a seventeen-year-old. Taking too little or too much could derail our research or at worst, cause you harm."

Seraphine folded her hands in her lap and bowed her head. "I turned eighteen in March. I am no longer a child."

"Are you disappointed? I don't mean to be harsh or unkind, just factual." He came closer and offered his handkerchief, crouching to her eye level. "Seraphine?"

She raised her eyes to look at him directly. "Disappointed for myself, sir? No. To tell you the truth, I am overcome with gratitude. You have shown me such patience and given me far greater opportunities than if we had never met. The reason for my discomposure is my mother. She is with child. I hoped to share my salt with her in order to prevent a recurrence of what happened to my half-brothers. They both suffered the affliction of this valley and I am more afraid than I can voice because it might happen again."

He caught her twisting hands in his. "You may rest easy in your mind. I am willing to visit your mother and on diagnosing the level of deficiency, prescribe the correct dose."

"No! Sorry, sir, but that will not do. Her husband, my stepfather, forbids it. Only by stealth can I assist my mother during her pregnancy. This must seem very provincial to a city doctor and I apologise. The fact remains she needs help. She has a goitre the size of a quince and already bore two boys incapable of the simplest functions. I am sure this is highly irregular, but can you give me what she needs? Forgive me, I am ashamed to ask."

He stood up and walked to the window, looking out at the

dusk. "I want to help you, truly, I would like nothing more. But never in all conscience can I administer any kind of medication without the patient's consent. It goes against all the principles of the Hippocratic oath."

In an instant, Seraphine was by his side. She had a matter of minutes before she was due to report for duty. If she didn't convince him now, she might never have another opportunity. "Herr Doctor, I swear to you, my mother wants the salt. It is on her behalf that I beg for your help."

He turned to her, his face stern. "Why not ask Dr Bayard? He knows everyone in this valley and is better placed to understand your mother's situation."

She dropped her eyes, searching for a way to express her thoughts. She could tell him the truth and say she found Bayard and his wife impossibly intimidating. But what a back-handed insult to Herr Favre. She opted for a half-truth. "I respect both you and Dr Bayard very much. The issue here is trust. You have shown me great kindness and discretion, which is why I confided my predicament. The doctor knows my stepfather. His wife knows our neighbours. The community is small and people talk. You are not local and besides, I already know you can keep a secret."

His gaze bored into hers. She forced herself to maintain eye contact, determined to show sincerity. The hall clock rang half past the hour.

Seraphine started. "I have to go. Frau Hediger expects me in the kitchen. I apologise for putting you in a difficult position and promise not to mention the subject again."

He placed a hand on her shoulder. "I will do what I can."

"Thank you, sir. Thank you." She ducked out of the door and pattered down the stairs, light-headed and flushed. Even the air in the kitchen was cooler than the doctors' surgery.

"Ah, Seraphine!" Frau Hediger was dragging a heavy hessian

sack across the kitchen to the sink. "You are returned from your walk and just in time. I knocked on your door some twenty minutes ago to say we have a party of mountaineers arriving at eight. Tonight's special will be *Rösti* so you'd better start peeling these potatoes."

14

He stepped down, trying not to look at her, as if she were the sun yet he saw her, like the sun, even without looking.

— Leo Tolstoy, *Anna Karenina*

July 1919

My dear Julius
    Can it really be two months since you visited your old friend Bastian and the Matterthal valley? The date insists this is the truth but my mind swears it was but a month ago. Perhaps because we made so many memories in that fortnight, it feels as fresh as yesterday.

    Or am I ashamed of my letter-writing capacity and making sycophantic excuses? I am certain you would deem it the latter. As usual, you are probably right.

    It is conventional to list the myriad reasons one is late to correspond, and I am not one to buck tradition. Since our adventures in the mountains, I am run ragged between St. Niklaus and the villages, not to mention sending telegrams between the good doctors and reporting all our activities to the relevant authorities.

It is my great good fortune to have a friend like you who came to see for himself. I need waste no ink on describing the dramatic changes we have seen in Cantons Valais and Appenzell Ausserrhoden since Dr Bayard's initial experiments. What I cannot impress on anyone who had not seen these villagers before we implemented the use of iodised salt is the transformation. By which I mean both in the measurable, physical sense and the other less identifiable but equally significant alteration in local attitudes.

Under the current circumstances, one hesitates to use the word 'revolution', but I know of no other to convey the immense shift in the quality of life. Schoolyards with over 75% of children presenting goitres are now fewer than 10%. New-borns with iodine-related mental deficiencies are in single figures. The village baker is using treated salt in his bread and more than one farmer is adding low doses to cattle feed.

We discussed on several occasions how your specialism matters so much to individuals threatened by the loss of their sight. The delicacy of the eye, our dependence on that particular sense and the progress made in ophthalmology is a triumph. I am proud to know a specialist in the field. Your name, I have no doubt, will go down in history.

Unlike your clear-eyed self (I did intend that pun, forgive me), I had no urgent desire to study and improve a single facet of the human body. My drive when studying medicine was an unrefined desire to do good for ordinary folk. Make a difference, my mother always said. Thanks to your generosity and the determination of far greater physicians than I will ever be, I have found a field where I truly can make a difference. I owe you the most tremendous debt of gratitude.

Do you recall that day we trekked to the Weisshorn? We tried and failed to express our wonder at the hue of the sky, pounding of the waterfall and taste of a simple slice of cheese we ate sitting among flowers in a meadow. Even when channelling Walter's unabashed grandiloquence, we fell far short. I recall little of our efforts but your laughter still rings in my ears at my painful metaphor of blue glacial lakes and the mantle of a nun.

Blue is a colour much occupying my mind of late. Whilst I feel most at home in Herisau, the little town of St. Niklaus holds its own lure. I reside and receive patients on the top floor of Hotel Lochmatter, where you stayed. My recollection of you and our host singing and toasting with that potent schnapps – was it Williams? – still makes me smile. Thankfully by the time the new girl got promoted from chambermaid to waitress, you were long gone. Otherwise I would most certainly have been eclipsed.

Julius, she is like a woodland flower with eyes the colour of a forget-me-not. Modest and hard-working, she listens with true curiosity and her polite attention teases stories from the most retiring guests. When not on duty, she sits at her window and reads novels. Can you imagine? She is a favourite with everyone, none more than me. I dread leaving for the winter for fear of some local chap asking for her hand.

Dare I prevail on this Alpine maid to walk out with me? Asking you is a waste of good ink because you are incorrigible. How is the lovely Nina, by the way? My guess is you barely remember her name by now. After all, it has been two whole months.

I sign off now, my dear and treasured friend, with every hope of seeing you in person on my next visit. The trip to Herisau in early October will include an overnight stay in Zürich, possibly two. I have no shame in saying I intend to make full use of Walter's media connections in spreading the word about Dr Bayard's work. Could I invite you for an indulgent dinner at a restaurant of your choice?

One last comment. Men besotted with their object of affection often describe them as angels. The object of mine bears the name Seraphine. Am I a fool to read this as a sign?

Until we meet in October, all my heartfelt good wishes for your health and continued success,

Your loyal friend
Bastian
St. Niklaus, 10 July 1919

N o place on Earth, at least in Bastian's opinion, could compare to summer in the Matterthal valley. The sun shone like a benediction, refracting from waterfalls and illuminating peaks. Flowers sprouted everywhere, dots of colour amid the grass, and the sky, not content with its infinite blue claiming the heavens, reflected from every river pool.

His perspective was skewed, he knew that. A man in love could find a muddy puddle romantic. Even so, customers at the bakery brimmed with good cheer while hotel guests spoke in breathless tones of plans, projects and new horizons. Against the background of world peace signed into reality by the Treaty of Versailles, a civil war in Switzerland narrowly avoided, the entire country bubbled with optimism for the future. Newspapers, ordinarily harbingers of doom, echoed hopeful notes counterbalanced by long editorials on lessons learned.

St. Niklaus had more reasons than most to feel buoyant. The medical trials were an undeniable success, drawing interest from major figures in university hospitals and the Federal Health Office. Rarely did a week pass without a visitor, more often than not a minion, sent to observe the activities of Dr Bayard and his assistant. Demonstrating the efficacy of their treatment was a matter of documentation, Bastian's personal area of expertise, so he had no cause to disturb the doctor. Occasionally he mixed business with pleasure by inviting Seraphine to stand beside the photograph he had taken before she commenced iodine consumption. Swollen thyroid versus smooth neck. It did not hurt to see a beautiful young woman with bright blue eyes as an advertisement for all they had achieved.

And she was beautiful. Those officious little men who came from Bern or Basel, Zürich or Geneva were transfixed, cynics turned believers after one glimpse of that slim white throat. He watched them mumble and stutter when she bobbed her head, smiled and flashed those lightning-bolt eyes. Seraphine's presence for two minutes outweighed an hour of documentary evidence. Truth be told, Seraphine's presence outweighed everything. When she entered the dining room each morning, it was as if someone opened a window to let in fresh air.

When taking his meals alone, Bastian always sat at the same corner table. There he could observe people walking along Dorfstrasse from behind lace curtains and watch the rest of the room, Seraphine in particular, via the mirror between the two windows. It was the next best thing to gazing upon her directly. He was careful to respect the boundaries of propriety. Frau Hediger had sharp eyes, alert to an individual paying her waitress too much attention. Bastian refrained from anything but the most banal small talk in the dining room. Only during their weekly checks while measuring the girl's throat did he enquire after her mother's health.

"She says this pregnancy is harder than the others, sir, but I suppose that is only to be expected at her age."

"Yes, to conceive at the age of thirty-four is quite a challenge. Has she had any adverse reactions to the salt at all?"

"I don't know that it is the salt, but she did complain of headaches last week. Headaches and a dizzy episode, she said."

Bastian frowned. "Is she sticking to the dosage I recommended?"

"She says so. But I am only there one day a week so cannot swear to it."

"Seraphine, your mother may be at risk of high blood pressure which an increased intake of salt can only exacerbate. I would like to examine her."

"She won't have that, sir. I already tried to talk her round, but she insists she has borne three children without a doctor's interference and this time will be no different. I mean no disrespect. She can be a little old-fashioned."

"In that case, you can tell her there will be no more treated salt unless she allows me to test her blood pressure and give her a general check-up. I can go to her if she will not come to me."

Seraphine's eyes widened in alarm. "Please don't say that, sir! The salt is working, I can see for myself. Her neck is much reduced. Even she admits that."

"That is neither here nor there. Prescribing iodised salt to a pregnant woman with such issues is a danger to mother and child. My words are no idle threat, Seraphine. I will not run that risk. In hindsight, I was foolish to enable it. You must convince her to see me, for her own sake."

She lifted her gaze to meet his. "I will do what I can."

Whether she chose her words as a deliberate echo of his own or it was coincidence, he could not be sure, but the urge to take her face in his hands and kiss her all but overwhelmed him. He stood up from his chair, turned to his paperwork and gave her a curt dismissal.

"See that you do. I will record today's measurements now. Thank you for your time."

She slipped out of the door, silent as a cat. Bastian heard voices in the stairwell and recognised Frau Hediger's strong Walliser accent, no doubt requiring some assistance in the kitchen. He sat at the desk and placed his head in his hands. This passion was foolhardy in the extreme. He had to make a decision and stick to it. Either he declared his feelings for the girl or stopped seeing her altogether. By behaving like a moonstruck schoolboy, he could lose his position or compromise her reputation, and for what? For a man of twenty-four, he was still absurdly immature.

M any people who came to the surgery masked their fear with hostility. Clothilde Widmer's hostility masked nothing but raging contempt. Rude and dismissive from the moment she entered the practice, she complained at such a volume that Dr Bayard left his patient to see what crisis was causing all the noise.

"Why must I see a wet-behind-the-ears junior with no experience of midwifery when I have already given birth to three children? I have a farm to run. The time and cost of coming here on the bus, it's ruinous! My health is my own business."

"Good afternoon, Frau Widmer." Bayard's soft tones soothed the situation like balm. "Your health is our concern, no more and no less than anyone else in this valley. However, if you do not wish to see a doctor, I wonder why you are here?"

Bastian swallowed. The woman was about to demand a further supply of treated salt, something Dr Bayard knew nothing about.

To his surprise, Nurse Dunant intervened. "Frau Widmer is here for a blood pressure test and general health check. I am perfectly capable of performing both. There will be no need to disturb either doctor unless I see fit. Gentlemen, I apologise for the interruption to your important work. For your information, madam, I am a midwife and I have successfully delivered more babies than I can count. Follow me and please, out of respect for other patients, keep your voice down."

Cowed by the woman's steely tone, Clothilde Widmer pulled her coat tighter and walked into the nurse's bay. Bayard blinked at his assistant and returned to his room. Bastian treated a scratched cornea, an ear infection and a case of trench foot before Nurse Dunant appeared in the doorway.

"Herr Favre? The Widmer woman is in decent health. Her blood pressure is at the high end, but otherwise she's sturdy as a mule and twice as stubborn. She wants to see you. Good luck."

Bastian washed his hands and straightened his tie. The woman was nothing more than a patient and he was a professional.

"Nurse Dunant tells me you are in good health, Frau Widmer. I am happy to hear that."

Her coat was folded in her lap, her handbag by her side and the goitre was prominent, even disguised by her garments. In a glance, he took in its texture, reminiscent of dried fruit. Seraphine had spoken of its reduction in size but her skin would never recover.

"Give me the salt and let me go. How dare you hold me hostage? Typical doctor, withholding help, wielding power for his own ends. I see you, Favre, don't think I'm blind." She almost spat the words.

"Let me assure you, my concern is for you and your unborn child. I want to help since I know a little of your history from your daughter."

"My daughter, yes. First you fill her head with empty promises and now you try to blackmail me. It won't work, Herr Doctor of the university. We are not dependent on your benevolence. Seraphine is young and stupid but I am not. The nurse tells me I can get treated bread at the bakery. Why do we need you?"

"Frau Widmer, my profession is dedicated to improving people's lives."

"Like Seraphine's? You are keen on her, that much is clear. Why else would you give the girl the special salt unless she batted her eyelashes and made you think she was under your spell? Well, you can forget about my daughter, Herr Doctor, because she is engaged to be married. A bus driver by the name of Niederer, you see. Sweethearts since childhood and they have their parents' blessing. Talking of the bus, I am in a hurry. Give me the salt and I will take up no more of your time."

In the galley kitchen which served as the pharmacy, Bastian filled a jar with a low dosage of iodised salt and wrote strict notes on how it should be consumed. He handed it to the nurse.

"For Frau Widmer. Thank you."

"You're welcome, sir. Are you ready for your next patient? That boy with the toes."

"Of course. Send him in."

W hen surgery was over, he and Bayard compared notes on the day, finished their paperwork and closed the practice for the night. Bastian assured his mentor that he would clear up and sent his warmest greetings to Frau Bayard. Once the doctor had departed, the rooms seemed echoing and noisy, despite the fact he was the only occupant. He turned off all the lamps and locked the door. In his own chair, he stared out across the street at the *Meierturm*, sifting through every recollection of Seraphine.

She batted her eyelashes and made you think she was under your spell.

Was he really that stupid to pin all his hopes on a pretty adolescent who had shown him no more attention than the rest of the hotel guests? Yes, he had treated her but only as one element of his medical findings. They were all recorded as part of the iodine experiment and he had no reason to be ashamed of himself. At least not in a professional sense. Infatuation, on the other hand, was embarrassing. He had allowed himself to grow close to the girl, allowing her space in his thoughts, fantasising about a future gazing into those hypnotic eyes.

A soft knock came at the door. Seraphine had submitted to her evening measurements yesterday so she had no cause to visit the surgery tonight. He stayed completely still, waiting for her to leave. Until he could calm the maelstrom of his own thoughts, he was unable to keep his countenance nor trust his articulacy. The footfalls descended after a full minute of waiting outside the door. He checked his timepiece and noted she had to start work in a matter of minutes. Dining at the hotel that evening was an insufferable thought. He waited until the clock struck the half hour, gathered his things and unlocked the door. An envelope fell at his feet – a telegram addressed to him. He tucked it under his arm and walked down one flight of stairs to his own room. There he lit the candle and read the surprise missive.

URGENT. US DATA PUBLISHED. FAVRE TO RETURN TO HERISAU WITHOUT DELAY. EGGENBERGER

No sooner had he sat on the bed to digest the news than someone thundered up the stairs to bang on his door. He opened it, his pulse already elevated.

Dr Bayard looked more excitable than Bastian had ever seen him. "You received a telegram, yes?"

"I did, sir, not five minutes ago."

"So did I. This is extraordinary news!"

"What is, sir?"

"Why the Americans, of course! Their findings correspond to ours. Now is the time to address the Federal Health Office. You must leave first thing tomorrow and take copies of all our records for Doctor Eggenberger. We shall examine all the paperwork together and gather it into a single bundle. I shall compose a draft letter for the *Bundesrat*. My wife is bringing a suitcase for the purpose. I took the liberty of asking Frau Hediger to serve us some *Siedfleischsuppe* as we shall require sustenance. Come along, young man, hurry upstairs. We have much work to do!"

In the bustle of collating documents, some further hurried packing in his own quarters and a broken night's sleep, Bastian had barely a moment to think of Seraphine's engagement, apart from every time he closed his eyes. He left the hotel early, intent on catching the first train down the valley. Herr Lochmatter stood at reception, tall and buttoned up, ready to prepare his bill.

Bastian peered into the dining room for a glimpse of Seraphine. "The ladies are sleeping in this morning?" he asked, signing his name in the visitors' book.

"That is correct, Herr Doctor Favre. Last night's carousing went past two of the clock and the women deserve their rest. I laid out bread, ham and cheese or I can boil an egg if you need something for your journey. May I pour you some coffee? No finer way to face the day."

"Thank you, I would rather reach the station a little early. The carter?"

"Waiting outside. I wish you a pleasant journey, good sir, and we all look forward to your return."

"Thank you for your hospitality. Please pass on my sincere gratitude to Frau Hediger and Fräulein Widmer. Excellent service at this hotel. Goodbye."

The train bore him down the valley as the sun crested the peaks, washing the shadows away and displaying all the colour, detail and scale of the Matterthal. Bastian drank in every detail and swore a solemn oath to himself. For the sake of his heart, he would never come back.

· · ·

P OST RETURNED

Dear Herr Doctor Favre

I regret to inform you the recipient of the enclosed letter is deceased. Herr Doctor Julius Willmann passed away due to complications after a bout of severe influenza on 10 September.

My most sincere condolences.

Sekretariat, USZ – Universitätsspital Zürich

29 September 1919

15

Oh, God and his good angels! Whither, whither Is shame fled human breasts? That with such ease, Men dare put off your honours and their own? Is that, which ever was a cause of life, Now placed beneath the basest circumstance? And modesty an exile made, for money?

— Ben Jonson, *Volpone*

Jan 1920

"She's serving breakfast in the dining room, Herr Widmer. Whatever is the matter?"

Josef barged through the double doors, still in his coat and winter boots. "Seraphine, your mother needs you! The child is coming! She suffers terribly and how am I supposed to help? Frau Hediger, please release my daughter so she might save a life!"

"Good gracious! There is no question she can be released, Herr Widmer. Seraphine, go to your mother without delay. We shall pray for them both, Frau Widmer and her baby."

In the scramble of apologising to the guests and her employers, taking off her apron and donning her winter garments, Seraphine reflected on Josef's use of the singular. *Save a life?* Whose?

Snow flurries whirled about her head as she followed her stepfather out of the hotel to see two horses stamping in what little light penetrated the morning mist. In all her years, Seraphine had never ridden a horse. The only means of transport she knew were the Postauto and her own two feet.

"Horses, Papa?"

"Borrowed from the mountain guides. It will cost me but there is no faster way to ascend. Your mother is in terrible distress. Now, Seraphine! Get on."

A woman's voice cut through the air. "Seraphine? Is something wrong?" Frau Bayard stood at the corner, so striking in the hazy light she seemed like a character from a fairy tale. "Can I be of assistance?"

"Thank you, Frau Bayard, but I think not. We must ride to our village where my mother is in labour. Papa says it is difficult and he does not know how to help."

"He may not, but I most certainly do. Herr Widmer, will you allow me to accompany your daughter? Together we can ease your wife's troubles. I require the use of your horse so that I can ride to her bedside and deliver your child safely."

Josef stepped backwards and held out the reins, unusually bereft of speech.

"Follow us on foot," said Frau Bayard, hitching up her skirts, "and be assured we will greet you with good news. I am quite capable of mounting this animal alone. Would you lend a hand to your daughter?"

Her stepfather's strong hands caught Seraphine by the waist and lifted her into the saddle. She found her balance, set her feet into the too-long stirrups and scooped up the reins. The horse began moving without hesitation, following its stable mate. Seraphine had never felt more vulnerable or exposed. She clamped her knees to the horse's flank and prayed Frau Bayard knew what she was doing.

The horses plodded up the track to the village, sure-footed and solid, puffing great clouds of warm breath into the wintry air. The animal's gait soon became as familiar as her own, and Seraphine's tension relaxed into a swaying motion, working with and not against the huge beast. A powerful equine body straining up the slopes exuded heat and scent, somehow reassuring and less lonely than ascending alone on foot.

Ahead, Frau Bayard clucked and commanded her steed onward, her cloak billowing in gusts of biting air. For a city woman, she handled mountain life with confidence. Seraphine stopped worrying and put her faith in the doctor's wife, trying not to imagine what her mother would say.

Their journey took a little under an hour. After a clumsy dismount in the yard, Seraphine was relieved to be on her own two feet.

"Fasten the stirrups high and secure the reins so as to give the animal his head, like this. We leave them to drink now and they will make their own way back to the village. They know what they are doing."

She copied the livery arrangement, left her horse at the trough and ran after Frau Bayard into the farmhouse.

Her mother lay on the kitchen floor, her face white and sweaty, her dress dishevelled. Glassy-eyed, she showed no recognition but spoke through gritted teeth.

"It won't come. I push and push and nothing. It will not come."

"I am here, Maman." Seraphine was at her side, gripping her hand in a second.

"Seraphine? Where is Josef?"

"He is on his way. Frau Bayard is here. She knows what to do."

Clothilde clenched her fists and made an animalistic growl as a contraction racked her body. "Then do it! For the love of God, do whatever you have to do!"

In a rush of purple skirts, Frau Bayard knelt in the pool of fluid surrounding Clothilde and offered her a vial. "Take this, Frau Widmer, it will help you relax and soothe the pain. Leave the rest to me. Seraphine, boil some water and bring a cool flannel for her forehead, please."

It took all of two minutes to set a pan on the stove and rinse a cloth in the trough where the horses still steamed. By the time she returned, her mother was limp as a rag. Frau Bayard poured boiling water into a bowl, rolled up her sleeves and wiped her hands with a moist towel.

"We cannot wait, Seraphine. It's possible the baby is at the wrong angle, or worse, the cord might be around the child's neck. I must examine your mother and her child if we are to have any hope of saving either. Light some lamps and stoke the fire. It's dark and cold as a tomb in here. Then hold her hand and reassure her all is well."

In the dim light of the stove door, Frau Bayard knelt between Clothilde's legs while Seraphine wiped moisture from her mother's lip, spoke comforting words, tilted her head if her breathing caught and caressed her face each time she winced. With a spasm like a dying fish, her mother grunted as if to vomit and something wet splattered into Frau Bayard's lap.

"You took your time, little man. Seraphine, come clean your brother. Make sure his mouth and nostrils are clear, wash him gently and keep him next to your own body for warmth. I shall attend to your mother."

The boy was tiny and a lurid shade of purple. His eyes tightly closed, his mouth opened and closed like a fish, but made no sound. Seraphine wiped his face of mucus, resting a palm on his fragile ribcage to check for breathing and rested him against her hand in the now cooling bowl of water. The baby's impossibly small limbs worked like a miniature mountain climber and his mouth puffed little gasps of air as Seraphine cleansed his body. A tuft of dark hair crowned his smooth head, exactly the same as Henri when he was born. But there the similarities ended.

Seraphine prayed this was a healthy child, free of the challenges her brothers had battled. She patted him dry and tucked him inside her blouse. Midday sunlight was strong enough to penetrate the gloomy kitchen, adding a celebratory glow to the scene. A sharp breeze blew across her neck and something brushed her elbow.

"Barry! Look, there's a new baby for you to mind." The St. Bernard sniffed the infant's head, his tail wagging incessantly.

Frau Bayard returned from the barn with a bucket. "The dog was whining so I let him in. They have an instinct for these things, don't you think? Your mother needs to rest but first she must feed the child. May I take him?"

With some reluctance, Seraphine eased the warm scrap of flesh from her chest and handed him to Frau Bayard, who examined him like a piece of porcelain.

"For the last year, every child has undergone the same examination, each attended by the same bated breath. Your brother is well, with no sign of a goitre. Whether he will develop normally remains to be seen." She wrapped the new-born in a clean cloth. "Fetch me another cushion, Seraphine, her back needs support. Frau Widmer? Wake up now. Frau Widmer, your baby is a healthy little boy who needs feeding. Can I give him to you?"

Clothilde opened her eyes to stare at the bundle. "It's not …"

"No, he's not. But he is hungry. Your son, *meine Dame*."

As if to reinforce the point, the baby opened his mouth and

after a few experimental bleats, released a loud wail, his face crumpled like a handkerchief. Frau Bayard placed him into his mother's arms and after a moment's wonder, she guided him to her breast. The sound ceased and Seraphine blinked away her incredulity.

Theory was now proven by practice. The concept of treated salt to which she had been so committed had borne results. Clothilde and Josef had a child of their own who needed no extra care or particular protection. It was a dizzying thought. In one brilliant instant Seraphine's head grew light and gave her fantasy wings. She was free to leave the valley. Free to make a difference.

Barry growled and paced to the barn door, his head cocked. Stamping boots and a loud cough announced Josef, who burst into the room, bringing wintry chill behind him. He stared at the women in turn, finally fixating on his wife. She pulled back the coverlet to reveal the infant's head.

"A boy. A fine, healthy little boy."

Josef seemed rooted to the spot and even Barry moved closer as if in encouragement.

"Are you sure?"

"I am not a doctor, Herr Widmer, but I have assisted the doctors of St. Niklaus, given birth to my own and assessed over a dozen new-borns. Your son shows no sign of any affliction. In my opinion, the boy is a little premature, but with good nursing and care, he should develop like any other child. I congratulate you on your happy event."

"Frau Bayard, I cannot thank you enough! You and Seraphine made a miracle happen. Please, have a glass of wine with us to wet the baby's head." Josef's eyes were dark with emotion.

"That is a generous offer, but as I am with child myself, I must refuse. Know this, Herr and Frau Widmer, I would toast your new arrival with champagne were I able. This is a truly joyous occasion and I am honoured to have played a part. Seraphine, your calm and capable nature makes me think you should train as a nurse. The way you supported your mother today was exemplary. I must leave you now and return to St. Niklaus."

Josef and Seraphine protested in chorus.

"It is nothing. Walking to the village is all downhill and my boots are stout. From there I shall avail myself of the Postauto and return to St. Niklaus in time to prepare the evening meal. I rejoice in your good news and wish you every happiness with your son."

Seraphine and Barry walked Frau Bayard to the end of the farm lane.

"Frau Bayard, I will never be able to thank you for such kindness. You and Herr Doctor Bayard have changed our lives."

"It is within everyone's capacity to enhance the lives of others. All of us must do what we can. I was perfectly serious when I said you should study nursing. From there you could specialise in childcare, midwifery or any discipline where your natural pragmatism and good nature can shine. You are a bright girl whose skills might benefit more than the clientele of Hotel Lochmatter. When you return to St. Niklaus, we shall take tea and discuss the possibilities. Good afternoon, my dear and once again, congratulations."

I n early 1920, while her workplace stayed the same, Seraphine's role changed completely. She accepted the position of trainee nurse under Frau Dunant at Dr Bayard's practice. The job involved a good deal of studying as well as practical duties, demanding long hours and a whole new vocabulary. It also required a change in her living arrangements. No longer a hotel employee, she had to vacate the maid's room in the attic. It was hardly a wrench in the bitter temperatures of January to take up residence with her old schoolteacher. Frau Fessler, now retired, still owned her small cottage next door to the school with three rooms she rented to guests or temporary summer workers. They came to an agreement under which Seraphine was entitled to stay until the end of May for a fraction of her wages. It suited them both very well, as Frau Fessler liked to spend her evenings reading by the fire, while Seraphine studied at the dining table.

Dr Bayard's experimental work with iodine interested Seraphine greatly, not only due to the substantial benefit it had brought to her family. Bayard was willing to explain at length when he had time and thus Seraphine learned much about the thyroid gland and its role in the body.

"Let us consider Frau Fessler," he said. "When she was head teacher at the school, she regulated your timetable. She listened and observed, rang the bell, instructed the caretaker, placed each child into the correct class and ensured every part of the organisation had precisely what it needed. Sometimes discipline, sometimes a spontaneous race around the school yard. The thyroid is the same. Inside your neck, that small butterfly-shaped gland sends out exactly the hormones your body needs. No more, no less. How you eat, sleep, breathe, digest, develop and reproduce is down to your thyroid. It regulates your day, just like Frau Fessler used to do."

"Unless it does not function, sir?"

"Unless it cannot function. Starved of iodine, it swells, trying to perform its duties with what little it can provide. In an expectant mother, there are barely enough hormones to serve one, let alone two. This is why we must feed that hard-working little gland. But with great care. Not too much, not too little. It is as delicate as a butterfly. We still have much to learn about this complex organism we inhabit."

He only once mentioned Herr Favre and that was in the context of a similar experiment happening in the east of the country.

"Dr Eggenberger of Herisau, the man who loaned me Herr Favre, is pressing on with a canton-wide initiative with a view to having the treatment implemented into law. Certain learned minds are sceptical, as is to be expected, but I am quite convinced the results both here in the Matterthal and Appenzell Ausserrhoden, in parallel with those of the Americans, speak for themselves. You yourself know the facts of the matter from personal experience."

"Indeed I do and I am most profoundly grateful. May I ask why it is to be expected that some are sceptical?"

Bayard looked at her over his round glasses. "There are many reasons. Previous attempts at treating thyroid imbalances in France were unpopular because the dosage was too high, causing problems of its own. Let us not forget that having a goitre was sufficient reason to exclude one from military service. With France at war, no wonder there was reluctance to cure oneself. Here in Switzerland, those who have an interest in the salt industry, those who have no direct experience of what an iodine-deficient diet can do, and those simply resistant to change have stood and will continue to stand in opposition. It takes great determination and a long time to change people's minds. But change they must. I have sincere faith in Eggenberger. If anyone can make this happen, it will be a man with his energy.

"That reminds me, my wife sent away for some reading material from the Red Cross. There is an organisation known as the Swiss Nursing Association, with branches in Zürich and Bern, where young ladies such as yourself can continue their professional training. Should you feel that is something you would like to pursue, I would be proud to sponsor you."

"Thank you, sir. I am most grateful. I had never thought of becoming a professional."

"You should. My wife was right about you. I can see you doing very well in the world of medicine."

It was with a strange mixture of fear and excitement that Seraphine walked through the snow towards the schoolteacher's house that evening. The thought of leaving St. Niklaus to study in a city was simultaneously terrifying and absolutely what she wanted. She decided to say nothing to Frau Fessler or anyone else, but to discuss the idea with Frau Bayard when she next had an opportunity. Deep down, she knew that was because Frau Bayard would be enthusiastic and see a way to overcome every obstacle. She smiled to herself as she hung up her coat and hat then unlaced her boots.

"Seraphine?" Frau Fessler's face was sombre. "A telegram came for you."

She read the words three times and each time they weighed heavier like a yoke. "This news is from my aunt in Montreux. My brother died on Monday. Henri, the one in the Bern boys' home, the only one I had left."

"Oh, you poor child! Sit down and I shall make some tea."

"I must tell my mother."

"Of course you must! But that is out of the question until tomorrow. The last bus to the village went an hour ago and even if you got that far, you would still need to walk up to the farm in the dark. Wait until morning, dear girl. Would you like me to accompany you?"

"Thank you, but no. I prefer to speak to her alone. Frau Fessler, would you mind if I went to my room? I want to pray for Henri." Her voice cracked and she could barely see her landlady through her tears.

"Take as long as you need, my dear. I am so very sorry for your loss."

C lothilde crossed herself. "God rest his soul."

Josef sawed at the bread. "God bless him, yes indeed." He looked from his wife to Seraphine, his manner hesitant. "Only eight years old, poor boy. Did Margot say anything about the funeral?"

"That is tomorrow. He will be put to rest in the family plot, with your permission, beside Anton. I cannot attend because of my duties at the practice but intend to pay my respects on my next visit."

"I meant about who is going to pay for it. This has been a very hard winter for us."

Clothilde turned her head and fixed her husband with a malevolent glare. "My brother and sister will foot the bill for our son, as they did for Henri's care, just as they did for Anton's hospital bills and funeral expenses. An expression of gratitude would be the civil response."

Josef had the grace to look humbled, but only for a moment. "Write them a thank-you letter. Seraphine can deliver it on her next trip, along with a pot of jam. Did your mother tell you about Peter? Not six months old but sitting up on his own and eating solids. He grows so fast he'll be out of that cot and running around in no time. The perfect child, he sleeps through the night, every night. He'll be awake soon enough and you can see for yourself."

Seraphine stood up and scratched Barry's head. "Not today. I took the morning off work to deliver the sad news. Now I must return to the village if I am to catch the bus. To see you both well and hear Peter is strong does me good. This Sunday I am cleaning the surgery to compensate for my absence today. That means I shall join you for lunch one week from Sunday. *Au revoir*, Maman. *Tschüss*, Josef, and give Peter a kiss from me."

No one responded and Seraphine turned to see Clothilde and Josef exchange a look.

"The bus, yes, of course," said her mother. "I was meaning to talk to you about that. Sit down for a moment."

Seraphine sat, discomfited at the way they were watching her. "About the bus?"

"About the bus driver," said Josef. At a furious glare from Clothilde, he held up his hands in defence and tucked them under his armpits.

"The Niederers have always been good neighbours to us, don't you agree?" Clothilde's voice had a wheedling edge to it.

"We hardly have anything to do with them."

"They allow us to cross their land for the mountain pastures, they brought potatoes while Josef was away and they are willing to sell us some cows."

"Whatever are you talking about? You farm goats. What would you do with cows?"

"Five cows would make us more money than an entire herd of goats," Josef replied.

"Josef." Clothilde silenced him through gritted teeth then returned her attention to Seraphine, rearranging her expression into sweetness. "Herr and Frau Niederer are getting older. Which of us escapes time? On one hand, they are lucky with two healthy adult sons earning good money driving the buses or fixing tractors. On the other, neither of those handsome boys wants to work the farm. This is why their parents want to sell some of their land and cattle. They think, and we agree, it would be a fine thing to forge closer ties between our two families. I should add that the price they are asking is extremely generous."

Seraphine absorbed the meaning behind her explanation and could find no words to express her horrified astonishment.

"Philipp Niederer has always been very fond of you. What we are proposing is a fortuitous union between two families. An honest local man is ready to provide for you so you no longer need to skivvy at Hotel Lochmatter. Our part in the bargain is to buy a parcel of land and half a dozen of the Niederers' milk herd. The arrangement makes all of us stronger and happier. Seraphine, you have always been a sensible girl. I know you will see the practical side and rejoice that our family's fortunes are changing."

Seraphine got to her feet, her fists clenched. "This is the year 1920. People no longer barter their daughters for livestock. If they did, I hope my future happiness would be worth more than six cows."

"Seraphine!" The anguish in her mother's voice had stopped her on the threshold on more occasions than she could count, but not today. She stalked out of the farmhouse, her head hot and muddled with anger and disbelief. As always, Barry escorted her down the farm lane with a proprietorial air. His muzzle was whiter than before and his ears were greying. Without warning, hot tears spilled down her cheeks and she knelt to cuddle the dog. Poor Barry. The tears his ruff had soaked up would fill a bath. She patted his head and strode off down the lane without looking up at the window to wave goodbye.

When she boarded the bus, she greeted the driver with the briefest of acknowledgments and moved to sit near the rear. Preoccupied by her parents' betrayal, thoughts of the brothers she had lost and her reluctance to bond with the newest addition to the family, she pressed her face to the window of the bus, staring over the white valley. *Spring will come. It always does. Things will change for the better. They always do.*

A wave of shame washed over her as she replayed her own words. *People no longer barter their daughters for livestock. If they*

did, I hope my future happiness would be worth more than six cows.
How could she be such an ingrate? Josef had taken her and her
mother in, gave them a home and treated her as his own child.
No matter how little he and Clothilde owned, Seraphine had
wanted for nothing. Even though Josef considered them a waste
of time, he gave her money to buy her beloved books. To dismiss
their suggestion with high-handed behaviour was unforgivable.

But Philipp Niederer? He was ten years older than her, surly
and unsmiling, with a predatory expression. The way he looked
at her made her uncomfortable. No, the thought of marrying
him was bleak and chilling. A week on Sunday, she would take a
peace offering to her parents, apologise for her ungrateful attitude and plead with them to let her go to the city and study
nursing.

She scuttled off the bus in a hurry, hoping to avoid eye
contact with Philipp Niederer. He must know her parents had
mooted their proposal. Normally she avoided the Postauto on
weekdays simply because he was driving. When she finally
passed the driver's seat, it was empty. She exhaled and emerged
into the cold, wrapping her scarf around her neck, only to come
face to face with the man himself.

"Hello, Seraphine. I hardly see you these days," he said,
blocking her path.

"Hello, Herr Niederer. No, I rarely use the bus now. I have no
need when I live and work in St. Niklaus. Nice to see you again."
She moved to walk past him but he stretched out an arm as if to
embrace her. She stepped away.

"Call me Philipp. I want to talk to you."

"Today is not a good time, I'm sorry. I should be at work.
Please excuse me."

He loomed over her. "Don't you want to hear what I have to
say?"

Normally, every single one of the gossips would be clucking

and squawking, sticking their beaks in and chastising Seraphine for inappropriate conduct. She would be blamed, not him, even though he was the one preventing her escape. Today, not a single busybody noticed.

"Herr Niederer, I have no desire to be impolite. Neither do I wish to disappoint the patients at the practice. Kindly move aside and allow me to proceed."

His brows gathered and he caught her wrist in his chilled, bony hand. "Ideas above your station, that's what your mother says. Time she settled down with a decent man who earns a good living, in Josef's words. Happens I agree with your folks. A practical family, the Widmers, much like ours. Good heads on broad shoulders with no airs or graces."

Cold air blew down the valley, dragging strands of Seraphine's hair across her face. Herr Niederer reached out a hand to sweep them away. A deep-seated revulsion forced her to act. She twisted her wrist from his grip and took a pace backwards.

"Yes, you are a practical man, Herr Niederer, one who keeps his options open. I wonder how many other girls in this valley received a pretty powder compact as a token of your affection. Or was it only me and Romy? Excuse me, please, I believe this conversation is over."

She ducked under his grasping arm and ran several paces until she cleared the narrow gap between the station building and the bus.

"*Guten Morgen*, Herr Lochmatter," she yelled, even though there was not a soul on the street. The footsteps behind her crunched to a halt and she skittered downhill, all the while addressing an invisible individual. "Yes, I am little late. Are you going that way? How fortunate for me. How is your son after his fever?"

Around the corner, the wood merchant was smoking with

Alois and complaining about the weather. Seraphine slowed her panicky run and risked a look behind her. Niederer was nowhere in sight. She acknowledged both villagers with a civil greeting and continued along Dorfstrasse to the hotel. So perturbed was she by the encounter with the bus driver that she failed to notice the travelling cloak on the hotel coat rack.

She was heading to the nurses' room when a shadow crossed her path. Directly in front of her stood Bastian Favre. The pressure of the last two days cracked her composure. She burst into tears and ran out of the practice, up the attic stairs and to her immense relief, found the key still in the lock of her old room. She went inside, secured the door and threw herself on the bed, still wearing her hat and boots. She cried for Henri, for Anton, for her mother and even for Barry. Finally, she cried for herself and only then did she sleep.

16

... jealousy gave him, if anything, an agreeable chill, as, to the sad
Parisian who is leaving Venice behind him to return to France,
a last mosquito proves that Italy and summer are still not too remote.

— Marcel Proust, *Swann's Way*

May 1920

O ver the last ten months, Bastian convinced himself he had forgotten his youthful infatuation with a blue-eyed mountain girl. Since then, he had begun walking out with a lovely widow called Teresa in Herisau, flirted with several daughters of local politicians and abandoned himself to a night of lust in Zürich. The woman was a friend of Walter's. Her name escaped him but her breasts were unforgettable.

When Eggenberger bade him return to St. Niklaus to collaborate with Dr Bayard on the masterplan, he accepted the order with equanimity. While Teresa's pleasant company would be lacking, they could resume their affections on his return. In fact,

SALT of the EARTH | 171

a change in routine suited him very well. He was in danger of settling for the easy option, something he despised.

Springtime in the Matterthal. What a pleasure! The company of Dr Bayard and his wife was always welcome. And to play a role in the reformation of Swiss society, scientific rather than religious, would be a privilege. That young waitress had faded from his memory to the extent he could barely recall her family name.

During the journey through the valley he renewed his acquaintance with every bridge, dramatic drop, sheer cliff face and village along the route, his anticipation growing the higher the train ascended. St. Niklaus appeared unchanged when he disembarked and he was able to greet half a dozen familiar faces on the way to the hotel. No one was attending reception, more than likely preoccupied with the lunch service, so he hung up his cloak and left his cases for the porter. A trunk was old-fashioned and unnecessary as his sojourn would last no longer than a sennight.

Female footsteps echoed down the corridor and Bastian squared his shoulders, a smile in waiting. A sour-faced woman carrying two bowls of soup gave him a nod.

"Be with you directly."

He waited until she came back, wiping her hands on her apron.

"You'll be wanting a room, I suppose." She opened a leatherbound book and fumbled in her apron for a pair of spectacles. No 'sir', no polite form of address.

"That is correct. My name is Herr Doctor Bastian Favre and I am here to work alongside Dr Bayard. I am a regular visitor, as Frau Hediger or Seraphine Widmer can attest."

The woman did not look up. "The Hediger woman cannot attest to much these days, I'm afraid, and Seraphine has moved up in the world. Not that it bothers me. Why shouldn't I do the jobs of three people? Several rooms on the second floor are available and I daresay more convenient for the practice. How many nights?"

Bastian's disappointment was unaccountable. What did he care about members of staff he recalled from earlier stays?

With affected formality, the woman spoke again. "Herr Doctor? How long would sir like the room?"

"One week from today, if you please."

"Sign here if you would be so good and the boy will take your bags. If you want to eat your midday meal in the restaurant, the menu today is barley stew with mutton. Here is your key. Excuse me, I must attend to the kitchen."

His welcome in the practice was of a different ilk. Nurse Dunant gave one of her rare smiles, Dr Bayard clasped both his hands around Bastian's, and two people in the waiting room greeted him by name. He and the doctor sat in his surgery drinking tea and exchanging information until Bastian grew concerned about keeping his patients waiting.

"No need to worry about that. Our new junior doctor deals with the everyday issues these days. You really must meet Herr Zanetti, he has a similar drive to your own. Dinner tomorrow evening, perhaps? My wife is impatient to see you again. As for our patients, Frau Dunant manages the rest. She is a little more under pressure than usual as Seraphine asked for a half day, but no one would be any the wiser. That Dunant woman is like a swan, serene on the surface and paddling frantically below."

Bastian calmed his urge to ask questions. "It would be an honour and a privilege to meet your assistant and reacquaint myself with your wife. Frau Dunant is a formidable woman any practice would envy. Am I to understand she too has an assistant? That girl who used to work in the hotel?"

Bayard raised one eyebrow. "Yes, I refer to Seraphine. The same girl you often used as living proof of our work." He smiled. "I may be old, Herr Favre, but I am not blind. Thus far she has proven herself to be most capable. Training her as a nurse was my wife's idea and she is rarely wrong about people. Now I think of it, we should invite both Frau Dunant and Seraphine to dine with us together. I shall propose the idea to the ladies. Let us walk down to the *Apotheke*. I am eager to show you the little laboratory in which we prepare the salt. A coat and scarf would be wise. Spring can be unpredictable."

Bastian agreed to meet the doctor inside the entrance so he might retrieve his cloak. The moment he closed the surgery door, a figure scurried along the corridor and almost cannoned into him. She lifted her face, widened her eyes and burst into tears, running in the opposite direction. Bewildered, he stood in silence until the sound of her footsteps receded.

Then he descended the stairs to don his outdoor garments. What earthly reason would Seraphine have to cry the instant she set eyes on him?

His composure collapsed. Did she love him? Did he love her? Or was this a case of momentary madness which would be over in a month? He had believed himself in love with Flora, and look how often he thought of her now. Whereas he thought of Julius every single day with a pang in his heart. The calendar reminded him it was approaching a year since his friend had joined him in St. Niklaus, eager to learn about the valley and Bastian's work within it, ready to share ideas, drink beer and laugh. He missed his friend with a sense of furious injustice. Of all the people who should have been taken early, Julius was the least deserving. Especially by a malady as mundane as influenza.

Bastian refused to call it by the popular epithet, the Spanish Flu, for the very sound reason it was incorrect. That deadly epidemic had swept across every continent, killing indiscriminately. Many countries were prohibited from reporting their catastrophic losses due to wartime propaganda and its effect on public morale. Whereas Spaniards, neutral in the conflict, were able to tell the unvarnished truth about their huge death toll. Thus, saddled with the unjust moniker, Spain was henceforth to blame.

Part of Bastian still refused to accept he had lost his friend. His mind played tricks, especially in those liminal states of early morning, reminding him a letter was overdue or assuring him it must have been a mistake. Somewhere, Julius was still alive, wondering why he and Bastian were no longer in correspondence. When he woke and faced reality, it pained him almost as much as that first blow to the solar plexus which stole his breath. How many times must he lose his dear friend? The letter from the hospital had come weeks after the funeral, meaning Bastian was not present to say his final goodbye. Even after visiting his grave at the family plot in St. Gallen, the fact of his friend's demise was repeatedly rejected by his brain.

If Julius were here, how would he advise his smitten colleague? He smiled. If Julius really were here, Bastian would hardly stand a chance at courting Seraphine. Women flocked to his handsome friend like birds to a bath. He could just imagine those eyebrows twitching, the sound of his voice as he poured more champagne. *Faint heart never won fair lady. Why not,* mon brave, *why not?* Bastian made up his mind. He would test the waters and ascertain whether her feelings matched his. Should her bright eyes and blushes transpire to be nothing more than politeness, he need trouble her no further. If she reciprocated, why delay a moment longer? Imagine Dr Eggenberger's astonishment if he returned to Herisau with a beautiful bride.

. . .

Bayard's laboratory was little more than one corner of a woodshed, where two men and one woman worked around a central table. Clearly used to observers, they nodded a greeting and continued with their measuring, sifting, packaging and labelling. Each person wore a leather apron and sturdy gloves, much like an ironsmith, with stout boots to protect their feet. The system differed from that Doctor Eggenberger had set up in Herisau in various ways but the concept was the same. Bayard explained each stage of the manufacturing process and described its distribution. A cottage industry designed to serve its community, but well-organised enough to expand.

The separation of the products was clear: one person was responsible for a single dosage, mixing, weighing and identifying every little sack with precise marks. The doctor's passion was tangible and all-consuming, distracting Bastian from his own concerns. They spent an hour in the small shed until a delivery cart came to collect the day's production. The cool air whirling through the workshop reminded both men that daylight was dwindling and they returned to Hotel Lochmatter, still in animated conversation.

Bastian's hope that the doctor would invite him upstairs once more was quickly dashed when a barefoot child accosted them in the street.

"Dr Bayard, they sent me to fetch you. A man took a fall and he's coughing up blood. They need you, sir, because the poor soul is in a dreadful state. Make haste, his condition is woeful!"

"Can I help in any way?" offered Bastian.

"Thank you, no. I will send word later." The doctor dashed after the boy, leaving Bastian at the junction. To his right lay Dorfstrasse, the site of his accommodation. To the left rose the lane to the train station and bus stop. Shadowed by the station building, the Postauto stood idle, its driver smoking a pipe in the last rays of sunshine. When the man looked up, Bastian tipped his hat but received no response. He walked on, shrugging off the slight, his thoughts returning to Seraphine.

G ood as his word, Dr Bayard issued an invitation the very next morning. The brutish woman shoved it in his face as he entered the dining room. What he deemed his 'usual table' was unavailable, occupied by two voluble young men speaking English. He opted for a spot near the unlit fire, indifferent to old habits. The only reason he had favoured that corner of the room was to gaze upon Seraphine. The rude graceless female who had taken her place excited no such desire.

Dr and Frau Bayard would like the pleasure of his company tomorrow evening to complete a party of six.

His hosts, the junior doctor, Frau Dunant and surely Seraphine. The girl could hardly refuse an invitation from her employer. He penned a reply to the doctor's invitation, expressing his thanks, and entrusted it to the porter. Then after some decent bread, cold meat, sliced eggs and cheese, accompanied by milky coffee, he returned to his room. He prepared his materials, ready to record the daily output of the shed behind the *Apotheke*.

He locked his room and hesitated in the corridor. The urge to run up the stairs, walk into the practice and check on Seraphine tugged at his head like a hand on a halter. But his role was no longer on the top floor at the surgery. He wrested control of himself and left the hotel, the sound of loud foreign voices still ringing in his ears. His morning was spent in a draughty outbuilding, noting numbers and observing systems. Outside the sun shone and birds sang, but Bastian and Dr Bayard's team were confined to a few square metres of back alley shade. At midday, they took a break and Bastian thanked them for their endless patience with his questions. He did not wish to eat at Hotel Lochmatter, due to the unpleasant replacement hostess, nor at the Weisshornstube with its gloomy interior. Nearby establishments offered alternatives but none were sufficient to tempt him. Instead, he bought some dried sausage, a crusty roll, a bottle of beer and an apple from the little grocery store and walked up the paths he knew from memory, seeking a sunny spot to rest.

He passed a drover with half a dozen sheep and raised his hat to the man. They wished one another a pleasant day and Bastian pressed against the cliff wall until the noisy ovine flock bleated, deposited their ordure and moved on. Further up the path, he found a stone the size of an armchair, if somewhat less padded. He sat, unpacked his provisions and nourished himself with food and natural beauty. The valley wore many disguises, some threatening, some startling and all impressive. He asked himself a blunt question. Did he love this valley because of an exceptional young woman who trusted him with her secrets but now ran away in tears? Or did he love the place for itself, its inhabitants and this breathtaking scenery?

By the time he finished his rustic meal, he was no closer to a conclusion. He wrapped his empty bottle, peel, core and sausage skin in a cloth bag and made his way downhill with the intention of reporting for his afternoon duties. The weather made every roof gleam and each stream glisten. Something in this valley tugged at his heart and it was not a person, a mountain, a village or an aspect. It was an instinct. *When you find yourself in the right place, you know. You can fight it and flee, but that location embeds itself under your skin like a splinter and will itch for eternity.*

"Herr Doctor?"

Bastian started, so absorbed in his thoughts he had not registered the shepherd sitting on the fence, watching his sheep graze beside the stream. "Good afternoon. Yes, I am a doctor. Does something ail you?"

The man's eyes, blue as the water flowing below his feet, reddened and he removed his hat. "No, Herr Doctor, nothing ails me. Not any longer. I take this opportunity, an impertinence and intrusion on your private moments for which I beg forgiveness, to lay my gratitude at your feet. My wife, my children and even my sheep have hope for the future due to you and your medical wonders. I thank you, Herr Doctor, and if I prayed for your health and happiness every day of the calendar, it could never repay what you have done for us. By us, I mean this whole valley. We are changed, sir, changed, thanks to you and Herr Doctor Bayard. I am a simple man. How to express feelings the scale of an Alp with words no bigger than a pebble? All I know is that I am forever in your debt." His voice grew hoarse. A sheepdog appeared by his side, its stance defensive.

"My good man, we are all of us indebted to Herr Doctor Bayard. In the same spirit, I applaud you and your fellow villagers for your courage. Without such faith and trust in his methods, nothing would ever have changed. You may not believe me, but honest opinions like yours matter more than you know. I wish you a fine afternoon."

"Likewise, Herr Doctor, and may your life be forever blessed."

Touched by the man's sincerity, Bastian's mind dwelt on higher things than the affairs of his own heart and he returned to the *Apotheke* with a light tread.

A little before six the following evening, he left the hotel and strolled up the street to the Weisshornstube. His reasons were complex. For one thing, he wished to avoid Seraphine until they met at the Bayards' dining table. Another urge propelled him to seek out locals, to embed himself in the community and take the pulse of the people. The shepherd could have been an anomaly. The basest reason of all was a phrase he had recently learned from an Englishman he met in St. Gallen: Dutch courage. His nerves made him clumsy and gauche when he desired to project the opposite impression. A large beer might soften the edges.

He greeted the patrons of the smoky room with a general 'Good evening' and took a seat at a table by the bar. When he had settled himself and ordered a glass of beer, he took in the other occupants. The clientele was mostly male, except for half a dozen ladies beside their husbands. Few of the villagers caught his eye but those who did nodded in friendly acknowledgement. The waitress placed his beer glass on the wooden table.

"Would you like something to eat, Herr Doctor? *Bratwurst*, perhaps?"

"Thank you, no. I am expected for dinner elsewhere. That will be all for now."

A young man limped across the wooden floor, his leg dragging behind him, making directly for Bastian's table. One of the hazards of his occupation was the assumption that he was never off duty. He took a sip of beer and groaned inwardly, already assessing the youth's gait before he came close enough to speak.

"Herr Doctor Favre, I suppose you no longer recognise me. Wilhelm Brigger from Grachen. I want to thank you all you have done for me and for my family."

"Wilhelm? The last time I saw you ..."

"I was small and spotty and around this high?" He put a palm face down beside his hip. "Yes, it's been three years. But thanks to you I am no longer affected by a goitre. Your treatment changed our lives, sir, and I cannot let the opportunity to express my gratitude pass." He held out a hand. Bastian got to his feet and shook it.

"It gives me great joy to hear you and your family are well. Credit is due not to me but Dr Bayard for his vision and determination. Wilhelm, your leg. What is the problem?"

"Oh, that was polio, Herr Doctor. It barely troubles me at all. I will disturb your *Feierabend* no longer. Let me just say that this evening you shall have no bill to pay."

He reached out to squeeze Bastian's hand again and turned to the now silent assembly with a bandmaster's flourish. "*Unser Herr Doctor Favre, ein Mensch.*"

The room burst into applause, with broad smiles and approving nods. Bastian bowed, raised his glass and returned to his seat, more emotional than when he had arrived. He emptied his glass in two swift gulps before anyone else could repeat the Brigger boy's gesture. With warm wishes for the rest of their evening, he left the bar, rather light-headed after rapidly consuming strong beer on an empty stomach. If this was the kind of reception he got, Dr Bayard must be greeted like a king.

He strolled up the street, his eyes drawn to the emerging stars and the night sky. *May your life be forever blessed*, the shepherd said, and Bastian dared hope that could come true. By the time he reached the stream, he realised he had gone completely the wrong way and hurried back up the hill.

A lantern flickered outside the Bayard family home. He was a little later than intended and hoped he would not be the last guest to arrive. A maid opened the door mere seconds after he rapped the heavy knocker shaped like a *Steinbock*.

"Herr Doctor Favre, welcome back." She took his jacket and showed him into the parlour, where Frau Bayard rushed to greet him with three kisses on the cheek.

"Bastian! What a pleasure to see you again! You deprived us of your company for far too long. Are you well?"

Over her shoulder, Bastian saw Bayard pouring drinks, Frau Dunant in conversation with a young man he assumed was his replacement and Seraphine, hands clasped as if in prayer, eyes on two children playing on the floor. "In fine health, thank you. And you? How are your little girls?"

Frau Bayard cupped her hand around his elbow. "A learned man like yourself must have read Stevenson's book, *Dr Jekyll and Mr Hyde*? I can only assume the man had daughters. Tonight, they will be all charm and convince our guests of their pure, sweet-natured hearts. Only to turn into shrieking harpies before bed. Let me get you something to drink. You know everyone other than Herr Zanetti, I think. Otto, introduce the gentlemen. They are sure to have much in common."

The instant Bastian set eyes on Herr Doctor Zanetti, he detested the man. Two metres tall with a high forehead and strong eyebrows, he had a confident smile, hazel eyes and enough presence to fill a room. The young women of St. Niklaus and beyond would trip over themselves to gain his attention.

"I'm sure they will. Marco Zanetti, may I present Bastian Favre? His reputation precedes him as you know, as my ally and messenger between here and Herisau. Herr Favre, this young gentleman studied in your home town of Fribourg. It is my great good fortune to have worked with two superlative assistants during the most intensive years of my life."

"You left large boots for me to fill, Herr Favre. Many of your patients still sing your praises. It is an honour to make your acquaintance."

"The pleasure is mine. What a happy coincidence we both studied at Fribourg!"

They shook hands and passed some meaningless pleasantries before Bastian excused himself to greet Frau Dunant and Seraphine. He had never seen Frau Dunant out of uniform, so her contemporary peony-blue dress caught him unawares. She was handsome and made him think of his mother. As usual, Seraphine wore a simple navy shift over a white shirt. Her simplicity of attire only served to emphasise the exceptional loveliness of her face.

"Good evening, Frau Dunant. May I say how well that colour suits you? Good evening, Seraphine, it is a pleasure to see you again. I hope you and your family are well? Does nursing please you as an occupation? I imagine you have the best teacher." He was babbling, so closed his mouth.

"It is quite the opposite, Herr Favre," said Frau Dunant. "I have the best student. Seraphine has a way with children. In fact, she has a way with most people and I am convinced she will make an outstanding nurse."

A flush crept up those pale cheeks. "You are very kind, Frau Dunant. I am glad you are returned, Herr Favre. To answer your questions, yes, I am lucky to be able to study as a nurse. My mother is in good health, as is her son, barely three months old and strong as a calf. Sadly, my brother who dwelt in the Boys' Home in Bern is recently deceased. A short life but it was as happy as possible. Do you plan to remain in St. Niklaus for long?"

With wonderful timing, Frau Bayard re-entered the room, pressed a glass of wine into Bastian's hand and drew Frau Dunant away with a question about herbs.

"I am truly sorry to hear about your brother. May he rest in peace."

Seraphine said nothing but sipped at her water.

"On the other side of the coin, the blessing of a healthy child must ease the pain, for you and your mother. Much credit for this joyful occasion lies at your feet."

"If that is true, why do I feel nothing but grief for the brothers who died and an absence of joy for the one who lives?"

"Seraphine," he murmured, moving closer. "Much like grazed skin, loss is painful and raw at present. Little can soothe the agony of grief other than time. Yet children see the world with wide innocent eyes and can renew our jaded views, making us laugh and love even when we believe our hearts incapable. Forgive me. In the Weisshornstube earlier, I drank a large beer at some speed and it appears to have loosened my tongue."

She laughed, her expression surprised and her face brighter. "You should have asked for a small one, as you did the night I first served you." She met his gaze with a guileless smile and moved to join the group beside the fireplace.

Around the dining table, they stuck to the conventional arrangement of male/female alternation. Thus Bastian found himself between Frau Bayard and Seraphine, opposite Zanetti. The consummate hostess, Frau Bayard introduced topics of conversation of interest to all, drawing everyone into participation. Her esteemed husband chimed in with his own opinions of Fribourg's august university, asked questions about the pleasures of Montreux, enquired about Frau Dunant's knowledge of English and shared several anecdotes about his time in Ireland. Herr Zanetti mentioned an Irish poet and quoted a few lines in English with a sonorous voice. He then asked Bastian if he had encountered another Irish fellow during his studies in Zürich. A writer by the name of James Joyce? To Bastian's immense annoyance, he was forced to admit he had never heard of the man. Perhaps he should have paid attention to Walter's endless babbling about notable figures rather than dismissing it as facile gossip.

The maid cleared away the soup plates and served each guest a portion of risotto. This gave rise to a discussion of Italy and its many merits. The Bayards had travelled some of 'The Grand Tour' for their honeymoon and reminisced about Florence and Venice with great fondness. For his part, Zanetti described his Tyrolean upbringing in the shadow of the

Dolomites with a mixture of pride and humility, all delivered with a raconteur's flair. Everyone at the table sat spellbound and Seraphine seemed rapt by his animated face in the candlelight. As a doctor, Bastian had sworn an oath to save lives, but at that moment it was fortunate the only weapon in his hand was a fork.

"It sounds quite idyllic," he said, as he laid down his cutlery. "Your love for your homeland rings true as a bell. Did you not consider giving South Tyrol the benefit of your talents rather than coming here to the Matterthal?"

"That is a good point, Herr Favre. One day, I shall return to the region of my birth not only from a sense of obligation but because it is the most beautiful place on earth." He held up his hands in mock defence. "We all make the same claim for our birthplaces, do we not? That said, I catch my breath daily when I wake up in this valley. Seraphine, you have grown up here. Is it true what they say, that one simply becomes accustomed to such beauty?"

Bastian's molars were in danger of cracking.

With a dab at her mouth with her napkin, she answered the question. "I doubt anyone 'simply becomes accustomed' to the Matterthal. How can we with four different seasons and an ever-changing landscape? Those who pass through, scaling a peak or admiring a gorge in April sunshine will never appreciate the full picture. We live here. We endure the winter snow, clouds, ice and brittle winds, with no other objective than to survive until spring. When it comes, and it always does, we wonder anew at the resilience of nature. We treasure the long fat days of summer when we can revisit pastures almost forgotten and fill our larders during autumn. Every year, this valley is a miracle. I do not wish to contradict you, Herr Zanetti, but in my humble opinion, this is the most beautiful place on earth."

The flash in her eyes, the jut of her jaw and the modest drop of her chin when the table burst into murmured agreement made Bastian's chest swell with emotion.

"Well said, young lady!"

"Brava! Wonderful!"

Frau Bayard patted her fingers to her palm. "You see, only a girl who reads novels can wield language like a weapon. Otto, my dear, would you ring for the maid? It is time for dessert. I think you might enjoy this dish, Herr Zanetti. It is an Italian speciality."

The women withdrew to the parlour after the fiddly biscuit and cream affair which Bastian found sickly and overly rich. Bayard poured port for his junior colleagues and without preamble, talked business. Here at least, Bastian had the advantage. As Eggenberger's second-in-command, he knew his superior's strategy in detail. A people's initiative could be put to a vote on condition it garnered enough signatures. Therefore, Dr Eggenberger and his assistant planned to address the community in small lectures, in order to convince them of their methodology. It would take time, as every tiny hamlet placed their faith in results above words. Nonetheless, Eggenberger sent his assurance that he could and would have iodised salt prophylaxis as a cantonal directive within two years.

Otto Bayard clapped him on the back. "Well done, Bastian, well done indeed. From Appenzell Ausserrhoden to the whole of Switzerland and beyond. A toast, gentlemen. To changing the world!"

"To changing the world!" Bastian knocked his glass against those of his colleagues, but remembered his manners. "The credit is due to you, sir, along with Herr Doctor Hunziker and our predecessors in the field. Herr Zanetti and I have the great good luck to swim in your wake."

They joined the ladies for coffee after which the party quickly broke up. Frau Dunant's boy knocked at the door on the stroke of ten, ready to escort his mother home. Frau Bayard spotted Seraphine's smothered yawns and asked if either of the junior doctors would walk her to her lodgings. Bastian was on his feet before she had finished speaking.

"It would be a pleasure. I too am ready for my bed. We can walk to the hotel together."

Seraphine blinked. "I was a serving girl when I lived at the hotel, sir. Since accepting the nursing apprenticeship, I made more respectable arrangements."

"Allow me," said Zanetti. "Seraphine and I are neighbours. I reside at the boarding house, not fifty paces from the school and Frau Fessler's home. Can I offer my most sincere appreciation of your hospitality, Frau and Herr Bayard, and it is indeed a wrench to leave such stimulating conversation. But the pleasure of Seraphine's company on the homeward stroll will be ample reward."

In somewhat less florid prose, Bastian added his thanks, assisted Seraphine with her coat and said goodnight to the Bayards by the light of the lantern. On the walk up the hill, Zanetti engaged Bastian with questions about the practice in Herisau, speaking above Seraphine who walked between them. When the road split, Bastian bowed to them both and rather than bid the pair a good night, said he looked forward to seeing them in the morning. Seraphine's face was as gentle as ever in the light of the moon, her tone crystal clear when she said, "Goodnight, Herr Doctor Favre. Sleep well."

He forced a smile onto his face and turned away, unable to find a reason to follow the pair along the shadowy lane. It was pointless to delude himself further. The girl showed little to no interest in him while being clearly dazzled by the chivalrous and exotic Zanetti. Apprentice nurse and junior doctor, the two worked side by side, giving him ample opportunity to whisper compliments, inevitably seducing the girl into his arms. Bastian's anger simmered just below boiling point to the extent he twice stopped and considered running after the pair to box his challenger on the nose.

What was he thinking? This was the 1920s. Men were no longer subject to barbaric practices such as duels to satisfy one's honour. Nor were women fought over in the street like chattels. He could almost feel the chill of disapproval from his mother and sisters blowing all the way from Fribourg.

Seraphine's words, mild and factual, lashed him for his insensitivity. *I was a serving girl when I lived at the hotel, sir. Since accepting the nursing apprenticeship, I made more respectable arrangements.* He was a crass, undeserving idiot and could scarce blame her for placing her affections elsewhere.

At the hotel, in a near-empty dining room, he ordered a whisky and slumped into an armchair by the fire. He would pay for such rash behaviour in the morning, having drunk a beer, two different kinds of wine and a decent measure of port. A party of three mountaineers were finishing their meal, regaling one another with exaggerated achievements. Bastian wondered how the hotelier and his sons, the best mountain guides in the Alps, could suffer this hubris nightly. That old fool who used the place as a free sitting room woke up and looked at the fire, his eyes focusing on Bastian.

"Your whisky, Herr Favre." One of the Lochmatter boys placed a glass at his elbow.

"Thank you, young man."

He lifted the glass and gazed through the honey-coloured liquid at the fire. Flames, phantoms, elusive desires and foolish visions were nothing but smoke. He could not mould Seraphine into his own version of Frau Bayard any more than the girl could have saved her brothers with the strength of her love. He was becoming maudlin and the whisky was unlikely to help. At least it would knock him out. He took a sip and winced as the rough liquor hit his throat.

"Herr Doctor Favre?" The old man addressed him, leaning on his Alpenstock. His face, wrinkled as an autumn leaf, creased into deeper folds when he smiled. "It pleases me to see you here once more. I know I am not the only one. My name is Alois, if you remember?"

Manners overcame Bastian's annoyance. "How could I forget? You are well, I trust?"

"No vaccines, potions or magic salt can match the relentless drag of old age."

Bastian disguised his groan as an appreciation of wisdom. "Wise words."

"Strike while the iron is hot. A trite platitude, you think? I have spent sixty-one years on this earth and met people from each of its corners. What have I learnt? That we think our time is infinite. The present passes while we plan our future. Herr Doctor, your selfless care is a noble calling but there comes a time when you must look to yourself."

"Quite. I shall finish this drink and repair to my room for a good night's sleep. I wish you the same, Alois. Goodnight to you."

The man made no move. "The Widmer girl wants nothing to do with that man. She told him so and he did not like what he heard. Not one bit. Right there, I was, doctor. With my own ears, I heard her refuse him in no uncertain terms. On the balls of my feet, I was, ready to run to her aid. The girl is bright as a button which is how she got away, feigning a conversation with someone he could not see. She will not have him, doctor. In my view, she needs a protector. Someone like yourself."

Bastian thrust himself to his feet, his head seasick. "Thank you for your advice, my friend. I am in your debt. Goodnight and God bless."

He staggered up the stairs, bilious and weary, drank a draught of cold water and took off his boots. Head in hands, he tried to remember the man's words. Seraphine rejected Zanetti? He looked out at the moonlight and laughed, before collapsing onto his pillow.

His hangover, as he had predicted, was crushing. He opened the window to the cold morning air and emptied half the ewer while still in his nightshirt. In the dining room, he consumed cheese, ham, eggs, a portion of Rösti and three slices of bread before he could face the day ahead. Only then did he recall the previous evening's conversation with Alois. In an instant, the pain in his head lessened and his spirits rose. His path was clear. He would find an opportunity to get Seraphine alone and enquire as to her future plans. If she was not, as it appeared, promised to another man, he would seek an understanding between them. That might entail a visit to her parents, something he dreaded after his previous encounter with that awful woman. But nothing could impede him as long as Seraphine was willing. He found he was smiling vaguely at the other hotel guests.

As he left the dining room, he checked again for Alois, who was yet to make an appearance. Not that it mattered. Drunk Bastian might have been, but the message had registered. With a spring in his step, he ascended the stairs to the surgery on the pretext of requiring some clarification on a minor point. Frau Dunant looked up from the nurses' station with a broad smile.

"Dr Favre. How fortuitous! I was about to send someone down to the *Apotheke* to fetch you. I'm afraid we must press you into service. An avalanche occurred on the Matterhorn and Dr Bayard is in attendance. That leaves Dr Zanetti to manage morning surgery alone. I am aware your reason for being in St.

Niklaus is for more important reasons than the usual villagers' complaints, but it should only occupy you for half the day."

Bastian hid his delight. Even a half day spent working alongside Seraphine was an unexpected boon. "An avalanche? Oh dear, that sounds very grave. Of course I will do my share. Should I take Dr Bayard's room?"

"You are most kind. Yes, if you would. I will do my best to apprise you of each patient's problems and recent history, but I too am on my own today, as Seraphine accompanied Dr Bayard to Zermatt as his assistant."

"Ah, I see."

In the event, Zanetti and Bastian worked until six, staggering their lunch breaks so someone was always on duty. The problem of gleaning any accurate information about the incident on the mountain was exacerbated by its remote location and obfuscated by gossip and hearsay. The two men wrote up their notes while Frau Dunant restocked the pharmacy. At six-thirty, they vacated the top floor for the cleaner. Bastian assured them his top priority was the practice, and if required he would throw his shoulder to the wheel the following morning. The nurse wished him a good evening and hurried home to her family.

Zanetti buttoned up his coat against the evening chill. "Do you have plans for dinner, my friend? I usually eat at the Weisshornstube, as the boarding-house fare is dull and the company similar. I would be glad if you could join me."

"I had no plans, other than the hotel, but that can become repetitive after three meals a day. The Weisshornstube is reliably hearty and a convenient place to encounter those with the latest news. Shall we go?"

The Tyrolean was an interesting conversationalist and since the two men had a good deal in common, the meal passed pleasantly. Until they ordered coffee. The waitress, a jolly girl with a sturdy frame, asked if the gentlemen desired anything else to round off the meal. Zanetti passed an off-colour remark, which seemed not to perturb the young woman in the slightest. She merely chuckled and prodded the man's shoulder.

"One of these days I shall say yes and then where will you be?"

"In Heaven, I daresay."

"Oh, get away with you," she laughed. "You know perfectly well I have a beau. Now behave yourself and tell me whether you do or do not care for a Kirsch."

Zanetti answered for them both and Bastian found himself once again having consumed more strong drink than he deemed sensible. Otherwise he might not have spoken.

"Do you think it wise to flirt so with a local girl? It may reflect badly on your professional reputation."

"Not at all. It's a harmless bit of fun and she knows it as well as I do." Zanetti grinned. "Getting in some practice, that's how I see it."

"Practice?"

"Indeed. I have no designs on Romy, good gracious, no. The object of my affection is cut from different cloth. But it never hurts to learn how to make a lady blush."

Bastian took out his handkerchief and blew his nose in an effort to look nonchalant. "Ah, now I see why you intend to return to the Tyrol. A lady awaits."

"More than one, my friend!" Zanetti let out a bark of laughter. "No, the truth of the matter is I plan to disappoint them all. Here in the Matterthal, I found the prettiest girl I ever saw." He leaned closer. "My heart is set on an alluring young nurse with beautiful blue eyes and lips like summer cherries."

Bastian bristled. "You surely cannot mean Fräulein Widmer? I understand she intends to study nursing and has no interest in husband-hunting."

"Who's talking about a husband? In any case, it's a lady's

prerogative to change her mind. She has already agreed to accompany me to the Spring Fair and from there it's only a matter of time. In fact, what would you say to a gentleman's wager? Five francs says the lovely Seraphine will be in my bed by Swiss National Day."

With a start as if he had been jabbed with a pointed stick, Bastian jumped to his feet. "I will not have you speak about one of the practice staff in such a disrespectful manner. From my experience, that young lady has far more sense than to get entangled with your sort. Please excuse me, it is getting late."

"No need to get hot under the collar, my friend, unless of course you have designs on the girl yourself. In which case, may the best man win." He gave a vulpine smile and motioned to the waitress to refill their glasses.

"Not for me, thank you." Bastian was about to leave but could not bear the idea of Zanetti viewing Seraphine as some kind of competition. "I have no interest in the young lady other than as a professional colleague. It is incumbent on you to treat her well."

There was no reply as Zanetti's attention was on the serving girl, as he made another comment about her figure to ribald laughter from the other customers and from Romy herself. Bastian walked out into the night, wondering how much he could achieve before he must depart.

I t soon transpired that where Seraphine was concerned, he would achieve nothing. Dr Bayard treated those injured in the avalanche and left his capable nurse in Zermatt to oversee their recovery. She would not return before the following week, long after Bastian's departure.

On the long journey north, Bastian made a grown-up deci-sion. No more idle fantasy or chasing blue butterflies. He sought a wife and family and there was one within his reach. He had tended to the noncommittal with Teresa, one step forward, one step backwards. No more playing games. She deserved better. After she lost her husband to the same malady that took Julius, they were destined to be one another's consolation. Her modest manner and patient fortitude merited more than being used as an inconstant companion. His behaviour hitherto had been reprehensible, not only to her but to her little boy. He swore a solemn oath. From now on, his courtship of her was his priority and he would make it his mission to win the affection of her fatherless son. In a year, perhaps two, he could achieve the stable family fundament he so badly wanted. This, he told himself, was maturity.

17

«*Man kann es nicht fassen, man will es nicht glauben und fragt sich
nur immer: Wie konnt' dies geschehen? Es könnte den Glauben an
Gott uns fast rauben!
Warum, Schöpfer, liessest die Tat du begeh'n?*»
*(One cannot understand it, one refuses to believe it. Over and over we
ask ourselves:
how could this happen? It could almost rob us of our faith in the Lord!
Why, O Creator, did You let this act take place?)*

— Poem published in an Appenzeller newspaper on 1
March 1922

7 March 1922

"Good afternoon, Dr Favre. That man over there is
waiting for you." The landlord of the *Rössli* restaurant
pointed to a corner table where a figure bent over a newspaper.

"Will you have the daily special too? It's *Käsefladen* with potatoes."

"Yes, that sounds good." He hung up his coat and approached the stranger. "Excuse me?"

The man turned. "Bastian! Here you are!"

"Walter? What on earth are you doing in Herisau? It's not like you to make a social call." His glance took in the main story on the front page of the paper. "Ah, of course."

"It's good to see you, my old friend. How are you? Let me buy you lunch and we can catch up on everything. What a peculiar little place this is! You are still content here, I take it?"

Bastian sat down, his pleasure at seeing his old friend overcoming any irritation at the cynical reason for his presence. "Very much so. How are things in Zürich?"

"Never a dull moment, as you can imagine. Although this month the big news is to be found in Appenzell. What a thing to happen!"

"And you are seeking more details on the story. I'll be happy to share what I know about Dr Eggenberger's initiative and the plans to introduce iodised salt across the country."

Walter grinned. "Bastian, come now, you know that's not why I am here. The whole of Switzerland wants to know what occurred up that mountain. As a doctor working at the hospital, you must be better informed than most. Look, here's the thing. You help me out with the double murder story and I promise faithfully to do a feature on your salt stuff."

His dismissive tone rankled, but fortunately their meals arrived, giving Bastian a moment to compose himself. "*En Guete*."

"*En Guete*. They don't hold back on the portions, do they?"

"No, they don't. Meals here are generous and reasonably priced, unlike in Zürich. As for the feature on my 'salt stuff', that subject is in the public interest and an important story in its own right. Any journalist worth his, ahem, salt would know that. But if you insist upon a *quid pro quo*, I can tell you what I know about the murders. To be honest, it's not much more than is already public but I'm privy to one or two items yet to be published."

Walter's eyes widened. "Really? Right, I have the basic facts. What I want to know, along with the rest of the country, is why? We won't get any answers from the killer, that's for sure."

"Before we go any further, I'll talk to you on one condition and that is anonymity. You can quote a vague source at the hospital, nothing more."

"Rest assured, my friend, your name stays out of print." Walter scrabbled for his notebook.

"Please, Walter. We can't appreciate our food and exchange information at the same time. Let's enjoy our meal then trade knowledge afterwards. Gossip upsets my digestion."

"It's not gossip, though. This is journalism of the highest quality. All right, all right. If you want. How's life in the sticks?"

"More settled of late. Over the past few years I spent the summer months in the Matterthal, assisting another doctor with his experiments. Those are now complete so I can stay here in Herisau, which pleases me greatly. This summer I have quite a different agenda."

Walter reminded Bastian of a groundhog. Always alert, nose and ears open, sensitive to the faintest hint of a change in environment. His eyes flicked to Bastian's left hand and registered the third finger was bare. "Unmarried, so it can't be an imminent child, but that mysterious smile hints at good news. Are you going to tell me a wedding is on the cards?"

"You surmise correctly. My marital status is due to change in June of this year. I gain not only a wife, but a son. My fiancée Teresa lost her husband to the influenza epidemic. Since then she has struggled to survive and raise her little boy. We've been friends for a few years, but now our mutual regard has blossomed into a deeper attachment. She and Magdalena Haas were close friends and as you can imagine, she is most dreadfully distressed by the news of her death."

"Well, congratulations! Can we toast your happy news with a glass of the local brew?"

"Unfortunately not. I am on duty this afternoon. But next time I pass through Zürich, I invite you to celebrate with me. Tell me about your situation."

Walter's plate was almost empty. He ate voraciously, like a locust. "Same as ever. Keeping my options open. Nearly snared by a devious vixen with a huge fortune and an enormous appetite. I was lucky to escape unscathed. There! Decent food, I will say that much. Now to the business at hand."

DOUBLE MURDER ON SÄNTIS!
Text by Walter Brunn

On 25 February 1922, Josef Rusch and two other mountain porters climbed the 2,500 metre peak of Mount Säntis. Their job was to find out why the telegraph office of St. Gallen had received no regular reports from the Säntis weather station for five days. Since the station operators, Herr Heinrich and Frau Magdalena Haas, were reliable and experienced meteorologists, the climbers assumed the recent storm had damaged communication lines.

Instead, what they found shocked the whole of Switzerland. Magdalena lay dead in the office, shot at close range. Her husband Heinrich lay face down in the snow on the summit with a bullet in his back. The calendar indicated they died four days earlier. Only their dog, Sturm, starving and frantic, survived.

According to Dr Bastian Favre, assistant to Dr Eggenberger at the hospital of Herisau and someone familiar with the case, it was a crime of passion. The identity of the murderer was no mystery. Magdalena complained of a visitor overstaying his welcome in a telegraphed message to a friend two days before her death. An expert Alpinist, Gregor Kreuzpointer had climbed the peak to visit the couple, still embittered by losing the position of weather operator to Haas. German-born Kreuzpointer shot and killed his victims, leaving their bodies where they lay and skied down the mountain. On 4 March, he hanged himself in a barn, leaving no explanation for his actions.

The geographical location of the murder complicated police activity. Three cantons converge at the peak of Säntis. Magdalena Haas died in Appenzell Innerrhoden. The body of Heinrich Haas fell in an imprecise area between two cantons. Therefore, administrative responsibility was shared. The next problem to vex the authorities was where to bury the killer. Kreuzpointer committed suicide in Urnäsch, whilst being a citizen of Herisau and registered in St. Gallen. None of the three municipalities wanted to 'desecrate' their cemeteries by interring such a monster.

Finally, the hospital at Herisau proposed an unusual solution. The corpse could be donated to the Institute of Anatomy at the University of Zürich. All three councils agreed to share transportation costs, achieving a compromise, an altruistic solution and a clear conscience.

The daughters of the murdered couple, along with Sturm the dog, were adopted by family members.

T he one thing Bastian had always admired about Teresa was her even temperament. That was why he was wholly unprepared for his reception the moment he opened her gate. She wrenched open the cottage door before he set foot on the path, her anger emanating like a force field. In her left hand, she clutched a newspaper. To see such fury in her eyes and the tension in her jaw made him wonder if he had even known her at all.

"Teresa? Is everything in order?"

"How dare you? How can you show your face here?" She marched towards him, brandishing the paper.

Bastian took a step backwards. "I'm sorry? How do I dare visit my fiancée and keep my promise of joining you for dinner? My dearest, is something wrong?"

"This is what I mean!" She rustled the paper in front of his face. "You sold my story to the press! I thought you were a decent man, Bastian Favre, someone my son would grow up to admire. I was grievously deceived by a base charlatan. Leave my house and never return. Any understanding we may have previously had is now over." Her voice caught but she did not shed a tear. "How much disappointment must a woman bear?" She closed the door quietly but firmly, taking the newspaper with her.

His head throbbing, Bastian walked to the train station where he bought a copy of the evening paper. There was Walter's story, on the front page, supported by the words of Dr Bastian Favre of Herisau. He folded it under his arm, took the back lane to his apartment so as to avoid other people, and cursed the name of Walter Brunn to hell.

18

In reality fantasies mean much more than that, for they represent at the same time the other mechanism—of repressed extraversion in the introvert, and of repressed introversion in the extravert.

— Carl Gustav Jung, *Psychological Types*

May 1922

The Swiss Nursing School or *Schweizerische Pflegerinnenschule* with its attached women's hospital was affectionately referred to by the people of Zürich as the 'Pflegi'. Despite battling frequent financial difficulties, the founders refused to compromise on standards. In fact, standards were their raison d'être. That was one of the key reasons Seraphine desperately wanted to study in Zürich.

The concept of a centrally recognised methodology in healthcare was accepted as normal for doctors, but when it came to nursing, far less rigour applied. Much like the differences in bedside manner or personal interest, people had no expectation of nurses having the same levels of training and knowledge. Anna Heer and Marie Heim-Vögtlin changed that by breaching established divisions. Why, they demanded, were doctors and nurses only ever male and female respectively? Leading by example, they overcame barriers. Heim-Vögtlin graduated as the first female Swiss doctor, while Heer became the first female Swiss surgeon. Seraphine had no such soaring ambitions but her horizons expanded as she saw how much was possible. Her admiration for their sheer stubbornness was one thing, but their talent and skills left her speechless.

By appealing to women's charity organisations, Anna Heer raised enough funding to establish a school of nursing. Alongside ensuring uniform levels of care, she and her head nurse Ida Schneider campaigned for appropriate pay and acceptable working conditions for their charges. Few men had any say in how the 'Pflegi' was run and the decision-makers were female. The nursing school and hospital espoused one theory: 'For women, by women'.

It was Seraphine's idea of heaven. She threw herself into her nursing training with absolute determination. For all her fears that she would fall short of expectations, she found herself in a supportive group of twenty young women, all of whom strove daily to help one another become a better nurse. Their schedule was relentless: rise at 05.30, breakfast at 06.00, a full day's theoretical and practical learning, followed by evening lectures by professionals. Seraphine was a good deal younger than most but, due to her routine on the farm and at the hotel, no stranger to early mornings or long days. Her experience under Frau Dunant – *if a patient sees your nerves, they will lose all trust in you* – gave her an air of confidence. When called upon to demonstrate a procedure, Seraphine did not hesitate, picking up a thermometer or a bandage with as much ease as if it were a knife or fork. She was accustomed to describing whatever she was about to do as reassurance, or distracting the individual with a well-timed question about family or livestock just before she administered a needle. Her progress was steady if unspectacular and the next step was a one-year apprenticeship at the hospital followed by a position elsewhere to apply her skills.

The city both frightened and fascinated her. She liked to take the tram on Saturday afternoons just to watch the people. At first, her nerves got the better of her and she did not dare step off until the last station. Then she got straight back on for the return journey. It took three Saturdays until she was brave enough to descend and face the streets. People, noise, banks, trams, cafés, motor vehicles, commerce, horse-drawn carts and cyclists intersected in an exhilarating melee. The only place she knew as a comparison was Montreux. The two could hardly have been more different. Montreux was sedate and comfortable, full of the rich and elderly, where everyone spoke French. Zürich was exciting and dangerous, a mixture of rebellious radicals, confident woman and men in suits, where people spoke Swiss German, Italian, English, Russian, French and languages Seraphine could not identify.

All the time she was crossing one of the bridges or wandering beside a thoroughfare, Seraphine searched for the tall figure of Bastian Favre. In her quiet moments, she imagined a chance encounter, perhaps an invitation to a coffee shop and an offer of employment in his own practice. For how else was she to find him again? Not once did Seraphine give voice to her innermost thoughts and fantastical hopes. Only when exhausted after a rigorous day's work, lying on starched sheets in the nurses' dormitory after lights out, did she allow her mind to wander, recalling his voice, his warm fingers on her throat, his deep brown eyes sliding away from hers. Bastian Favre. She reminded herself it had been two years since they met. He might well have married, moved to another canton or forgotten about a silly little mountain girl he once cured of a goitre. She caressed her neck and fell asleep with a smile on her face.

O n Dr Favre's last visit to St. Niklaus, he had been kind enough to offer reassurance regarding the death of Henri. She had hoped for further conversation, perhaps even a chance to walk to one of the farms together for a medical visit. It was not to be. By the time she travelled down the mountain after the avalanche, his short stay was over and she had missed her opportunity.

Frau Fessler noted the change in her lodger's demeanour and correctly surmised it was due to affairs of the heart. Where her supposition stumbled was over the object of her affection. Dr Zanetti, for heaven's sake? In Seraphine's view, that man was far too full of himself, convinced his charm was irresistible. He had won over the entire village and had his pick of companions, but shortly after her return from Zermatt, he asked her to accompany him to the Spring Fair. He made it sound as if she had won a raffle. She refused, grateful for a previous commitment to mind the farm in order that her parents could attend. He wheedled and cajoled but she stood firm, eventually asking him politely not to raise the topic in the future.

"You're making a mistake, Seraphine."

"Maybe so, but it is my mistake. I dislike others telling me what to do with my life."

That was only half true. She only disliked certain people telling her what to do with her life.

The doctor's wife invited herself for tea one afternoon, bringing papers from the Red Cross and Nursing Association. It was time, said Frau Bayard, for Seraphine to consider her future. Seraphine agreed without demur.

"My husband tells me you have real aptitude for patient care and is willing to pay your fees. Your arrangement with Frau Fessler is due to cease in May. What better time to take up a place at an educational establishment? Your family has connections in the capital, if I'm not mistaken?"

"My uncle Thierry is a trustee at a children's hospital in Bern, yes."

"Perfect! One of the two centres of nursing excellence is in Bern, founded by Walther Sahli and supported by the Red Cross. The other is in Zürich, established by Anna Heer and run entirely by women. I'm quite sure your uncle can use his influence to get you accepted in Bern." She shifted uncomfortably in her armchair, her pregnancy nearing the end of its third trimester.

"Would you like another cushion for your back?" asked Seraphine.

"Thank you. This sort of thing is supposed to get easier after the first couple, so they tell me, but I find it quite the opposite. Shall we write to your uncle this very afternoon? Seraphine?"

"I was wondering ... all the material Dr Bayard gave me concerned the work of the women's hospital and nursing school in Zürich. Naturally, I would be grateful to go wherever I can secure a place. It is simply that I had hopes of working in an institution like that, alongside pioneers in the field."

"Zürich? Well, why not? In your shoes, I would do the same. It's such a thrilling place to be, bursting at the seams with ideas and energy and yes, pioneering when it comes to the female cause. In that case, we can compose an enquiry to the head nurse, supported by letters of recommendation from my husband and from your guiding light, Frau Dunant. You know, the more I think of it, Zürich would be wonderful for you. On the occasions I am in the city, we can take tea at Brasserie Lipp and catch up with each other's news."

Seraphine blushed and a jolt of anticipation ran through

her. Frau Bayard talked as if they were equals and nothing could be more natural than two women taking tea at a French-sounding establishment. Not only that, but the chances of crossing paths with Dr Favre when Frau Bayard was in town increased significantly. "I scarcely dare believe it," she said, her voice small.

"Let us clear away the tea things and sit at the dining table. It's better for my back. Bring me some writing paper, nothing fancy just yet, and we shall draft your application. How is your penmanship? Fear not, we can work on that. Lend me your arm, my dear, getting out of an armchair these days is like heaving a sack of potatoes out of a well."

M idwifery and childcare attracted many of her peers. Their reasons were clear to Seraphine. Most girls in her school year were the oldest daughters in a large family, meaning they had raised and even delivered some of their siblings. She herself had assumed the role of carer for her two little half-brothers. *Three brothers*, she reminded herself. Peter was also her mother's son. Yet somewhere deep inside she knew Peter would never mean as much as Henri or Anton. Because he had no need of her.

Perhaps the onerous responsibility of having tended two unusually demanding children weighed against the pull of paediatrics. Or maybe she knew better than most the toll of such emotional investment. Whatever the reason, Junior Nurse Widmer removed herself from a crowded field. Her passion came from personal experience and moved her from the outside in.

Seraphine chose skin.

The field of dermatology had held a fascination ever since she had seen her own body react and change under Dr Favre's ministrations. Her curiosity only increased after attending a February lecture at the University Hospital with Lotte Volger, a German moulaguese. The concept of moulage, or skin casting, was entirely new and enthralled her from the start. Until then, Seraphine had taken the wooden skeletons and two-dimensional diagrams of the human body as the best she could get. Accurate wax representations of skin conditions showed students, who had thus far only encountered theoretical descriptions, how diseases such as tuberculosis and leprosy actually looked.

Lotte Volger demonstrated models of afflicted arms, legs, faces, mouths, nails and hands, all in detailed colour. None of the trainee nurses would have ever admitted to squeamishness, but everyone except Seraphine left as soon as the lecture was over. The delicate reproductions were susceptible to damage and required sealed boxes when not in use. Lotte Volger rolled up her sleeves and began the job alone.

"Frau Volger? I found your introduction most educational, thank you. May I assist you in packing your moulagen? I promise I have a gentle touch."

Volger's gaze brushed over her face and rested on Seraphine's hands. "Yes, that would save me some time. The box for each piece is directly under the table. Make sure the identification labels match, place them within the markers and please take extreme care. What is your name?"

"Seraphine Widmer. I am nearing the end of my first year of studies. Next, we all put our training into practice at the *Frauenspital*."

"Very well. Start at that end. They sometimes offer me a porter to help with packing. I may as well throw each piece out of the window."

They worked in silence for a few moments, Seraphine handling each piece with great reverence. Even as she placed it in its glass-fronted box, she tried to memorise the Latinate names defining each condition. *Pemphigus vulgaris. Syphilis. Ichthyosis congenita. Borreliose.* Every model represented a human being's suffering and she treated it with the respect it deserved. Her urge to shy away from symptoms of infection rang warning bells and she wondered at the ability of mind over natural instinct.

"You have no doubt chosen your branch," said Volger, watching Seraphine close the final lid on a reproduction of a man's face ridden with smallpox. "Few nurses see dermatology as an alternative. Fewer still possess the blend of scientific steel combined with artistic talent to learn the skill of moulage. Thank you for your help. I bid you goodnight."

She waited for Seraphine to leave, her hand on the door.

"Goodnight and thank you for this evening's lecture. Such talent is humbling and much to be admired." She bobbed a curtsey and walked out of the room, her head filled with images of blisters, wounds and flaking skin.

"Fräulein Widmer? If you have any questions, you may visit my rooms. Ask the Schneider woman for directions." She closed the door.

Seraphine pocketed that offer. She didn't yet know what she didn't know, but one day, she planned to knock at the door of Lotte Volger and beg to learn more.

F riends were a novelty to Seraphine. In the Matterthal valley, she had colleagues; her schoolmates and co-workers, or older women who showed her a kindness, but not someone to call a friend. She never had spare moment to idle time away discovering commonalities. At the nursing school, it happened without her even noticing. Edith and Vroni were close to her age and although different in temperament, both approachable and warm. They came from large families: Vroni was the eldest of five sisters and Edith's surviving siblings numbered eight. Well-versed in the language of girlhood, they gravitated to one another, and somehow Seraphine got caught in the middle. The fact she contributed less to their conversations seemed not to matter because when she did dare to share her thoughts, they met with fulsome approval.

"Is that not precisely what I said, Vroni? Did I or did I not express the very same opinion as Seraphine after barely a week at this school?" Edith's voice was a spitting hiss, like a posturing kitten. Her furious whispers often had the opposite of the desired effect, drawing fellow student nurses to enquire about the cause of her disgruntlement.

Vroni replied in her usual calm drawl as she sewed up a tear in her outdoor cloak. "More than likely. You did make a big fuss about the timetable, that much is true. Nevertheless, I believe Seraphine addresses a different question. Minds are fresher in the mornings. That is a scientific fact."

"Not at half past six! My mind is still asleep!"

"If I may continue, Edith? Seraphine's point was that learning about innovations in complex branches of medicine at eight o'clock in the evening is counterproductive. We're exhausted. Our concentration is mainly on keeping our eyes open and whether there'll be enough hot water left in the urn for a bedtime cocoa. I am fully in agreement with her. Lectures of this magnitude ought to take place mid-morning, giving us the lunch hour to discuss new concepts."

Edith shook her head. "The lunch hour is nowhere near long enough to queue for food, eat it and manage a civilised discussion afterwards. Our timetable is not conducive to good health and that is that."

Seraphine intervened before Edith launched into her long list of complaints. "You are quite correct, Vroni, and in an ideal world that would make perfect sense. The reality is that surgeons and specialists work equally long hours and the only time they can spare is an hour in the evening to share their expertise. The fault lies not in the nurses' schedule or that of the doctors. Both are part of the uphill struggle to establish women in the medical world."

"*Brava*!" said Vroni, in her St. Galler accent. "A woman's work is never done."

"Not here it isn't! They're training us to be skivvies, up first, to bed last. I ask myself if they intend us to learn anything more than bedpans and bandages. Nothing will change."

"I do not believe that is true, Edith." Seraphine rarely challenged her friends, but the ethics of the founders had lit a torch in her belly. "Things can change. It takes conviction and a fierce will from brave individuals. Only then do people begin to hope. I have seen this in my own village. This is why I want to prop open my eyelids with matchsticks to be present at the evening lectures, no matter how much I need my bed. If I miss my chance, it won't come again."

"Saint Seraphine!" exclaimed Edith, with a gentle nudge to show she was teasing. "I suspected you of trying to curry favour with our superiors in the hope of gaining a place in the Pflegi. Not that I would blame you. We all want the same thing. It will be such fun if the three of us can work together, don't you think?"

Seraphine smiled but said nothing. Her dreams of working as an assistant to Dr Favre of Herisau were so unrealistic she dared not admit them even to herself.

"As I always say," said Vroni, "aim high. If we miss our target, at least we can hold our heads up with pride." She shook out her cloak. "There! I'll warrant no one can see the repair, so fine is my needlework."

Seraphine examined the woollen fabric. "Worthy of a surgeon, Vroni. You could be the next Anna Heer!"

"Invisible. You have nimble fingers," said Edith.

"Thank you both. Now I am respectable enough to be seen in public once again, why don't we plan an excursion? Next Saturday morning, our half days coincide. The three of us are free to do as we wish, since we are not required to show our faces before noon. Some might wish to remain in bed. I am not one of them."

Edith opened her mouth and closed it again.

"No, indeed," Vroni continued. "Who would malinger abed when we have the whole of Zürich within our reach? I yearn for the bustle of society, to observe the latest fashions, listen to bright conversation, admire all the colourful hats and gaze through shop windows at beautiful objects I can never afford. Shall we three stroll up Bahnhofstrasse, take morning tea at a pretentious café before crossing the Limmat and walking back alongside the river?"

"I declare that is a wonderful notion!" Edith beamed. "Let's hope the weather is kind to us. Then we can sit outside and watch the passers-by. Will you come with us, Seraphine? Please say yes! Don't tell me you want to be holed up again with that German woman, painting poxes?"

Seraphine longed for fresh mountain air, the sound of cowbells, an absence of people, a decent work of fiction and all the colours of an Alpine hillside. Yet if there was any chance of encountering a tall doctor with kind eyes, Zürich's Bahnhofstrasse was the place to be.

"No, Frau Volger cannot spare me time this weekend. In any case, I devote far too much of my time indoors alone, being studious. What better way to spend a Saturday than outdoors with my friends, being frivolous!"

· · ·

Nurses-in-training had precious little free time. Seraphine chose to use hers 'holed up with that German woman, painting poxes', although that was not how she would describe it. Lotte Volger occasionally granted her a couple of hours on a Saturday to watch and learn by observing the master moulaguese at work. The skill of rendering a skin disease in wax, duplicating its colour and textures as accurately as possible, while sitting beside the afflicted individual, took intense concentration. Frau Volger made conversation with the patient if it helped him or her relax; otherwise she remained focused on her work, rarely addressing Seraphine at all.

Some patients, especially those suffering from venereal diseases, were not willing to add to their embarrassment and discomfort by having a young nurse in attendance. Three weeks might pass without her receiving an invitation in Volger's neat and tiny handwriting. Whenever she did, no matter if the sun shone or it was her turn to do the laundry, Seraphine snatched her opportunity to observe a master at work.

From the beginning, Volger made it clear that every moulageur or moulageuse had a fiercely defended secret recipe. She had learned hers from the great Fritz Kolbow in Berlin and she had no intention of sharing it with Seraphine. Nonetheless, she was willing to demonstrate her artistic techniques. No lesson was the same because no skin complaint was the same. Blisters, tick bites, eczema, tumours, shingles, lice, melanomas and fungal infections each required careful examination and replication in wax. Once again, Seraphine rejected her natural impulses to recoil from symptoms of disease to concentrate on its cause. The one thing she could not suppress was her sympathy for the victim.

Each of Volger's creations was a work of art, valuable beyond estimation. These pieces would be used as teaching tools in the best university hospitals and therefore ease suffering, aid treatments and save lives. Seraphine admired and respected the rendition of such conditions, but her interest lay in the next stage.

When one identified what it was, how to treat it? In her heart, she knew her destiny was not as a moulageuse, but as a nurse.

19

Nobody knows you.
You don't know yourself.
And I, who am half in love with you,
What am I in love with?
My own imaginings?

— D.H. Lawrence, *Collected Poems*

May 1922

I n a small Swiss town, twenty-six-year-old bachelors with a respectable profession were like Italian truffles – highly prized and rooted out by an expert nose. Since Bastian was once again eligible and free of commitments, he was fair game. Not a week passed without an invitation to some gathering or other hosted by a determined mother of marriageable daughters. It was a nuanced dance, paying respectful attentions to the ladies while giving no signals of false hope. More recently, Bastian had good reason to refuse such engagements.

Based on conclusive tests in the Matterthal valley, the Swiss government formed the *Kropfkommission* or Goitre Commission to share findings and advise on public guidance. In January 1922, sixteen experts convened in Bern, ranging from army officers to hospital directors. Hunziker, Bayard and Eggenberger were all present. The results were incontrovertible. Measured dosages of iodine could prevent the blight of goitre, cretinism, deafness, brain fog and exhaustion, a plague more prevalent in Switzerland than any of its neighbouring countries. However, every canton controlled its own salt production and distribution. The government could not impose dietary reform across the country, only issue a recommendation. If people wanted iodised salt, they would have to vote for it.

Dr Eggenberger immediately filed an initiative with his own half-canton, Appenzell Ausserrhoden. He and Bastian took turns at driving the ambulance to remote villages and small towns to explain the importance of consuming iodised salt. Even there, keen-eyed maternal figures found a reason to approach Bastian with questions, more often than not with a daughter in tow.

It was an honour to support the doctor's endeavours, albeit hard work during the long winter months. Eggenberger insisted on his attendance at over a dozen meetings before allowing him to carry the message alone. The tide was turning. Medical journals declared themselves astonished at such phenomenal results, neighbouring cantons were willing to entertain the concept of a publicly decided initiative and most importantly, the evidence spoke for itself. Letters flew between Herisau and St. Niklaus, containing undeniable proof of the treatment's success. Eggenberger and Bayard had proven themselves right, yet neither doctor wished to aggrandise their status. Rather, they hoped to convince the government to extend the benefits to the whole of Switzerland. Under a federal system, this would be a mighty challenge.

"Tell me, Bastian, what is an avalanche?" Eggenberger dipped his cervelat in mustard before taking a bite, leaning back in his office chair.

Used to similar oblique angles of enquiry from his mentor, Bastian chose to broaden the question. "An avalanche is an unexpected excess with the danger of overwhelm. If we are speaking metaphorically, I would offer as an example the number of unmarried ladies presented to me at the *Fasnacht* Ball. Literally, I define an avalanche as a displacement of a snow field, where tonnes of snow, ice and other material dragged in its wake descends from a mountain. The causes of such events are unpredictable and nothing can stop them."

Eggenberger wiped his beard with a napkin. "An unstoppable force, yes?"

Bastian nodded, with a wry smile. An unstoppable force was exactly how he would describe his employer. "Yes. Unless it encounters an immovable object."

"No object is immovable, merely reshaped. Huge slabs of snow slide downhill, mighty and merciless, changing the landscape. How are these deadly behemoths formed? From tiny snowflakes floating from the sky, so fragile they melt on your tongue. En masse, however, they become a weighty power against which we are defenceless."

"The husband-seekers of St. Gallen could be described the same way. I see your point, doctor. In sufficient numbers, snowflakes may create an avalanche and raindrops can form a flood. People, insignificant in isolation, can come together in an act of collective will to change our circumstances. I understand. We need more raindrops."

"We need every raindrop, every snowflake and every single

vote to influence the cantonal government. We cannot cease our efforts until the consumption of iodised salt is as normal as drinking milk." Eggenberger smoothed his moustache and laughed. "As for single ladies, I'm afraid that battle is yours and best fought alone. We all regret things went sour with Teresa, but you are still young. Choose well, Bastian, and do not tarry too long."

A rap came at the door. Both men recognised the impatient knuckles of Frau Neff even before she walked into the room.

"Philosophising can be done in the café, gentlemen. You have patients waiting and some cannot wait. May I recommend opening the window to clear the air before receiving anyone? A pungent scent of mustard and onions gives a distinctly unprofessional impression. Here is the post."

Eggenberger apologised and waited till she closed the door before shaking his head. "She is right, of course. A nurse par excellence, although I sometimes wonder if she missed her calling. What an asset she would be to the military." He sifted through the letters. "Ah, here's one for you. From St. Niklaus and in a feminine hand! Pity the poor ladies of Appenzell Ausserrhoden."

From the other side of the desk, Bastian's spirits performed an acrobatic leap of hope, only to fall, bounce and stabilise as he recognised the handwriting. He took the letter, tucked it into his jacket and returned to his own surgery, ready for the afternoon's ailments. Frau Bayard's long-awaited missive must wait till after dinner.

M*y dear Bastian*
At last I am at leisure to write. The children and I are returned from Ticino, restored to health and happiness by dint of

sunshine, blue skies and the indescribable joy of white peaks reflected in clear water. We thrived in warmer climes, all seasonal coughs, colds and general malaise forgotten. Are you familiar with Lago Maggiore? If not, I can recommend it. One can wave to Italy from the shores of Brissago. Imagine that!

Otto tells me that as a national commission and via local teams you are making colossal strides with regard to progress. As you know, my husband regards hyperbole with great antipathy, which leads me to believe what he says is true. The local government of Appenzell Ausserrhoden accepted a people's vote on iodised salt as cantonal directive within a week? I had to take two turns around the room after writing that sentence, merely to contain my excitement. How far we have progressed under the most trying of circumstances!

The health of the people in the hands of the people, is that not as it should be? A dream is come true. I would be remiss not to offer you my most sincere congratulations. Now then, I will accept no modesty, young man. Dr Otto Bayard and Dr Hans Eggenberger broke new ground on the foundations of their predecessors. You were instrumental in their work, in practice as well as theory. Indeed, you will carry their torch into the new decade. We were all part of this, Bastian, and should never forget how lives have changed for the better.

Daily I look at my daughters with a new confidence. I entertain immodest hopes that they too seek to enhance the existence of their friends, neighbours and compatriots. Is that not every person's responsibility? To serve others?

I wax lyrical. After all, in the last four weeks I have spoken nothing but Italian. I find it is the best kind of language for dramatics and I often make several exaggerated pronouncements before breakfast. The customers of the Weisshornstube now regard me with a combination of suspicion and sympathy.

My dear boy, I had every intention of taking a trip to Zürich next month to satisfy my curiosity. That is not to be as I am expecting another child. Our joy is untrammelled, naturally. Therefore, I must *quash my butterfly urges until a later date. On my list was a long lunch with two favourites: Dr Bastian Favre and recently qualified Nurse Seraphine Widmer. Would you believe the first two letters in my post pile were from you and dear sweet Seraphine? She is on the cusp of graduating from the School of Nursing in Zürich and a student of Dermatology.*

If I was not with child, I would swear this swelling is a pure burst of pride. Since I cannot travel to see you, perhaps you might embark on another epic adventure into the mountains? I am quite sure Seraphine would be glad of the company. Otto's forehead clears for a full five minutes when he hears news of your arrival.

Arrivederci, my friend

F. Bayard

St. Niklaus, 6 May 1922

H e placed the letter on the table but fearing the candle might set it alight, folded it once more and tucked it in his jacket. Seraphine was studying nursing in Zürich? Why had no one mentioned it? What a waste of time when he could have visited on his occasional trips. He would seek her out, an old friend from a previous practice, and invite her for an innocent cup of coffee. They could travel together to St. Niklaus, comparing notes on a medical education. He bolted his dinner and checked his schedule. He had community duties on Friday evening and was on call the whole of Sunday. But on Saturday, he was completely free.

He grabbed his pen to write on the calendar and clasped his forehead in dismay. In capital letters by his own hand, there was a blunt reminder: ELOISE, 09.30, ZHB. LUNCH?

How could it be he had no private arrangements for weeks on end and now a diary conflict in Zürich? He took a deep breath. This was ridiculous. He had no claim on Seraphine's time. All he could do was leave a note at the nursing school, suggesting a time to meet. On Saturday, as agreed, he would meet his sister and hope she read his agitation as nothing more than the delight of a reunited sibling. He sighed at the futility of the idea. Of all the people in the world, Eloise could read him like a picture book.

Zürich Hauptbahnhof on a Saturday morning was an opportunity to observe the world in all its variety. Bastian was early, with ample time to sip coffee and study his species in its urban habitat. The station, he noted, was full of alarming sights and sounds. Everyone was in a hurry, carrying too much, herding too many and rushing to beat the relentless clock. He crossed his legs, drank his bitter brew and warded off memories.

He did not succeed.

Flora cried and Walter yelled a cheerful goodbye. 'Uf Wiederluege,' said Julius, doffing his hat with a knowing smile. Young Bastian swallowed hard and waved farewell, fooling no one.

Was there anywhere in this city which did not harbour recollections of how naïve he used to be? He blinked at the pigeons strutting like grey-uniformed inspectors beneath his table. Soon Eloise would arrive. Then he would attempt to play the knowledgeable brother with an insider's guide to the city everyone was talking about. What a fraud.

A group of women passed his table, their conversation lively. His gaze skimmed each face but none came close to the unadorned simplicity of Seraphine. Painted and powdered, each of these women had the same sharp eyes of a farmer's wife at market. One gave him such a calculating look he almost expected her to march over and inspect his teeth.

He left some coins on the table and strode away to meet his sister's train.

Of all his sisters, Eloise was closest to him in both age and temperament. The entire family had a studious and quiet nature, taught to equate pleasure with learning. Only Eloise, two years older than him, sought pursuits with no other objective than laughter or exhilaration. Every scratch and scrape on his ten-year-old body could be attributed to one of her impulsive schemes. She pushed the swing dangerously high, jumped into the river first, skied off piste to chase 'wolves' and raced him downhill on her bicycle. In almost every case, he came off worst. But the very next time he saw that gleam in her eye, he threw himself into the adventure without a backward glance.

Married now and a mother of two, she gave the external impression of dignity and poise. An impression Bastian did not believe for a second. She stepped off the first carriage with a brilliant smile at the conductor and raised a gloved hand at her waiting brother. Eloise assumed everything in the world was arranged for her pleasure, and the world obediently fell into line.

"My dearest, how lovely to see you! Was the journey a dreadful bore?" he asked, taking her holdall and kissing her cheeks three times.

"A bore? Quite the contrary. I sat opposite a pair of stuffy sorts. You know the type, disapproval leaking from every pore at a lady travelling alone. Well, I cannot resist a challenge. With all manner of allusions and hints as to my top-secret mission, I more or less convinced them I was Mata Hari. Ha, ha! They'll be talking about me the entire weekend."

"What on earth is in this holdall? You're only here for the day. As a matter of fact, Mata Hari was executed by firing squad during the war."

She stopped and fixed him with a quizzical stare. "So they say. But can one ever really trust the French? Come along, I am in desperate need of fresh air. My holdall is overflowing with presents for you and a few little essentials a lady must never be without. Where are you taking me for lunch? Will we have time for a boat trip? I do so love the lake!"

They perambulated up one side of Bahnhofstrasse with a pause for coffee and confectionery at Paradeplatz. Eloise insisted on sitting outside, despite the noise of trams and a chill May breeze.

She took off her gloves. "When will you come to Fribourg again? Papa rails daily against your absence while we, that is Mami, my sisters and I, try our best to convince him you are at the forefront of medical advances. You have a niece and two nephews you are yet to meet, one of whom is your godchild. We are still waiting for you so we can baptise the boy. Surely you have the occasional free day?" She stirred her coffee, a dainty finger and thumb clasping a silver spoon.

"I apologise, Eloise. I do have free days, usually one or two at the weekend, but my circumstances are unpredictable. More so than ever now we have the initiative to promote. If I made a promise to visit next week, for example, a crisis might occur at the practice and I would be forced to cancel."

She said nothing, examining her fingernails.

"Do not pout. How about this? One month from now, I shall take a holiday, come hell or high water. If I combine my trip to Fribourg with some collegiate exchanges, Dr Eggenberger will undoubtedly support my endeavours. That way, everyone is satisfied."

Eloise reached out a hand to stroke his cheek, her eyes sparkling. "Thank you. That means so much to me."

He caught her hand in his and pressed it to his lips. "I know, my dearest. I hereby promise to be a better brother, son, uncle and godfather from this day forward, amen."

She spluttered with laughter, tugging a lace handkerchief

from her sleeve to pat her eyes. A tram rattled past and a cloud obscured the sun. He was oblivious, basking in his sister's smile.

"Very well. Therefore the only thing remaining is ..."

He finished her sentence, partly to deflect the inevitable. "For me to take you to lunch?"

"A gentleman never interrupts a lady. The only thing remaining is to make your parents and sisters even happier by becoming a good husband and father. Only you can continue the Favre family name, you know."

"Ah." He sipped at his cooling coffee.

"And now who pouts, my darling pup? Listen to your older, wiser and fully matured sister. You can have no shortage of admirers, of that I am convinced. Handsome, well-dressed, tall, charming and a man of means? There must be a queue stretching from Herisau to St. Gallen. You are busy with important medical work, granted, but no one is too busy to find a bride. Time is ticking, Bastian. All the most desirable ladies will get snapped up while you hide away in remote valleys, buried under books. Your sisters are ready and willing to assist. Indeed, we have drawn up a list of the bright and beautiful of whom we approve. A liberty, perhaps, but taken with the best of good intentions."

"You do know what they say about the road to Hell? Your list will not be necessary, Eloise. After I have seen you safely onto your train this afternoon, I intend to pay a visit to a certain young lady and issue an invitation." On seeing her eyes widen, he forestalled the inevitable enquiries. "Since I have no idea whether she is likely to accept, I shall say no more on the subject and neither will you. Let us be optimistic and hope your list is surplus to requirements. Now, can we talk of other matters? Tell me tales of Fribourg society including every scurrilous rumour."

"All in good time. I will ask no more questions about this

certain young lady, for now, but I refuse to move another step until you tell me the inside story about the Säntis murder!"

"Eloise, you too? Why must everyone scratch around for the unedifying details?"

"Because knowledge is power, Bastian. Your knowledge gives me power." Her gaze fixed on him like an inscrutable cat and his resistance crumbled.

S ome days last for an eternity. Others pass like bubbles, a fleeting moment of weightlessness and rainbows, before disappearing into nothing. They ran for her train, laughing like magpies, and found the platform with two minutes to spare.

"Take this," he gasped, handing over her bag.

She brushed stray hairs from her face. "No, you take it. It contains all your presents. I must dash or be stranded here for all eternity!"

"But what about your lady's essentials?"

She blew him a kiss. "Mata Hari will find a way! Until next month!" She swanned along the platform, where a conductor waited beside an open door. In an instant, she trotted up the steps, leaned out to wave and disappeared inside.

He waited until the train departed, his heart both full and empty, wondering what mischievous yarns she would spin for her fellow passengers this time. On leaving the Hauptbahnhof, he was surprised to see the sun still shining and warmth radiating from the pavements. Whenever Eloise left, he expected rain.

He had one more task to do before he caught his own train to Herisau. The note, the fifteenth draft to hit exactly the right tone, was sealed in a plain envelope with her name on the front. He took the tram to Hottingen and the nursing school, where he resisted the temptation to open it and read it one last time.

Instead, he slipped it into the letterbox. He glanced up at the building, willing her to appear at a window, but berated himself for behaving like an idiot. A return tram rattled down the hill to the lake and he got on, carrying Eloise's absurdly girlish holdall. All he could do now was wait for Seraphine.

20

June 1922

At a town hall meeting in Bern, an assembly of over fifty cantonal representatives discuss a proposition by the government Kropfkommission (Goitre Commission). The final speaker draws his address to a close and opens the floor to questions from attendees. A man near the front stands, one hand in his pocket, the other punctuating his speech.

Herr Fuchs: I stand here, horrified to my bones by the proposals of this commission. My outrage is such I can barely speak. To impose a national directive in this manner is unacceptable. Does this chamber not trust the housewives of this country? Do we doubt they feed their children adequately? Do we consider ourselves better informed and more knowledgeable than these good women regarding the needs of their offspring?

Applause and nodding heads indicate the general mood. Before Fuchs has taken his seat, another voice resonates around the room.

Herr Bircher: This country is founded on good faith and direct democracy. The people know best. If that is our central tenet, who are we to meddle with what they serve on their tables? Whether they be farmers, bankers, servants of God or of the state, each man is free to choose what he consumes. Other religions refuse comestibles they deem unclean and that is their God-given right! I will defend a man's refusal of an imposition on his own plate until my dying breath.

The crowd echoes its agreement and several men stand, each raising a hand. The chairman indicates a stout fellow near the door.

Herr Schaffenhauser: My colleagues are correct in rejecting this unwelcome intervention. To dictate what citizens may or may not eat presages a dark chapter in Swiss history. The proponents of the *Jodsalz* initiative have short memories. A blight recorded innumerable times in France, Austria and the Italian Alps, the pernicious condition known as *Jod-Basedow* is also widespread here. Yes, here in the Helvetic Confederation, gentlemen. Wretched victims tremble, spasm, bulge and die due to an overdose of iodine. The very same poison these physicians wish to inflict on our people!

Calls of 'Never!' and 'Shame!' are audible over the cheers. The chairman holds up a hand for silence and points at a whiskered man leaning on a cane.

Herr Mangel: Hear, hear! Short memories indeed. We are scarcely recovered from the Great War. Four years ago the people of Switzerland faced the deadliest threat to our geographical location. Our hardy country folk, resilient and courageous, survived despite the deprivations. To insist these brave citizens submit to medical experiments, which must be paid from their own pockets, is nothing short of an abomination.

The audience echoes his final words amidst their clapping. When they finally quieten, the chairman, seated at the head of the table opens his hand, inviting further contributions. Other than mutters and grumbles, no one speaks. The chair indicates the guest speaker may respond.

Herr Favre: Thank you all for your well-expressed and intelligent comments. With your permission, I will address each objection in turn. Herr Mangel, you object to the initiative because people must pay more for a household necessity, if I am not mistaken? That is incorrect. The salt producer serving almost all of Switzerland – Vereinigten Schweizer Rheinsalinen – guarantees iodised salt will be priced the same as untreated and available everywhere.

Whispers rustle through the rows, with many frowning at the unfortunate Mangel.

Herr Favre: Medical experiments, Herr Schaffenhauser? Yes, we call them that for reasons of accuracy. The three doctors I referenced in my speech addressed one of the worst afflictions in Switzerland. How? By testing small communities with tiny doses and measuring the results. In every case, goitres reduced to almost nil, women bore far fewer deaf-mutes or cretins, and crucially, the common complaint of 'brain fog' disappeared. Every single person tested was a volunteer and even those unable to give consent, such as infants, were not coerced. To tell the truth, we had more willing test subjects than we could handle. Those brave souls who made this simple dietary adjustment benefitted not just themselves, but their entire communities.

A thoughtful silence descends on the room.

Herr Favre: The oft-invoked *Jod-Basedow* condition you mention, sir, is indeed a reaction to an excess intake of iodine. However, I refer you to my earlier comments. Medical tests, given at gradually increasing doses, involve no danger to the patients. Not a single case of poisoning has been reported in any of the valleys. The decrease in thyroid-related malformations, on the other hand, has disappeared. We in the medical profession document physical phenomena. To my knowledge, no chart or record exists to quantify improvements in quality of life.

All I have is the evidence of my eyes: the heartfelt handshake from a shepherd, the laughter of children in the schoolyard, sparks in the eyes of pregnant women and whole villages transformed from defeat into hope.

With my hand on my heart, I can tell you the change is nothing short of miraculous, a word I never use lightly.

People shift in their seats, looking to one another for an objection.

Herr Favre: No man could contradict Herr Bircher when he says a government should advise but must not impose when it comes to choices regarding one's health. That is why we propose public initiatives in every canton. One cannot compare Valais with Ticino, or Bern with Graubünden. It is up to the people to make the best decision for their particular circumstances. As we have seen in Appenzeller Ausserrhoden, with sufficient information and evidence of their own eyes, people make the right choice.

Herr Bircher: You are talking of a rural half canton. Those country folk are easily swayed under the influence of a powerful doctor.

Several listeners take an intake of breath and one or two direct a stern scowl at the man.

Herr Favre: Far be it from me to generalise, but Appenzell Ausserrhoden is regarded as one of the most conservative communities in the whole of Switzerland. Its people are known to be resistant to change and suspicious of false promises. The reason the half canton voted to ensure the provision of iodised salt for their families, their cattle and even their bakers is because they had incontrovertible proof. Farmers watched their livestock, men noticed their wives, women observed their children and everyone acknowledged the difference. The same is true of the Matterthal valley. It is a grave error to underestimate 'country folk', Herr Bircher. I was born, raised and trained in a city. But only in the mountains did I receive an education.

Herr Bircher sits down with a snort. No one meets his eye.

Herr Favre: Regarding your question, Herr Fuchs, I am in complete accord with your assertion. Mothers are the experts on the well-being of their infants. Women bore the brunt of this symptom of malnutrition, suffering physical deformity, mental exhaustion and the harsh reality of caring for deficient infants. Yet there is an irony here. Women have no say in whether or not we implement a cure. Why? Because they have no vote.

I put it to you, gentlemen, the responsibility lies with us. Our duty is to study the results from St. Niklaus and Herisau, acknowledge the improvements in public health, choose to become champions in medical history and release our fellow citizens from a curse. This is a fresh new decade in a young century. It is imperative we look forward to a better future, and only backwards to learn from our mistakes.

21

Beyond a certain point there is no return.
This point has to be reached.

— Franz Kafka, *Die Zürauer Aphorismen*

July 1922

S he cut out every single newspaper report bearing his name
and tucked it in the worn envelope alongside his note. It
was quite foolish to keep it since there was no question of
answering him. Even so, she could not quite bring herself to
throw it away. Her humiliation no longer stung. Rather it itched
like the long-healed burn on her shin. The blame for her pain
lay squarely at her own door. His good manners were commend-
able, hers were sadly lacking. The very thought of her girlish
delusion was pure mortification.

Seraphine prided herself on being resilient in operating
theatres and on crowded wards. She never failed to perform her
tasks even after seeing the most dreadful sights. What use did it

serve if she fell apart? The day she had seen Bastian Favre with his wife, she had no duties other than making frivolous conversation with her friends. At that, she had failed dismally.

The scene played out again, like a series of gaudy postcards that refused to fade. Of all the times she had searched the faces, scanned the crowds, hoping to spot him, it happened when she was not looking.

On a bright Saturday in May, Bahnhofstrasse was crowded with glamorous browsers and serious shoppers, lively accordion players and smelly sausage stalls. The sun was shining with intent, as if this time it was serious and April's unpredictability was a distant memory. Sensory stimulations distracted and entranced the three young nurses, meaning their progress was as erratic as children in a fairground.

"Oh, look here! That cape would look so fetching on me!"

"Lovely colour, I agree. That man is selling the prettiest posies. Shall we try charming him into a bargain?"

"Do you see that lady in blue? Now that is how one wears feathers with style."

"Gaudy, if you ask me. She looks like something from a Parisian nightclub."

"Watch out for that horse manure, Vroni!"

"Thank you, Seraphine. Do you remember that perfumery I mentioned? Here it is."

Seraphine's head rotated from left to right as if she were watching a badminton match, but Vroni had already moved on. "Good heavens, that child almost fell under an automobile. Parents should be more careful."

"There's Confiserie Sprüngli! Can we stop for tea and watch the beautiful people pass by?"

"Have you taken leave of your senses, Edith? That place is far too expensive for the likes of us. In any case, I cannot see a single unoccupied seat. Let us not dawdle."

Acquiescent as ever, Seraphine followed Vroni along the pavement on the opposite side to the famous café, with a curious glance at its clientele. She spotted him immediately, right in the centre, gazing at a beautiful woman. As she watched, the lady reached out a hand to caress his cheek. He took her pale fingers, the third bearing a wedding ring, and pressed them to his lips. The look of love between them was unmistakeable. He had chosen well. His wife was elegant, animated and beautifully dressed, rather like Frau Bayard. Clouds threw shadows over the street, a tram rattled past and the happy couple were hidden from view.

"Seraphine! Do buck up, we only have two hours before we're back on duty." Edith scuttled in the direction of the lake.

Vroni cupped a hand around Seraphine's upper arm. "Are you feeling unwell? It's the heat, I expect, we're not accustomed to it after months of winter. Let's sit in the shade and take a glass of iced water. Edith, will you slow down! You're like a poodle off the leash. Turn left here, Seraphine. I know a quiet spot in the courtyard."

Her friends attributed her silence and withdrawn behaviour to sun and exertion, and soon resumed their bright conversation. Meanwhile Seraphine sat in front of a fountain, watching a bonfire and all her fantasies burn to ash.

N o one thought to collect post on a Sunday, meaning Seraphine did not receive his note for two days. She was heading to the bathroom on Monday morning when Vroni handed over the envelope, her expression alert. Seraphine took it into the lavatory and locked the door.

. . .

Dear Seraphine

I trust this finds you well. Only recently in correspondence with Frau Bayard did I learn of your presence in Zürich. What excellent news that you are studying to be a nurse, and in a much-respected establishment. I offer you my most sincere congratulations.

As you may recall, I am currently employed in Herisau and greatly occupied with extending the iodised salt therapy at a cantonal level. However, I visit the Matterthal occasionally. Frau Bayard suggested we might travel together the next time we both set off for St. Niklaus. I would be honoured to accompany you. If this arrangement suits you, send a note to the address above informing me when you intend to travel. I will endeavour to join you.

I wish you every success with your nursing career and look forward to renewing your acquaintance.

Yours respectfully

B. Favre

His words compounded her injury. He was proper, formal and polite, just as he should be. How foolish and ridiculous was she? To entertain hopes of his affection was naïve at best and arrogant at worst. His wife, so refined, so polished and a thousand leagues away from herself, was exactly the woman he deserved.

She shed a few hot tears at her own stupidity, then tucked the note into her pocket and washed her face in cold water at the basin. She would not reply. The gesture was clearly provoked by Frau Bayard's kindness. Why else would a happily married man offer to escort a plain little nurse to the other side of the country?

Her disappointment and shame was wholly her responsibility and she had no reason to resent him. She would wish the man well and forget he had ever existed.

The day she moved out of the nursing school seemed the right time to let go. Unlike her friends, she had not gained a hospital place after her internment. Skilled paediatric nurses such as Vroni and capable midwives like Edith were always in demand. An average auxiliary with an interest in skin complaints was not. She received her certificate and a positive reference for applications elsewhere.

On her behalf, Edith was distraught and Vroni was furious. Seraphine expended as much effort comforting her friends as she did sending job applications. Finally, with tearful farewells, the two future nurses departed for a fortnight's holiday before commencing their new roles. Seraphine packed up her trunk and faced the return journey to St. Niklaus alone and defeated. It was possible Dr Bayard might re-employ her as a return on his investment. If not, Herr Lochmatter might require a chambermaid.

In their empty dormitory overlooking the hospital garden, she knelt at a window ledge, rested her head on her forearms and cried over every dashed dream. As her mother had so often repeated, life is not fair. *Pride is the best teacher of humility, Seraphine, learn that lesson young.*

She wiped her cheeks and registered the green space and walled garden below, where two burly men were piling fallen blossom, grass cuttings and dead branches onto a bonfire. She fumbled for her tapestry bag of keepsakes. There it was, her name written in his confident, cultured hand atop some folded newspaper cuttings. The time was right. She had no need to read his words again since she could recite the entire thing from memory. Instead, she slipped a light shawl over her summer dress and walked the long way around to the garden. The maddening winds from the south were even worse than yesterday. Hot breath from an invisible dragon.

Under the stone archway, she sheltered from the gusts and waited. The gardeners finally returned to the shed, leaving the aroma of tobacco in the air. She crept through the gate and stood in front of the glowing embers, the scent of burning wood filling her nose and mellow heat warming her face. Instinctively, she turned her scarred leg away from the fire. There was no one to watch her. Junior nurses were in class or at the hospital; graduates had all left for a holiday. Dry-eyed, she tossed the envelope into the centre of the fire. In an instant, it caught light, blazing for a few seconds as if it still had something to say. She watched it crumble into flakes of ash, borne away on the breeze. Gone. As if Bastian Favre had never existed.

She wandered into the main building with the faintest hope of finding good news in her post box: a letter, a job offer, a cheery missive from Vroni or Edith? Contrary to expectations, the box was not empty. A handwritten note lay on top of a stamped envelope. The tiny letters were familiar. Lotte Volger wrote so neatly and small, her letters could have been written by a mouse. Seraphine unfolded the note, her breath shallow.

D*ear Fräulein Widmer*
    Thank you for your enquiry.
    Unfortunately, I have no need of an assistant at this time.
    With every confidence you will find a suitable position, I wish you well.
    Yours sincerely
    Lotte Volger

· · ·

The other item was a letter bearing a St. Niklaus postmark, her address scrawled in a clumsy hand. The sender was registered as Clothilde Widmer. Her mother wrote so rarely, Seraphine had not recognised the handwriting. Whatever had provoked the letter could not be good news. She tore it open, her pulse thunderous.

Dear Seraphine
        It seems I owe Josef a franc. He wagered you wouldn't come home for the 1st August holiday and he was right. For myself, I am disappointed but not surprised. You've barely shown your face these past months and the only news I hear is from that gossipy doctor's wife. Perhaps it is for the best. What with the way things are on the farm and Peter growing so strong, we barely have enough to feed ourselves. I am quite sure Margot and Thierry will provide you with a full plate and more sophisticated entertainment than our humble village celebrations.
        Friendly greetings
        Maman
        P.S. Barry is dead.

After twenty years of her mother's self-interest and withheld affection, she had grown accustomed to the pattern. The tone of her letter hurt Seraphine as intended, though more of a graze than a wound. Clothilde's callous rejection was designed to make her daughter cry tears of shame, hurry home and plead for her mother's love. Even the cruel postscript knowingly inflicted hurt.

Seraphine pushed open the door of the nursing school and sat outside on the steps, tucking her dress under her knees and shielding her eyes from the sun. In biology lessons, she had learned how certain species grow a carapace to defend themselves against attack. Inside, they remain tender and vulnerable. The soft underside of Seraphine welcomed memories of the big furry dog, his gingery eyebrows and unswerving loyalty.

Another part hardened and detached. Her mother's vicious barb against her own sister tipped the balance. Until now, family connections had always been a last resort. If a newly qualified nurse could not find a position under her own steam, she would do exactly what her mother assumed and fall back on the generosity of her relatives. A thought crossed her mind. If anyone in her acquaintance had a telephone, it would be her aunt and uncle.

Next month, she could be walking the streets of Montreux, speaking French with her aunt, weighing prospects with her uncle and strolling down to the lake to read her book. What better way to start a new chapter in her life?

She dropped her hand from her forehead and stared down at the street, filled with energy and determination. Barely ten metres away, a hatless man stared back, his eyes locked on to hers.

22

We can never give up longing and wishing while we are thoroughly alive. There are certain things we feel to be beautiful and good, and we must hunger after them.

— George Eliot, *The Mill on the Floss*

July 1922

In the relatively small community of Herisau and the half-canton of Appenzell Ausserrhoden, fame or notoriety were rare occurrences, generally unwelcome. Recent events had changed that. For the salacious, Dr Favre's tangential involvement in the most shocking events in living memory drew intense but thankfully short-lived interest. Meanwhile Dr Eggenberger's achievement of galvanising the populace into demanding the manufacture and provision of iodised salt drew medical attention from across the globe. The significance was greater still in Switzerland as Appenzell generally was regarded as the least radical region in the country. People flocked to the town with questions on their lips. Eggenberger and most of the community saw it as a chance to spread the word. Bastian Favre threw himself into the publicity drive with patience and good will. His heart, however, was absent.

Their strategy was working. No one could deny the effects on the populace; reduced goitres, almost no underdeveloped babies and a proud, robust population. Local governments put the question to a public vote. Government and salt manufacturers were ready to make treated salt available by law. Hans Eggenberger, along with Otto Bayard and Heinrich Hunziker, had successfully changed the face of Switzerland forever.

Bastian played his part but this was not his fight. Not his glory. He was fast approaching twenty-seven. Most men in his circumstances would have their own practice by now, along with a home, wife and child. At least that was what everyone said. His parents and sisters mentioned it at least twice in every communication. In the town, the subject of Teresa and the brusque end to their relationship was tactfully avoided. Bastian spent his days at the hospital shaking hands and patting backs, dodging invitations and dreaming of escape. Not a day passed without his revisiting a lost and hopeless scheme. His note to Seraphine, so carefully crafted and polite, had disappeared into the ether. He spent weeks imagining the reason she had given no reply, conjuring the most extraordinary series of events until he accepted the obvious. Her silence was a polite refusal and a sign he should move on.

Therefore, he made a point of avoiding Zürich. He told himself the city of his youth held too many emotions, regularly ambushing him with a poignant recollection or flush of embarrassment. He spent a week in Fribourg, visiting his ever-expanding family of nieces and nephews. Three times he travelled to Bern to deliver documentation to the Federal Bureau of Public Health. Once or twice he changed trains at Zürich Hauptbahnhof en route to Luzern or Basel, but saw no reason to dwell longer than necessary.

Until July, when Dr Eggenberger sprang one of his non sequiturs.

"If this weather continues, our National Day celebrations should be blessed by sunshine. How would you like your own practice by a lake?"

Bastian thought before he spoke. "Sunshine is a blessing indeed. Let us hope it continues, for everyone's sake. A lake, a mountain, a forest or a valley, I can be content in any environment. The difficulty of establishing my own practice anywhere in Switzerland is a lack of reputation."

"Quite so, quite so. Ordinarily, you could succeed me, reassuring our long-term patients that nothing has changed. Our success has entrapped us, you see. The political nature of our iodine initiative means I must remain in post for a good few years yet. Ideally, I would employ and train one to three juniors to assume my place when I retire. Bastian, believe me when I say no one is better suited to such a role than yourself. However, to step down now to make way for you is to leave a job half finished. You are an excellent physician and retaining you here in Herisau, in my shadow, does you a disservice. A man of such skill and intelligence merits a practice of his own." Hans Eggenberger's gaze softened into a smile.

"If I am not mistaken, you wish me to leave your employ."

"Wish? Certainly not." Eggenberger massaged his forehead. "You have been the most reliable partner, research fellow, sounding-board and dare I say, constructive critic through the greatest challenge of my career. The battle is far from won. That is why my selfish side balks at relinquishing your contribution. My unselfish side says it is time for you to shine, and shine you undoubtedly will. Have you ever visited Brienz?"

Bastian's mind was still processing the compliment. "Brienz? I know the name."

"A lake, mountain, forest or valley would make you content, unless I misheard. Brienz in the canton of Bern has them all. Enough with vague hints and allusions. An old friend from my university years is due to retire from a very small practice outside Brienz. He seeks a trustworthy pair of hands to take control. I recommended you."

Bereft of speech, Bastian stared at his feet, nodding his thanks.

"Only one concern remains. His is a well-established family practice, run by a local couple. My colleague is the doctor, his wife the nurse. His ideal replacement would be a married man, whose spouse would complement his skills. Failing that, you might be able to hire a qualified nurse to work alongside you. As you well know, Frau Neff has been a stalwart support to me and this hospital, usually nurturing, occasionally fierce, and always appropriate. What do you say, Bastian? Are you ready to spread your wings?"

Without warning, a flock of sparrows clustered on the plum tree outside the doctor's office, adding a crescendo of chirps. The two men laughed, appreciating a moment of levity.

"I am honoured by your trust, Herr Eggenberger. This is a rare chance and I would very much like to visit the doctor and the community of Brienz as soon as you can spare me. If he finds me satisfactory, I will place newspaper advertisements for nurses until I find one suitable for the post. On a personal note, working alongside you has been a pleasure and a privilege. Julius gave me a priceless gift."

"We both owe Julius a debt of gratitude." The doctor rummaged around in a desk drawer. "I may have been presumptuous, but I collected a folder with all the relevant information on Brienz. Study it carefully. I can release you from daily duties whenever you need to travel. Regarding the nurse, save yourself some time by enquiring at Zürich's *Pflegerinnenschule*. Those women know what they are doing."

"Thank you, sir."

"Thank you, Bastian. This is the correct course of action but I want you to know this: I shall mourn the loss of my loyal right hand."

O n the train to Zürich, he resigned himself to the fact he was already too late. Good nurses had secured positions months ago and those without were not the kind he sought. His best hope was to ask a senior nurse to suggest a rising star from the latest intake. Why a girl with an optimistic future would drop her studies for a tiny practice beside an undeniably pretty lake was uncertain. As for Seraphine, her year had already graduated, so she must be long gone. He was glad of the fact. Encountering her after sending that letter would have been excruciating. He shook himself as he stepped off the train and resolved to be positive.

On the bridge across the Limmat, a blast of warm air dislodged his hat. He caught it with one hand and scowled, searching for the infernal machine which caused the expulsion. Then he realised. The *Föhn*, a powerful wind from the south blew over the mountains, playing havoc with the natural order of things. Often blamed for inexplicable behaviour in animals and uncharacteristic acts by human beings, the *Föhn* was a force of nature. Bastian strode onward, his hair whipping around his face, praying he too was capable of uncharacteristic acts. Fighting a force of nature was a waste of energy.

He took the tram to Hottingen, just as he had done the day he dropped off his ill-fated note. Today it was a good deal less busy, with fewer than a half-dozen passengers aboard. He elicited one or two looks of respectful approval and sat in the rear, rehearsing his speech to the sister in charge. Outside, two boys cartwheeling down the street attracted his attention. Their exhilaration and high spirits drew smiles from his fellow passengers. At his stop, the boisterous wind teased at his clothes and attempted once again to part his hat from his head. He gave up the battle and carried it in his hand.

Once the tram had departed, he absorbed the scale of the *Pflegerinnenschule*. The new hospital building stood grandly alongside the original, a testament to its success. Bastian shook his head in admiration. How much a small group of indomitable women could accomplish! His gaze fell to street level, where a figure sat on the steps, her hand over her eyes. Blonde hair blew around her face, her dress billowed in the breeze and she clutched papers in her lap. He stood frozen, unable to take another step. The *Föhn*, he reminded himself, plays tricks with the mind.

The girl lifted her head and stared directly at him. Those eyes could belong to none other than Seraphine. His mind froze, unable to think of the correct way to handle such an awkward situation, while gazing at her unforgettable face.

"Herr Doctor Favre?" She wiped her cheeks, stuffed her papers in her pinafore dress and scrambled to her feet. She was out of sorts, he could discern that much, and not only due to his unexpected appearance.

"Seraphine!" Bare-headed and heedless of decorum, he crossed the street and raced up the steps to greet her. "Are you quite well? Is everything in order?" His eyes fell on the envelope poking out of her pocket. "I pray you have not received bad news."

Her face was flushed and her expression bleak. She struggled to maintain control, swallowing and blinking through several deep breaths. "Why are you here, sir, if I may ask?" Her gaze remained resolutely on the ground.

"You may. I am here to seek a well-qualified nurse to join my new practice." He ducked his head to try to catch her eye. "I don't suppose you know of anyone?"

She lifted her eyes, but only as far as his hands. "Congratulations. The influence of Dr Eggenberger, Dr Bayard and Dr Favre is the talk of the nursing school. I am always proud when I read about your achievements in the newspaper. My family and I owe you our thanks. We benefitted greatly from your work."

She was avoiding the question and still would not look at him. "Your family? Are your parents and brother in good health?"

"It seems so." A flicker of pain crossed her face for an instant. "Yes, the Widmers are well, sir, thank you. I hope the same is true of your wife."

The huge gust of wind buffeted them from the side, Seraphine staggered and Bastian caught her arm. "My goodness but the *Föhn* is maddening today. Shall we go inside?"

She stood her ground and wrenched her arm out of his grip. For the first time she directed her blazing blue glare at his face. "I asked about your wife."

"My wife? I am unmarried." He studied her face, the pink blooms of anger on her cheeks, the furious frown and tensed fists. "If some loose rumour reached your ears, it is untrue. I am a bachelor."

"No loose rumour. Less than two months ago, I saw you with a female companion drinking coffee outside Confiserie Sprüngli. An elegant lady in a feathered hat, wearing a wedding ring, with whom you appeared to be most affectionate. If she was not your wife, I can only assume you must be some kind of faithless dilettante."

Had she chosen any other word, Bastian would have

defended his honour with sincerity and passion. Instead he laughed, the wildness of the wind an encouragement to throw his head back and release his mirth.

"The only time I have ever drunk coffee outside Confiserie Sprüngli was with my sister. Eloise is indeed fond of large flamboyant hats. Since her marriage, she wears an ostentatious symbol of her marital status." He recalled the events of that day and his laugh withered in his throat. "You are quite correct. It was May when I spent half a day with my sister, made sure she caught the train and took the tram here with the express purpose of delivering a letter to you."

Her anger took some time to deflate. Her jaw and fists unclenched gradually and her gaze flicked between his eyes, seeking the truth. She did not speak.

"Seraphine, I promise you I am no dilettante. When I learned from Frau Bayard that you were in Zürich, I wrote you a note, intending to rekindle our friendship. I delivered it myself, with a view to our travelling together to St. Niklaus, conversing companionably as we used to do." The tail of his coat flicked upwards, slapping him on the back like a teacher clipping a thoughtless pupil. A fatal recklessness overcame him and he spoke the truth. "I confess I had hopes we might eventually form a different kind of attachment. When you did not reply, I accepted those hopes were unrealistic and swallowed my disappointment."

She blinked, her hair blowing like wild grass about her face, but she uttered no word.

"Receiving a letter from a man you presumed married must have seemed quite improper. I see that now and apologise most sincerely. Valedictions on future letters shall bear not only my medical qualifications but also my marital status."

That raised a hint of a smile. The first since he'd caught sight of her. Yet still she did not speak, her focus on his shoes. A phrase echoed through his head. Whenever he had done something to upset his sisters, they often adopted a reproachful tone and said, *how do you think I feel?* He tried to put himself in Seraphine's position. Her anger suggested something more than indifference towards him. But he had come upon her whilst already in some distress and had merely made it worse. Her face was pale, her eyes red and her posture spoke of exhaustion.

"The last thing I wish to do is upset you, Seraphine. Tears in your eyes pierce my heart like shards of glass. On the other hand, now that I have found you again, I cannot bear to let you go."

She stood like a statue, her blue eyes searching his while the wind tugged impertinently at her dress.

His poetic muse deserted him. "Perhaps we might go indoors and drink a glass of water?"

She nodded and led the way up the steps.

The wind whipped up pink and white blossoms, showering them like confetti.

23

Neither fish nor fowl, nor good red herring

— John Heywood

October 1938

"Our topic today is a man whose influence on nutritional science in the United States is impossible to ignore. Yet his name is known from east to west for one medical trial. Just one. If anyone in this room plans to replicate the clinical standards applied, you will be struck off the physicians' register."

Laughter echoed around the lecture theatre.

The professor continued. "The principal character in our story is one David Marine, born and raised in Maryland. A young man who showed promise at an early age and excelled at Johns Hopkins University. He spent his first year studying zoology which you may very well think signifies very little, but as our tale unfolds I dare say you will understand the relevance. His interest in biology soon became more general and he transferred to the faculty of medicine. Believe me when I say it is not hyperbole to state that he shone in his field, graduating in the top half dozen of his year.

"With grades that high, it is easy to assume every hospital in Maryland and beyond was warming him a seat. They were disappointed. A hospital in Cleveland, Ohio offered him a residency and a lake view. Who was David Marine to refuse?

"They say, and this may be little more than rumour, the good doctor had no burning desire to pursue any particular specialisation in medicine. I cannot vouch for the truth of the story but it is a good one so I shall repeat it.

"On his first day at the hospital, his new employers had high expectations of research papers, publication, grants and glory. Don't we all? The young doctor thought on his feet. In his first few days in the city of Cleveland, he had noticed a considerable number of dogs with lumps at the neck. Locals told him this feature was commonplace, and not only in four-legged beings. David Marine believed the condition, known as a goiter, was related to the thyroid gland. There, he stated, was where he would direct his energies."

A series of hmms and nods animated his audience.

"Indeed. Now you see the reason I drew your attention to Marine's first interest. Where else would a man trained in zoology begin his work? Why, the animal kingdom and in particular the very species which first caught his attention. Dogs. Treating ailing canines proved his theory correct. Street curs, wizened and listless, became active and robust after Marine dosed them with iodine. Sheep farmers reported notable results in their flocks after adding iodised salt to their feed. Even fish! I scarcely credited the story myself, but a trout hatchery pleaded for assistance. Marine perceived the fish were indeed lacking in some kind of nutrient and ruled out the common assumption of a contagion. He suggested changing the diet from chopped pigs' organs to a fresh sea catch, and lo and behold, the lumps dissolved and the creatures thrived."

The professor paused, watching the action of scribbling hands. This was the time to rein in their understandable extrapolation.

"Tall talk and wild claims held no thrall for our modest doctor. Certainly not. He never presented his results as definitive nor attributed the cause of endemic goiter to any individual reason. He asserted it appeared to be 'a compensatory reaction to some deficiency' and iodine was 'the most single important factor'. Do you not marvel at his caution? The man was a scientist to his bones and a student of the latest advances across the world. News came from Europe on similar lines of thinking, sadly interrupted by the onset of war. I often wonder how many more lives could have been saved had the communication between brilliant minds not been interrupted."

The atmosphere cooled. Professor Mulcahy was no fool and steered away from anything verging on the political.

"David Marine then turned his focus on the complex human organism, pledging to address the problem of widespread goiter and infant underdevelopment in the Great Lakes. He began at his own clinic. Initial introductions of sodium iodide for children were positive and contradicted nothing in his previous findings. He rallied support for a public health exercise with the intention of treating and testing schoolgirls over a three-year period. Like many a forward thinker before him, Marine encountered intractability and entrenched ideas, not just from the general public, but also fellows in his own profession."

Mulcahy eyed the audience with a hooded glare. "It so happened that the chairman of the school board was a physician. This man maintained iodine had toxic potential and wielded his power to prevent the scheme. Thwarted in Cleveland, Marine met a medical student by the name of Oliver Perry

Kimball. Together, these pioneers secured an agreement with the board of education in Akron, Ohio, and the trial began."

A hand went up in the third row. Mulcahy clenched his teeth. Had he not explicitly stated questions must wait until the end?

"Sorry, professor, but I believe you said school*girls*?"

"Indeed I did and had you waited a moment longer, you would have learned why. Incidentally, raising one's hand is a request for attention, not a licence to interrupt.

"As I was saying, why only girls? Did not boys, women and men suffer the same affliction? I can tell you that in the year 1916, when this project was mooted, the growth of goiters was 50% greater in girls than boys. With regard to fully grown adults, Marine and Kimball planned a high dosage of iodine with a view to *preventing* the development of such swellings in addition to treating those already in existence.

"I mentioned parallel advances in Europe. Some of you paying heed to yesterday's lecture may recall the reason why iodine treatments as proposed by Coindet in the early 19th century fell into disrepute. Anyone?"

Hands sprouted and out of sheer perversity to deny the eager young bucks at the front, Mulcahy picked a woman in one of the topmost rows. "Yes, young lady?"

"If I understood right, Coindet proposed his patients took 165mg of iodine daily. The potential for toxic effects caused a controversy and public opinion turned against him."

"You quite clearly did understand right. Bearing that in mind, let me tell you that Marine and Kimball had those fifth-graders take 200mg per day for ten days. Girls in the eighth grade and over took double that amount. This dosage was repeated at six monthly intervals."

The gasp was predictable.

"Ladies and gentlemen, out of 2,000 girls, how many do you

think succumbed to iodine poisoning? Let me tell you. Not one. The results were unmistakeable. Over 60% of girls with an enlarged thyroid saw a decrease in size or complete disappearance. Of those with no visible enlargement, 0.2% saw any swelling. Marine and Kimball had proven their theory only to find, once post-war scientific publications resumed, they were not the first. In similar tests, two doctors in Switzerland achieved staggering results by adding iodine to simple table salt.

"No matter. There are no competitors in the race for human health, only winners. Those are the people. Marine and Kimball changed people's bodies, and let us not forget, minds. Laying the blame for physical or mental deformity at the feet of the sufferer is lazy, unfair and the poorest application of scientific knowledge. The clock tells me our time draws to a close. I entreated you to leave questions until my lecture was complete. Thank you and I give you the floor. Please raise your hands, wait until called upon to speak and when you do, stand up."

24

I'm not sentimental—I'm as romantic as you are. The idea, you know, is that the sentimental person thinks things will last—the romantic person has a desperate confidence that they won't.

— F. Scott Fitzgerald, *This Side of Paradise*

August 1922

In the event, Seraphine did return to St. Niklaus for Swiss National Day. Not to cry tears of shame and plead for her mother's love, but to ask permission to marry. Tradition dictated the suitor must present his case to the father while mother and daughter await the decision with excitement and trepidation. This sat uncomfortably with Seraphine. She had every intention of accepting the proposal regardless of her parents' opinion. Nevertheless, she chose to abide by convention.

She answered Clothilde's missive with a cheerful note, announcing her intention to travel to the valley for the 1st of

August. Therefore, Josef had lost his bet after all, and she hoped he would forgive her. Rather than impose on her parents and her brother, she would stay in the village, most likely in her old accommodation with Frau Fessler. She looked forward to seeing them for the celebrations and would hopefully bring good news regarding work prospects.

It was light, both in tone and content, exactly what Seraphine intended. Plenty of time to spring her surprise in person.

The night before the journey, she barely slept two consecutive hours. Worried he would not be there as promised, convinced she was deluded about his words of commitment, fearful of her mother's sharp tongue and nervous he might change his mind, she finally succumbed to her over-wrought nerves after the bells rang three. Trainee nurses rose at half-past five, with much banging of doors and morning chatter, making it impossible for Seraphine to rest another hour.

The first connection was due to depart from Zürich Haupt-bahnhof at nine-fifteen. Seraphine was on the platform by eight-thirty. To her astonishment, he was already waiting.

"You are early!" he said, leaping up to take her bag.

"You are even earlier," she said, with a relieved smile.

"I caught the first train. Couldn't sleep, you see. Tossing and turning the whole night, terrified you would change your mind. But you came and you are looking lovelier than ever. You have not changed your mind, have you, Seraphine?"

She glanced at his face before dropping her gaze. "No ..." She could not yet call him by his first name. "No, I have not, although I too slept badly. It seems we suffered from similar fears. Nevertheless, here we are." She looked into his eyes.

"Here we are." The intensity of his stare made her blush.

"And since both of us had a rotten night's rest, we require the strongest coffee. I know an excellent Viennese place across the road. Shall we?" He offered his arm and she took it, her calm countenance hiding the thrill in her stomach.

Three trains later, the ease with which they had passed the last few hours dissipated once they boarded the last connection in Visp. Their private bubble of reassurance and anticipation would soon break open to include the wider world, leaving them exposed to uncertainty. Bastian suggested they travel in separate coaches for the final leg in case someone they knew observed their closeness. Gossip travelled up and down the Matterthal valley faster than the wind. He bowed politely and promised to see her later that evening, as he had invited the Bayards to join them for dinner.

He was only sitting in the next coach, but the lack of his presence beside her affected Seraphine keenly. It was as if someone had removed her coat, leaving her comfortless and vulnerable to the elements. She chose a seat opposite two women, clearly mother and daughter, who were travelling to Zermatt to see the Matterhorn. Their friendly inclusion of her and easy conversation between themselves only exacerbated Seraphine's dread at seeing her own mother.

She gazed out at the valley she loved so much and asked herself why she was dragging her own little rain cloud behind her. Her dreams were within her grasp. She had qualified as a nurse. The man she loved wanted to marry her. Together they would run their own practice in a beautiful part of the country. She had every reason to spill over with joy. Why did she persist in feeling unworthy? The train rolled alongside the Vispa river, verdant foliage decking the valley with greenery while summer flowers garlanded the river banks. After the penultimate stop before St. Niklaus at Kalpetran, two little boys ran along a road parallel to the train track, waving homemade flags at the passengers. One was the classic Swiss flag, the white cross on a red square. The other sported red and white stars on a contrasting red/white background, representing the thirteen districts of Valais. Seraphine recalled art lessons where she and her classmates tried to recreate those stars, usually getting covered in a pink mess of paint.

Unlike the train, the boys soon ran out of steam, slowed down and disappeared behind a copse of trees. Without warning, tears slid down Seraphine's face. She retrieved a handkerchief and blew her nose, keeping her head towards the window.

Henri and Anton, had they lived, would have been far older than those straw-headed tykes. Still Seraphine imagined them running beside a train, laughing, waving flags and turning to see Barry in pursuit, wagging his own proud flag. What would she not give to have her brothers back again!

The older woman opposite reached out a hand to pat her knee. "Are you in need of something, my dear? We have a flask of tea."

"Thank you, I am quite well. Perhaps a little overwhelmed at the thought of coming home and seeing my family after a long while apart. You're very kind."

The women gave understanding nods and Seraphine wiped her face with her handkerchief. After a near-sleepless night, an emotional journey and a waterfall of memories, her discomposure was understandable. She was only glad Bastian was not here to see it.

You do have a little brother. The voice seemed to come from her bones. *His need of you is not as great as that of Henri or Anton, but he too is deserving of a sister's love.*

A whistle announced their arrival in St. Niklaus. Seraphine saw clear blue skies and a way forward.

. . .

F rau Fessler was delighted to welcome her old lodger. So much so, she met her from the train.

"Seraphine! Over here! How are you, my treasure? I am beside myself with happiness you are returned. You are surely fatigued after the journey. Let us walk, take tea and then you will likely need to rest. Gerhard can handle your bag."

A burly man with an overgrown beard bowed his head and lifted her misshapen holdall onto his shoulder. Seraphine turned to the train, lifting her hand for one last wave to her good-natured travelling companions, and allowing her eyes to slide away, following the tall figure of a doctor heading down the hill.

Frau Fessler followed her eye line. "Isn't that Herr Doctor Favre?"

"No, I think not. I recall the doctor as being considerably shorter. Oh, Frau Fessler, to be in St. Niklaus again is a joy! You are so kind to host me once more, especially at this time of year, when your guest house is in great demand. Since the railway is repaired after the flood, you are surely up to full capacity." She judged the large man to be sufficiently out of earshot. "Pray tell, who is your gentleman friend?"

"Ah, I see you have grown mischievous during your time in the city! Gerhard is my handyman, gardener and reader."

They followed the man down the road past the school and along the lane to Frau Fessler's pretty boarding-house.

"Your reader?" echoed Seraphine.

"I see perfectly well here in the daylight. For instance, I recognised you the second you stepped from the train. Yet my eyes are weakening with age. In the evening, my chief pleasure is to read great storytellers. Surely you recall how I adore a dramatic work of fiction. It was one of the things you and I always had in common. Gerhard has a similar penchant for a good yarn. We sit by the fire in my parlour, he reads, I listen and we talk about the tale. I must say, he has the most instinctive nature for character. The man should have become, as I often tell him, a teacher of literature."

"Good afternoon, Frau Fessler." A farmer's son Seraphine knew by face but could not name tipped his hat. "Fräulein Widmer, good to see you again!"

"Where better to spend the 1ˢᵗ of August?" Seraphine replied. "It is very good to see you too and please give my regards to your family."

When he had gone, she whispered, "I've forgotten his name."

"Wilhelm Brigger from Grachen. His wife gave birth to twins last month. Both perfectly healthy, thanks to Dr Bayard," she added before Seraphine could even form the question. "This valley has much to be grateful for. Tell me, have you eaten? There are cold meats and cheese or perhaps would prefer some soup? As for dinner, do you plan to visit your family this afternoon and if so, shall I keep you a portion of *Älplermagronen*?"

"That's very kind of you but we ate in Visp."

"We?"

Heat crept up Seraphine's neck. She hated telling untruths to her ex-teacher, even lies of omission. "A mother and her daughter were my travelling companions. That's who I was waving to on the train."

"Oh, how nice. Women are very good at looking after one another."

"Very true. The journey was long and I would rather not do any more travelling today. I also have a dinner engagement this evening with the Bayards. I shall see my family tomorrow at the celebrations and visit the farm before I leave. If it does not offend you, my preference would be to lie down awhile. Last night I had a barely a wink of sleep. Anticipation about coming home, no doubt."

"That is understandable. Travelling is tremendously taxing. You must gather your strength before all the excitements tomorrow." She opened the gate and led the way up the garden path. "I put you in your old room. Draw the curtains but keep the windows open for the breeze. Gerhard mowed the lawn this morning, so you shall not be disturbed. It is a great pleasure to have you home again."

"It is a great pleasure to be here." Seraphine meant it. Butterflies still danced in her stomach, but Bastian's reassurances had calmed the worst of her fears. Just as soon as Josef and Clothilde had given them her blessing, Seraphine would tell Frau Fessler the truth. But until her engagement to Bastian was official, they could tell no one. Except the Bayards.

S he was a little late arriving for dinner due to Frau Fessler's insistence that Gerhard walk her to the Bayard residence. Since she was not going to the Bayards' home but to Hotel Lochmatter, that was out of the question. If she gave in and accepted his escort to the venue, he would obviously expect to be present for the return journey.

"That will not be necessary, thank you. The offer is kind and I appreciate the sentiment. However, I navigated the city of Zürich by myself for two years and came to no harm. From the age of five, I roamed this valley alone. I am now twenty years old and more than capable of walking across the village."

"In daylight, perhaps. Walking unaccompanied at night is unheard of!" Frau Fessler's tone bordered on querulous.

"Herr Doctor Bayard is a respected gentleman and will guarantee my safety. I categorically refuse to deprive you and

Gerhard of your reading evening when it is quite unnecessary. Incidentally, what particular work are you reading?"

Gerhard cleared his throat. "*Der Prozess*, by Franz Kafka. My choice and I admit it is a challenge. Next we read an English writer, no?"

"Yes." Frau Fessler's forehead smoothed. "The book is called *The Rainbow*, by a new author called D.H. Lawrence. By all accounts it is rather scandalous, so I have been eagerly awaiting the German translation. Seraphine, it will take Gerhard fewer than ten minutes to walk you across the village. I know you modern girls think I am a fusspot, but my mind would be easier."

Seraphine glanced at the clock. She should have left a quarter of an hour ago. Now she would be in a rush and arrive flustered and glowing. "Thank you, but I really must refuse. Walking alone allows me to clear my head. You and Gerhard enjoy your dinner and your book. I promise to take the greatest care. Have a lovely evening and I will see you on my return." She slipped out of the door, forestalling any further protests, and scurried down the path. As she closed the gate, she saw the pair of them standing in the doorway, their faces a mirror image of concern. She waved and walked sedately along the lane until she had turned the corner. Then she hitched up her skirts and ran.

She slowed to a rapid trot on Dorfstrasse when she saw another couple coming down the lane. Aware of her rosy cheeks and dishevelled hair, she kept her head down, hoping not to be recognised.

"Good evening, Seraphine."

She looked up to see Philipp Niederer arm in arm with Romy Seethaler.

"Hello, Herr Niederer, hello, Romy. Nice to see you again. Are you both well?"

"My wife and I are very well and looking forward to the birth of our second child."

"Please accept my heartfelt congratulations."

Romy wore her typical good-natured smile. "Thank you! What about you, Seraphine? How do you like the city? It must be so exciting."

"Exciting, but terribly warm. It is a relief to be here again during the summer. Tonight I am late for an engagement, so I wish you a lovely evening and hope to see you tomorrow at the village celebrations."

"We'll be there. It would be such fun to talk to an old friend. Goodnight."

"Seraphine!" Frau Bayard's face lit up. "Look at you!"

Seraphine mistook the greeting for a reproach and ran a hand across her brow. "My apologies, I was in a hurry."

Frau Bayard stood up to kiss her cheeks. "You look radiant, my dear! Does she not, Otto? How grown up and graceful you are! When Bastian mentioned your attendance at this weekend's celebrations, I rejoiced. Then I hear you are to join us for dinner! My cup quite overflows."

Seraphine struggled to keep her emotions in check. "I am so happy to be here with you all. Herr Doctor Bayard, it is a pleasure to see you." She offered her hand to Bayard, who had stood to greet her.

He shook it warmly. "Two of medicine's next generation visiting at once is truly a tonic."

Only then did she turn her attention to the tall man beside her chair. "Hello again, Herr Doctor Favre. Thank you for the invitation and I apologise for being late."

His eyes shone and he tried in vain to suppress a smile. "You are not late in the slightest. We had barely taken our seats.

May I?" He pulled out her chair and ensured she was comfortable.

There was no mistaking his expression and Seraphine dared not look at his face for fear of giving too much away.

Too late. Frau Bayard, who had highly sensitive antennae for changes in atmosphere, twitched like a March hare. "Do you realise it is almost two years since we sat at the same table? How much has changed in that time! My husband's work is nationally recognised, Dr Eggenberger's initiative is voted into law and your presence at the board of health is powerful, Bastian! As for we ladies, Seraphine is a fully qualified nurse. For my part, I have another beautiful, healthy and very noisy daughter. We have a great deal to celebrate, do we not?"

Bastian glanced at Seraphine, an enquiry in his eyes. She dipped her chin.

"There is still more to celebrate and I hope you will not mind that I have ordered a bottle of champagne. This is yet to be confirmed, since I have not yet spoken to Herr Widmer. Therefore we must keep our countenance in public. I am due to assume control of a general practice in Brienz and have asked Seraphine to join me as my head nurse, assistant and beloved wife. To my boundless delight, she has agreed."

Before Frau Bayard could open her mouth, her husband spoke, his voice restrained but his language less so. "I knew it! Yes, my dearest, you have an infallible feminine instinct. But this one I claim as my own. I wished for such a union from the very beginning. Bastian, Seraphine, I congratulate you with a full heart. To trust us with news of this ilk is an honour. My wife, in her wisdom, would have engineered circumstances to bring the pair of you together. Whereas I allowed nature to run its course and look at the result!"

Frau Bayard raised an arch eyebrow at Bastian. "Engineering circumstances? As if I would dream of such a thing. My dears, I am struggling to hold myself in check. I want to leap from my chair and embrace you with indecorous abandon. You asked for discretion and I will abide by your wishes despite my extraordinary delight. When the news is public, however, I need no permission to weep tears of joy. You are the most perfect couple." Her eyes became moist and she patted a lace handkerchief to her nose.

A waiter Seraphine had never seen placed a silver bucket on their table. "Would you like the champagne now, sir?"

While the process of uncorking and pouring went on, Seraphine ached for Bastian's reassuring touch. That was quite impossible without revealing their secret. It was true that most patrons were strangers or foreigners. Nonetheless, Dr Bayard had garnered a certain respect and renown from far further than the Matterthal valley. Alois dozed in his usual position by the fire, eyes closed but ears open. Waiting staff, the receptionist and even Herr Lochmatter himself, who passed occasionally through the dining room, knew Seraphine and her family.

A hand rested on hers. Frau Bayard inclined her head to Seraphine and whispered, "This is better than giving birth. All the wonder and none of the pain, with the added benefit of drinking champagne! I wish you all the luck in the world, you wonderful, deserving girl."

Seraphine clutched her hand and swallowed the lump in her throat. "I already have all the luck in the world and I believe, even if I'm not sure how, you are responsible for much of it."

"Ladies, a toast?" said Dr Bayard. "Let us drink to the future. To you, to us, to the whole of Switzerland! To the future!"

The meal was a lively affair with no gaps in conversation and frequent interruptions by people passing by to pay compliments to Dr Bayard. It was over far too soon and at the same time, well timed because Seraphine's inexperience with alcohol combined with a long day caused her to wilt. Bastian paid the bill and after protracted goodbyes in the street, they bade farewell to the Bayards. In the dimly lit streets, it seemed safe enough to link arms and converse in low tones.

Bastian's euphoria, and possibly champagne consumption, made him less conscious of his volume. Twice Seraphine pressed a finger to her lips to quiet him. The third time, on the corner of the lane, he took her finger away and pressed his lips to hers instead.

25
———

To be loved by a pure young girl, to be the first to reveal to her the strange mystery of love, is indeed a great happiness, but it is the simplest thing in the world. To take captive a heart which has had no experience of attack, is to enter an unfortified and ungarrisoned city.

— Alexandre Dumas fils, *La Dame aux Camélias*

August 1922

As it was not officially a public holiday, each canton or community made up its own rules for what happened on Switzerland's birthday. In the cities, many people worked as usual on the 1ˢᵗ of August, perhaps leaving early to toast the founders of the nation. In more rural areas like the Matterthal, people completed all their tasks by midday and devoted the afternoon, and more often than not the evening, to joining their neighbours in a show of communality. Children wore national dress and performed folk songs, sometimes accompanied by an Alphorn player. Farmers grilled sausages, housewives baked cakes and handicraft makers sold their wares at little stalls around the school yard. Colourful bunting comprised of the Swiss and cantonal flags fluttered in the summer breeze. Long trestle tables covered in white cloths took up the centre of the yard, where friendships were renewed and acquaintances formed, lubricated by local beer.

Never one to buck tradition, Bastian offered his services at Dr Bayard's practice for morning surgery. It was an opportune moment. Many valley-dwellers had chosen that day to travel to St. Niklaus, consult the doctor for minor ailments and spend the rest of the day carousing. Bastian diagnosed, bound, cleaned, lanced and prescribed for four hours. At lunchtime, he returned to his room, changed into his Sunday best and strode out into St. Niklaus with one aim in mind: Seraphine.

The memory of last night's kiss returned for the hundredth time, no less potent than the first. He had read the clichés of weak knees in fiction and attributed the phenomenon to the fairer sex. Last night proved him wrong. One moment his legs lost nearly all their power; the next, they carried him home on wings. Seraphine.

From the centre of the village came the sound of yodellers and the scent of frying onions. Bastian hesitated for a moment at the end of the street, gathering his courage.

"Herr Doctor Favre?"

The old fellow who whiled away his hours in the Hotel Lochmatter was standing on the opposite side of the street, beckoning him to approach.

Bastian crossed the street, hoping the man would not require an impromptu consultation. "Ah, hello again. Albert, isn't it? Or do I misremember?"

The man clasped both Bastian's hands in his own. "Alois, Herr Doctor. My name is Alois. See here, I know your news is a secret and rest assured, my lips are sealed. I want you to have an

Alpenstock as a present. I am not good for much at my age, but I can still craft a solid walking stick. I watched that sweet girl grow up and blossom. I said to myself, Alois, she deserves a decent man. Not Niederer the bus driver or that Tyrolean rogue Zanetti. A good, kind, honest man like yourself. That is why, and I hope you will excuse me, I had a word in your ear that particular night. I am sure your recall our conversation, despite your being a little worse for wear. When you announce your engagement to the world, sir, it would be an honour to give you one of my finest walking sticks. Consider it my blessing on you both."

"Why, that is a most unexpected and touching gesture, Alois. However, I must beg your silence on the subject until ..."

"Trust me, Josef Widmer will agree before you even ask the question. Now then, Clothilde is a difficult woman at the best of times. I advise leaving her to Seraphine." He smiled, his eyes disappearing into his wrinkles. "I have a feeling about people. The first time I saw you, I knew you would bring favourable luck. My Alpenstock will carry it with you into your future."

A horn sounded. Alois cocked his head. "That is the bus coming down the valley, more than likely with the Widmer family as passengers. I shall delay you no longer. Good luck, Herr Doctor." He held out a hand for Bastian to shake.

"Thank you, Alois, I am in your debt." He strode along the street, buoyed by the kindly words and somewhat humbled at his underestimation of the old man. When he neared the end of the road, he was startled to see Seraphine and the Fessler woman coming out of the Weisshornstube. He doffed his hat.

"Good afternoon, ladies. It pleases me greatly to you see you again, looking very fetching for today's festivities. I trust you are well?"

"Herr Doctor Favre! Did I not say, Seraphine, I thought it was him descending from the train. We are indeed well, thank you for your enquiry. How about yourself? Are you in St. Niklaus for long? Do you not agree the weather could not be finer for our village party? Seraphine and I are on our way to meet the bus. My sisters have made the journey today, as have the Widmers. We are all quite giddy with excitement."

"With good reason. I will not keep you from your family reunions. Have a wonderful day, and I hope to see you later. Perhaps Fräulein Widmer might be willing to dance?"

"Perhaps." Her smile flashed, but only for a second. He could sense her agitation and instantly panicked. He should never have kissed her. His attentions were smothering the girl. She was desperate for a way out and he had ruined everything.

"I like dancing, that much is true. But foremost in my mind at this moment is my family. I am eager to spend an hour or two in their company before anything else." Her steady gaze underlined her message.

"It does you credit as a loyal daughter to put your family first. Good afternoon, ladies, and happy Swiss National Day!"

They swept away, arm in arm, to meet the Postauto which had just halted outside the train station. Bastian stepped into the shadow of the Weisshornstube, observing the scene whilst keeping out of sight. The vehicle was clearly full to capacity and a large group of locals were already waiting to greet their visitors. It took several minutes for the bus to disgorge its load and another quarter of an hour before the crowd dispersed. For the first time since that comment by Alois, Bastian paid attention to the bus driver. The man sat on the fence overlooking the town, smoking a cigarette and surveyed the families, neighbours and friends as they reunited. He wore a cap to shade his eyes, which made his expression unreadable even if one was closer. His body language, however, bristled with hostility.

Frau Fessler and her sisters bustled down the lane, chatting with great animation. Then a small boy, blond and wearing short trousers with decorative braces, tore down the hill. At the crossroads, he skidded to a halt and shouted, "Which way, Seraphine?"

"Wait for me and I'll show you," she called.

"You're too slow!"

"Too slow, am I? We'll see about that!" She broke away from the couple she was talking to, lifted her skirts and feigned a run. The boy screeched with delight and crouched like a goalkeeper trying to guess her trajectory. She veered right and he took off ahead of her, passing within arm's reach of Bastian.

"Wrong way," she laughed, swerving left and running towards the school.

The boy ran after his sister, his little legs pumping and his face red with laughter and exertion. He caught up with her easily and she lifted him into her arms, placing a kiss on his cheek. Herr and Frau Widmer followed, watching the scene with indulgent smiles, thus missing their silent observer.

Josef Widmer reminded Bastian of a stray dog. His posture was watchful and opportunistic, always wary of his surroundings. Seraphine's advice to wait until he had drunk at least two beers made sense. Clothilde, on the other hand, looked as if smiling was a rare event. Her sharp eyes glanced in his direction and he slid through the open door of the Weisshornstube, intending to drink some coffee and give the Widmers some time alone. He had forgotten the tradition that children took over the restaurant for the day, while the adults occupied the schoolyard. The memory of young Seraphine struck him so powerfully he simply drank an espresso at the bar and left.

His pulse throbbed at his clavicle. The coffee on top of his nerves might have been a mistake. He wandered among the stalls, wishing he could somehow remain anonymous – an impossibility amid so many people of the region. Every other person wanted to express their thanks, if not for themselves, for a family member. Many had discarded hats and jackets under the afternoon sun, and Bastian wished to do the same. Yet he had to maintain formality until his duty was complete.

He stalked the schoolyard, sweating with shaking hands and waited for his moment. At one point, a brass band assembled to tune up. Children ran to the front, intrigued by the spectacle. As the music began, Seraphine and her mother moved closer, standing protectively behind the little blond boy. Josef Widmer sat alone at the table, rocking from side to side with the music.

Now was the moment. Bastian bought two steins of beer and ducked between the tables to sit next to the man.

"Herr Widmer, may I introduce myself? My name is Bastian Favre, an occasional assistant to Dr Bayard. I would like to buy you a beer to toast our nation's birthday."

Widmer's eyes widened, narrowed and focused on the stein. "Very generous. Wait, I remember you. You treated my wife. Yes, you were the one who gave her the special salt!"

Bastian tensed. "The salt was for her baby, Herr Widmer."

"I know that! Everyone knows what that salt did for this valley. I am man enough to admit I was suspicious at first but no one can miss the difference in our wives and our children. That lump at her throat was a monstrosity. Thank you, Herr Doctor. *Prost!*"

"*Prost!* In truth, Dr Bayard is the one who deserves your gratitude. He is one of three great men who effected a huge change in our country. My role was simply an assistant. On that note, I am due to take control of my own practice in the canton of Bern. I would very much like to offer the position of head nurse to your daughter. This is not merely a practical arrangement, sir. My affection for Seraphine is sincere." The band came to a crescendo, forcing Bastian to lean closer and shout over the final chorus. "I seek your permission and blessing for us to marry. With my hand on my heart, I promise to do everything in my power to make her happy." It was hardly the quiet *tête-à-tête* he had envisaged, but he would not miss his opportunity.

Josef reached out to clasp Bastian's right hand in both of his own, his cheeks lifting to reveal a wide smile. The music ended with stamping and cheering worthy of the Oktoberfest. The knocking together of Josef and Bastian's steins was nothing out of the ordinary.

"You have my permission, young man, and my blessing a hundred times over. That girl deserves the best. You sir, are indeed a fine young man with a bright future. I am proud to welcome you into the family." With one large hand, he patted Bastian's shoulder and with the other waved a hand at a serving girl. "Giuliana! Two more beers, two Kirsch and a half bottle of wine for the ladies!"

For a second, Bastian could not speak, overcome by relief. Across the yard, he spotted Seraphine and Clothilde, each holding one of the little boy's hands and swinging him into the air. She shot him a worried glance. He gave a single definitive nod and her eyes widened.

"What a day! Where are those women? I must tell Clothilde the news. I must tell everyone the news!" Josef beckoned his wife, whose eyes were already hooded with suspicion as she wove a path through the villagers. They arrived just as the waitress set a heavily laden tray on the table.

"Sit, Clothilde. Fill a glass for yourself and our dearest daughter. Herr Doctor Favre asked my permission to marry Seraphine and I said yes!"

"Is that true?" Seraphine clutched her hands to her mouth, her eyes sparkling with tears.

"Did you ask *her* if she wants to marry *him*? My daughter is not just a goat you can trade in the market." Clothilde glared at her husband, not making a second's eye contact with Bastian.

"Seraphine?" Josef poured two glasses of wine. "Are you

willing to accept this fine young doctor as your husband? It's not just a domestic arrangement, you know, but paid employment. In my opinion, you could do a lot worse."

"Maman, Papa, I can scarce believe my luck. Nothing could make me happier than to marry the man I love, with the blessing of my parents, and let's not forget, my little brother. Peter, what do you say? I say yes!"

"YES!" echoed Peter. "I'm hungry."

Clothilde pulled a cloth pouch from her bag. "Eat some nuts and we'll have a cervelat soon. Seraphine, Herr Doctor Favre, I am very glad for you both. I wish you joy." Over the head of the boy, she leaned into Seraphine. They wrapped their arms around each other's shoulders and, foreheads touching, closed their eyes.

Once news got around, everyone came to their table with congratulations and the band struck up a happy tune. Seraphine lifted Peter onto her hip and went to meet Frau Fessler, insistent on delivering the news herself. Neighbours, relatives, colleagues and total strangers made a point of shaking hands with Bastian. The only person who barely acknowledged his presence was Clothilde Widmer. At one point, Seraphine returned with the Fessler sisters and Peter asleep in her arms. Bastian's eagerness to greet his fiancée caused him to tread on the heel of Clothilde's shoe.

"I'm sorry, Frau Widmer."

She dropped her gaze and spoke in a strangled whisper. "No, I am sorry. When I told you about the bus driver, I was trying to protect her. To my mind, you were toying with my girl, using her as an experiment. I was wrong. You have been good to my family and I hope you will continue be good to Seraphine. Let us not speak of this again. Hallo, Frau Fessler, have you heard the news?"

. . .

The party lasted long into the night. When the last bus had left, taking the Widmers home, a late guest arrived. Neither Dr Bayard nor his wife had shown their faces all afternoon, an unusual phenomenon which went generally unnoticed amid the melee surrounding the engagement. When the doctor emerged from the shadows, a cheer erupted from the remaining men. Most of the ladies had retired to bed, including Bastian's fiancée. Even though he had consumed an inadvisable amount of beer, Bastian knew something was wrong.

"Herr Doctor? Is everything in order?"

"Good evening, one and all. My wife sends her regrets that she could not attend. Our daughter Elsa was taken quite suddenly and violently ill this afternoon. Hence my delay was unavoidable, I'm afraid. She is resting now and her fever has abated. What a shame to miss all the diversions and dancing. Have you all had a grand day?"

After expressing concerns and good wishes for little Elsa, people clamoured to tell the doctor of the announcement. He feigned surprise so well Bastian could almost imagine he had forgotten he already knew.

Bayard sat at the table in a pool of candlelight and pipe smoke, offering his congratulations along with everyone else. "Brienz? I would say you landed on your feet, young man. A charming and capable young bride, a plum location for your practice and a convenient position from whence to visit your old friends once in a while. I wish you joy. Nothing more than you deserve. Alois, the fire is fading. Another couple of logs, perhaps a Kirsch and one more round of congratulations, before we retire to our beds. Tell me, were Seraphine's parents pleased?"

Bastian had no hope of being heard over the local opinions, so rested his elbows on the table and listened to everyone else.

"Josef Widmer couldn't have hoped for more!"

"He said so himself. A son-in-law who is an ex-army man? He is perfect!"

"Herr Doctor Favre could not be better, not unless he has a secret herd of goats!"

Their laughter echoed around the dark schoolyard. Dr Bayard's teeth flashed in the firelight as he returned their grins.

"It must be strange for Frau Widmer. For quite some years, Clothilde and Seraphine had no one but each other. Yes, the girl is now grown, trained for a professional role and safe in the hands of her future husband. Yet not one man at this table can deny the wrench when a child leaves home, no matter how high our hopes. Herr Doctor Favre, promise us you will bring her home on occasion. On Swiss National Day, for example. You are also part of this village. Your successes are our successes and in a way, we are all family. One more *Proscht*, my dear friends, and I shall escort this young man to his hotel. It would never do to find the groom-to-be in the gutter."

"No chance of that with Alois around." Herr Lochmatter's voice rumbled from under the yew tree. "That man's a sheepdog. Never leaves a lamb unattended."

"Quite partial to a nap by the fire, too," said Alois, to general laughter.

The party drained their glasses, clapped shoulders and wended their various ways home. When Bastian found his room, he noticed something leaning against the door. A beautiful burnished Alpenstock, the icon of the mountain guides. He caressed its smooth strong curves. This was a talisman, his staff and protector, key to the Alps. He took it inside, threw off his coat and fell onto his bed, proud, emotional and exhausted.

26

April 1923

*D*ear Seraphine
I hope this finds you and Bastian well. You must be well into your third term by now. From all you said in your last letter, I feel sure you are carrying a boy. Whether that is true or not makes no difference. I pray it goes easy for you. How could it not for a nurse with a fine doctor for a husband?

Does Brienz still please you as much as your first impression? You used to say nowhere compares to the Matterthal valley, but that was when you had little knowledge of anywhere else. I used to say the same of Montreux when I was young, but now wild horses could not make me return. For my part, this is my home and I seek no other.

At the farm, things are very good indeed. The cows have already earned their purchase price and our goats have been up at pasture since April. Josef bought a new dog, a German shepherd, can you believe? Even worse than that, he named him Beau. The man is a fool, but the animal is trusty. The picture enclosed is a drawing of Peter's.

The dog is black and brown, not blue and red, but otherwise the likeness is accurate.

Peter grows stronger and hungrier by the day. He asks after you often. He drew a picture of his sister to show to his friends which he will not part with, not even for a Zimtstern. *I am optimistic you can visit us when the baby is fit for travel. Perhaps the first of August?*

You surely have friends and neighbours around you, as every new mother should. My help is likely unnecessary. Just know that I am willing to leave the farm with Josef's blessing and travel to Brienz, if you think I can be of use.

While I was carrying you, Seraphine, people often said they hoped the baby was a boy. I am quite sure they will say the same to you. Ignore them. The best thing I ever did in my life was bear my little girl.

With loving greetings to you and Bastian
Your mother, Clothilde

27

There is no happiness like that of being loved by your fellow creatures,
and feeling that your presence is an addition to their comfort.

— Charlotte Brontë, *Jane Eyre*

May 1923

May was not an easy month for Seraphine. The temperature rose but rain drizzled almost every day, swelling the streams, which in turn, filled the lakes. The atmosphere was humid and the air moist. It was near impossible to dry washing, her hair became unmanageable and her back ached day and night. Worse, she cried at the smallest thing. One day she trod on a ladybird, a well-known symbol of luck, and was inconsolable for over an hour.

Since she had retired from work for the remainder of her pregnancy, she was mostly confined to the house with very little to do but clean and cook and wash clothes. A little voice inside her kept whispering, '*Make the most of this time. When the baby comes, you will not have a moment to yourself.'* Which was all very well, but with barely enough energy to get up and down the stairs, she alternated between activity and rest. The one pastime she loved the most was the same solace she had sought as a child – reading novels. An entire hour could pass in the company of *The Count of Monte Cristo.* Injustice, revenge, learning, amity and an understanding of the self were lessons she was willing to learn. She anticipated with great curiosity the discussions with Frau Fessler and the wise Gerhard on her next visit. Presuming, of course, she could finish the book. Her concentration flittered like a moth.

She missed the medical practice dreadfully. She missed the sense of purpose, the constant flow of people and conversation, and most painfully of all, the proximity of her beloved husband. The whole day long, they worked in separate rooms. But every time they passed in the corridor or when she had cause to bring him supplies, there was a look or a touch or a smile. Without words, he told her he loved over a dozen times a day.

Now she had been replaced. A very capable woman from Thun had taken over her role until September. Her own time with Bastian was reduced to a few hours in the evening, when more often than not she was worn down by inertia.

His tenderness increased in direct ratio to her discomfort. The simple fact of his presence calmed her and in the hours of darkness, he spoke soft words of reassurance. He continued after she fell asleep, his voice sending vibrations through the mattress. Every evening, he brought home snippets of news, a posy of wildflowers, handmade gifts from their patients and sometimes a letter.

Vroni's correspondence was regular and uplifting, thanks to her dry wit. Frau Bayard wrote to them as a pair, including news to entertain both husband and wife. Tante Margot's letters always came in a package: eau de cologne in a pretty bottle, hand cream scented with lavender, a packet of herbs from Provence, olive oil from a Greek island. They were postcards from her travels, in a way, and a sign she was not forgotten. Seraphine's spirits lifted at the mere sight of the handwriting and exotic stamps.

D*earest Seraphine*

New York is the most extraordinary city in the world! I wish you were here and that is no idle platitude. All the sights from skyscrapers to shoe-shiners are better shared with a companion and Thierry is constantly in meetings with loud men who shout. You, my sweet niece, would love everything about America. Every detail we have read of in works of fiction is brought to life.

Can you conceive of how hard your uncle had to work to persuade me onto a transatlantic liner? That dreadful disaster occurred a decade ago but continues to haunt my imagination. I am of a nervous disposition in a sailing boat on Lac Leman. Therefore you can guess at my near hysteria as we boarded a cruise ship to follow the same route.

According to Thierry, icebergs are less common in summer and other than a stormy night or two, our voyage was smooth. The ship was quite extraordinary with all possible comforts provided, including nightly entertainment and notable chefs.

On arrival we took a suite of rooms at the Iroquois for the duration of our stay. People here are unrestrained in their pursuit of pleasure. At times, I find it rather overwhelming; at others, inspiring. One can almost forget there ever was a war.

My single regret is that I am not in Switzerland for one of the most exciting events in our family history. Your time surely draws near and I hope your nursing experience allays any natural nerves. Good luck, my darling, and I cannot wait to meet my little great-nephew or niece.

With my fondest regards to you and the charming Bastian. I hope the enclosed book of photographs with droll epigrams amuses you.

Your affectionate aunt, Margot

On May 15, Edith arrived in Brienz. Seraphine's relief caused her to burst into tears. Her friend was to stay for a month, employed by the practice to consult with new mothers. The true reason for her attendance was to deliver Seraphine's child. There was no one she trusted more. Edith had changed little, alert and bright-eyed as a blackbird, always finding something to laugh at or delight in. She settled into the nursery, became instantly popular at the practice and spent evenings soothing Seraphine's concerns.

On the first Saturday after Edith's arrival, the sun sparkled off the lake, a breeze caressed the town and people ventured out to remember why they loved where they lived. Seraphine joined in with Bastian and Edith's enthusiasm, and despite the weight she carried, she was eager to take the air. Just as she sat on a stool to lace her boots, a spasm ripped through her like a lightning strike. She gasped, clenching her fists, shocked by how her body could inflict such violence upon itself. Her nurse's mind recited the ritual procedures but somehow got them all muddled up.

"Bastian?"

"I am here, my angel. Edith too is at your side. Do you think it is your time?"

Her body still reverberated with the aftershocks of the agony and her hand trembled when she reached for her husband.

"Can we sit for a while? It might have been nothing more than ... oh!" Inside her, something seemed to pop and fluid soaked her underskirts. "Yes! It is my time."

Edith clutched her shoulders. "From this minute onward,

you listen to me, you do as I say and no matter what you think, I know better. Bastian, bring the bath chair and make haste. Someone is in a hurry!"

Seraphine said nothing because pain robbed her of speech.

Childbirth was an extraordinary journey through agony, exhaustion and the torturous knowledge there was still more to come. Each wave threatened to kill her until she began to believe they actually would. She heard Edith's voice, she felt Bastian's hand, but her whole world centred on the life she was desperate to push out of her body. Another contraction twisted her insides like a housewife wringing a dishcloth. The urge to urinate, vomit or defecate convinced her she had some control. She wept, defeated.

"I can't. It won't come."

"Seraphine Favre, you can and you will." Edith's voice was so stern, Seraphine could have laughed if her face was not a rictus of agony. "Push when I tell you. The baby is crowning. Take my hand and we will push together. One. Two. Three!"

Somehow, she detached from her body, feeling the tearing wrench and observing it from a distance. Edith cleaned the infant, Bastian checked its vital signs and they rested the tiny thing on her still panting chest.

"Here he is." Edith gave a happy sigh. "Your baby boy."

Seraphine wiped her tears away so that she could see the infant. "A boy? My mother said it would be a boy."

"He is indeed a boy," said Bastian, his eyes glittering. "Our little boy, whose name is Julius."

There were two classes of charitable people:
one, the people who did a little and made a great deal of noise;
the other, the people who did a great deal and made no noise at all.

— Charles Dickens, *Bleak House*

May 1924

On his return home from the train station, he was greeted by the most delightful sight: his wife, his mother-in-law and his son, sitting on the lawn. Bastian had to stop at the gate to compose himself. Julius was sitting up on his grandmother's knee and working his gums on a slice of apple. Mother and daughter were deep in conversation, Seraphine's head bent over her sewing. The creak of the garden gate made them look up.

"Good afternoon, ladies! What say you to this glorious weather?"

"Bastian! Home so soon!" Seraphine put down her needlecraft and took the baby from Clothilde. "Look, Julius, Papa is home. Here is your Papa!"

Julius clenched a fist around his soggy bit of apple and laughed his toothless chuckle, reaching for his father. Bastian dropped his bag on the path and embraced his little family, the cares of the day falling off his shoulders like raindrops off duck feathers.

"Hello, Clothilde, have you passed a pleasant few days?" He kissed her cheeks three times.

"We have, thank you. What with wandering around the lake, visiting the surgery, shopping at the market and keeping this little chap entertained, my stay has passed in an instant. This afternoon, we were plucked a chicken, peeled potatoes and apples, and have not long sat down. How was your trip to Bern? I hope it was a success."

"Unfortunately not. No matter. I will keep banging on the door until these people open their minds. Did you mention chicken and potatoes? Dare I hope that means what I think it means?"

Seraphine and her mother exchanged a satisfied look. "Yes, it does. I thought as it is Maman's last evening with us and you must be weary after your travels, we would dine on roast chicken and potatoes with gravy and garden vegetables. We even made apple strudel for dessert."

"Perfection! This is why I should never leave home. Clothilde, please take your grandson while I go and change out of this stuffy attire."

He changed, washed in the basin, unpacked his travelling bag and combed his hair. Her tread was light but she came upstairs as he knew she would. He kissed her the moment she closed the door, taking comfort from her body warmth, her gentle strokes down his back and the scent of roses in her hair.

"Your pallor is almost grey," she whispered. "Dreadful meetings or a miserable journey? Heaven hope it was not both."

"The journey was pleasant. However, I left my wife and son for three whole days to be lectured in medieval ways of thinking and therefore achieved less than nothing."

"Less than nothing? How is that possible?" Her hands rested on his shoulders and her upturned face was full of concern.

"Because their positions are even more entrenched than before."

He smoothed a stray hair from her face and noted how her skin glowed from the sun. Why was he dragging the dusty air of stale and stubborn meetings to spoil his peaceful home?

"Let us speak of this no more. I am weary of the subject and you should not concern yourself. What time does Clothilde's train leave tomorrow? Shall the three of us walk her to the station?"

"That is a kind thought. Her train departs at a quarter to ten, when you really should be at the surgery. Not only that, but I think our farewell will be more truthful if we are unobserved. Why not say goodbye after breakfast, go to work and leave the rest to me?"

"You are right, as so often. Have you enjoyed her visit, my love? From my standpoint, all seems harmonious but I can often be oblivious to feminine undercurrents."

Seraphine looked out of the window, her expression pensive. "Yes, I have enjoyed sharing my home and my son with her. The ties that bind us are now voluntary and that makes all the difference. Shall I leave you for an hour to read the post while I feed Julius and put him to bed? Then we can eat your favourite dinner together with my mother."

"The day I married you, I told myself I was the luckiest man alive. Every day since has proven me right."

.   .   .

He lay awake, his eyes closed, trying to shut off his brain. Why sleep eluded him, he had no idea. A fine meal, pleasant conversation and a quiet walk to the lake alone all soothed his spirits. Added to that, the pleasure of his wife's body, the necessity of silence exciting him more than usual. Normally, he fell asleep immediately after conjugal relations. Not tonight.

He tried not to shift and disturb the bedclothes. Seraphine slept lightly, always with an ear for Julius's cries, and she instinctively knew when something was troubling her husband. He opened his eyes and stared at the beams. Anything to remove those intractable expressions, overgrown eyebrows and smug sneers from his inner vision. He thought of Julius, his cheeks as plump and smooth as proven dough, his turquoise eyes bright with curiosity, always ready to laugh. A sharp exhalation escaped him.

Seraphine rolled over and rested her head on his shoulder. "Some people used to believe a swelling in the throat was caused by unvoiced anger. An old wives' tale, of course, as you know better than most. Even so, it is better to speak about what worries one, if only to lighten the load."

He drew her closer and wrapped his arm around her back. "You need your rest, my angel."

"As do you. What is it, Bastian? Your body feels like that volcano in Italy, ready to erupt. If you have no wish to discuss the matter, I will hush and let you sleep."

He swallowed, trying to order his thoughts. "The Swiss medical profession boasts some of the most brilliant minds in the world. It also houses malignant toads whose only desire is to amass and cling on to power. Over the past three days, I met them all."

Her hand caressed his chest but she said nothing.

"It is two years after Bayard's experiments, since Eggenberger's triumph and the Goitre Commission's recommendations. Our country is changing and only the wilfully blind cannot see it. Eugen Bircher, that pompous sheep's bladder, still maintains we are deceiving the public. He practically accused me of treason!"

"Hush, my love. We have no wish to wake the house. Was not Bircher himself part of the Goitre Commission?"

Bastian turned to his wife, his outrage barely containable, but dropped his voice to a whisper. "Yes, he was present at the meeting of 24th June 1922 when the decision was taken to recommend iodised salt. At the time, Bircher kept his mouth shut. One month later, he published an article stating promotion of iodine was unproven, exaggerated and borderline criminal. Too cowardly to state his objections in front of those with hard evidence, he put his unjustified complaints in print."

"That seems to lack conviction. If one continually repeats one's own arguments without fear of a challenge, progress is impossible."

"Exactly! Had he only repeated his fossilised views at every *Stammtisch* in Aargau, I could overlook his arrogance. But no, he wrote this piece in the medical weekly. Doctors all over the country rely on that for accurate and current information. He sabotaged our work. I said as much when I met him yesterday."

"Oh."

Bastian allowed a laugh to escape through his nose. "Oh, indeed. He and I did not part on cordial terms."

She thought for a moment. "Doctors often hold conflicting opinions, as far as I have seen. Simply because this man opposes your view, in contradiction of the evidence, why would anyone give greater weight to his judgement?"

"Because of who he is, who his family are, his role in the military and his influence in politics. He is no ordinary doctor. Nor is Hegelin, Wolff, Frankel, Vogt or Finkbeiner. They are a poisonous group whose influence is immense. At the same time, they care only for their reputations and nothing for their people. These men do not merit the title of doctor!"

"Bastian." She placed a finger to his lips. "You will upset yourself and wake Julius."

He pressed his lips into her palm and kissed it. She stroked his face, tracing his lips with her thumb. He tried to relax, reminding himself of his great good fortune: his wife, his son, even his mother-in-law in the room across the hall. But all three of his joys were tainted by what he had heard in the meeting rooms of Bern.

"Finkbeiner is the worst of those toads. He does not recognise our achievements in the Matterthal or Appenzell, instead regarding them as another failed pipe dream. His theory, which has substantial support, is that Switzerland must aim for racial purity."

Seraphine was silent.

"He gave a speech, two days ago, elaborating on his ideas in his book, *Die Kretinische Entartung* or The Cretin Degeneration. I read it on it publication last year and dismissed it as the ravings of an unwell mind. He believes in prevention, as do we. However, his perspective differs drastically. Rather than giving women in afflicted areas sufficient nourishment to bear healthy children, he wants to ensure they no longer reproduce. Herr Doctor Finkbeiner is an advocate of eugenics."

"I am unfamiliar with that word."

"Selective breeding. His view is that cretinism is hereditary. Any woman associated with a cretin in the family, no matter how distant, must be not permitted to propagate the defective gene. That would include your mother and you. Meaning no Peter and no Julius and our future daughter would not be allowed to have children."

Her fists clenched and her whole body grew tense as a wire.

"But it is not a defective gene, Dr Bayard has proven that. They cannot forbid women from bearing children."

"He goes further than that, my love. Making it illegal for women with a cretin in the family to reproduce is not enough. Finkbeiner stood up and said it in plain words: forced sterilisation."

Seraphine sat bolt upright, staring at him in the moonlight. "That is inhuman."

"Hush, my angel, hush." He sat up and folded her into an embrace. "We will stop this, I promise. They may have power, but we have proof. Children now run and sing and hear and breathe without impediment. Every single man, whether father, brother, son or soldier, has a voice and a vote. Canton by canton, people are seeing the light after centuries of darkness. In a few dank and miserable corners, toads still croak. Yet up in the mountains, down in the valleys, by the lakes and through the forests, the clean air is coloured with children's laughter and the wings of butterflies."

AUTHOR'S NOTE

Switzerland

On 24 June 1922, Switzerland's Goitre Commission took a historic and courageous decision in the face of furious objections. It officially recommended every canton should make iodised salt (containing between 1.9 to 3.75 mg iodine per kg) available to its people. Dr Eggenberger stated the dosage was too low, but it was a significant step forward. Consuming iodised salt was a voluntary measure and non-iodised salt remained on sale. For many, this was the first time a government approved additives to food as a preventative health measure.

Two complementary approaches ensured an even distribution: iodine supplements to children at school and treated salt (at the same price as untreated thanks to the Swiss Rhine Salt Works) for the whole population.

The results were decisive. Within one year, in those cantons which did provide iodised salt families reported a dramatic decrease in the size of children's goitres (as much as 66%). Newborns with goitre and/or deaf-mutism disappeared. Cretinism was eradicated within eight years.

Military records show the numbers of men unfit for duty due to large goitres, severe mental deficiency, or shorter than 156 cm decreased significantly between 1920 and 1950.

Some effects of long-term iodine deficiency could not be reversed, but as a prophylaxis and early treatment in young people, it was cost-effective, efficient and changed the landscape forever.

Iodine deficiency persisted into the 1930s, as shown by tests on urinary iodine excretion, but the Goitre Commission was unable to agree on higher dosage amounts. Finally, in 1955 all cantons agreed to make treated salt available although many insisted on keeping the iodine content as low as possible. It was not until 1962 that the Swiss Rhine Salt Works took matters into their own hands and increased the iodine dosage from 3.75mg/kg to 7.5mg/kg.

In the mid-sixties Professor Franz Merke offered geological reasons for poor iodine levels in Switzerland and beyond. Glaciers shifting through several ice ages forwards and backward, moved large strata of soil and washed away mineral deposits with melting water. The geographical pattern of this 'denudation' corresponds exactly to those places most affected by iodine deficiency. Areas such as the Jura in Switzerland, which was a natural barrier for the ice, consequently had no issue with a lack of natural iodine. This pattern can also be seen in areas of the USA and Scandinavia.

The United States

A similar fortification occurred in the US. Based on the work of Marine and Kimball, and thanks to the work of David Cowie, chairman of the Paediatrics Department at the University of Michigan, the state began introducing treated salt in 1924. The dosage was 100mg/kg and due to the fact the 'goiter belt' was severely deficient, there was an outbreak of thyrotoxicosis in 1926.

The Department of Agriculture initially wanted iodised salt marked as poison, but relented. In 1948, the US Endemic Goiter Committee tried to get a bill passed making iodised salt mandatory for all citizens. The bill was defeated. Since the 1950s, the percentage of American households using exclusively iodine-treated salt has remained at between 70-76%.

The World

Every country in Europe committed to eliminating iodine deficiency at the World Health Assembly in 1992. However, the World Health Organization identifies Europe as having the lowest coverage of salt iodisation of all its regions. Changes in dietary habits such as veganism or avoidance of dairy products exacerbates the issue, since plant-based milk, for example, is not fortified with iodine.

An estimated 2.2 billion people still live in iodine-deficient areas. One hundred years after the introduction of food fortification in Switzerland and the US, a lack of iodine remains a global public health issue.

JJ Marsh

Dear Reader

Thank you for reading SALT OF THE EARTH. I hope you enjoyed discovering more about Switzerland's past. If you are interested in more historical fiction, you might like my novella.

AN EMPTY VESSEL is the 1950s story of an ordinary British woman on death row for murder.

In a different time and place, this book tells a story you're unlikely to forget.

ACKNOWLEDGMENTS

Sincere gratitude for historical fiction guidance from fellow authors Jane Davis, Lorna Fergusson, Clare Flynn and Liza Perrat. Many heartfelt thanks to Dr Maria Andersson (ETH/Kinderspital Zürich) and Professor Peter Kopp (University of Lausanne) for expert advice. Perennial appreciation for Florian Bielmann, JD Smith and Julia Gibbs.

Any errors or omissions are entirely my own.

ALSO BY JJ MARSH

The Beatrice Stubbs European crime series

BEHIND CLOSED DOORS

RAW MATERIAL

TREAD SOFTLY

COLD PRESSED

HUMAN RITES

BAD APPLES

SNOW ANGEL

HONEY TRAP

BLACK WIDOW

WHITE NIGHT

THE WOMAN IN THE FRAME

ALL SOULS' DAY

TRUE COLOURS

SIREN SONG

The Run and Hide series (International thrillers)

WHITE HERON

BLACK RIVER

GOLD DRAGON

PEARL MOON

My standalone novels

AN EMPTY VESSEL

ODD NUMBERS

WOLF TONES

And a short-story collection

APPEARANCES GREETING A POINT OF VIEW

For occasional updates, news, deals and a FREE exclusive novella, subscribe to my free newsletter www.jjmarshauthor.com

Printed in Great Britain
by Amazon

40573101R00172